Falcon Finale

Don't miss the other books in the
Bob White Birder Murder Mystery Series

A Boreal Owl Murder

Murder on Warbler Weekend

A Bobwhite Killing

Carolyn & Corry,

Enjoy!

FALCON FINALE

Jan Dunlap

Jan Dunlap

NORTH STAR PRESS OF ST. CLOUD, INC.
Saint Cloud, Minnesota

Cover image: Corinne Dwyer

ISBN: 0-87839-448-6
ISBN-13: 978-0-87839-448-7

First Edition, September 2011

Printed in the United States of America

Published by
North Star Press of St. Cloud, Inc.
P.O. Box 451
St. Cloud, Minnesota 56302

www.northstarpress.com

Falcon Finale

Chapter One

Asking a birder to name a favorite bird is like asking a parent to name a favorite child. It can't be done . . . unless you've only got one kid. Then it's probably easy, although I have met a few students during my tenure as a high school counselor who may have pushed the envelope on that one.

(Appalled parent: "Are you telling me that my baby deliberately released all the lab mice in the school just for the fun of it?" Me: "Yes, I'm telling you that." Appalled parent: "I'm going to ground that kid forever!" Me: "Can you wait till he rounds up all the mice?")

According to the people I know who do have more than one child, however, it's impossible to choose one over another, and I think it's largely the same thing with birders. We've got a world full of avian species, each one special in its own way. Sure, you might prefer ducks to geese, or sparrows to finches, but coming up with one favorite?

Not gonna happen.

Honestly, I've been birding since I was five years old, and I can't think of a single bird I don't like.

Except for pheasants.

I hate pheasants.

They scare the bejeezus out of me.

You can be walking through a gorgeous stretch of open fields, enjoying the heady smell of the earth and listening to the songs of a choir of grassland birds, and a pheasant will explode out of the grass right in front of you. It's like a feathered grenade blowing up. All you can see are feet, bills, and big wings, and all you hear is this frantic rush of flapping. Intellectually, I know it's afraid of me, and it's making a flight for its life, but I still have this recurring vision that the bird is going to launch itself right at me and tear my head off.

With its little feet.

Pathetic, I know.

Anyway, it's kind of funny in a way that I hate pheasants so much, because if I had to name my favorite bird, I'd fudge a little and say it's any bird of the prairie.

Except a pheasant, of course.

And that's why my fiancée, Luce, and I were out so very early on a sunny August morning in southwestern Minnesota looking for birds of the grasslands.

In particular, I wanted to find a Gyrfalcon. According to the species occurrence maps that the Minnesota Ornithologists' Union has on its website, no one had ever seen a Gyrfalcon summering in the state, though they did show up sporadically later in the fall. The reason I thought I might find one more than a month early was the unseasonal weather pattern we'd experienced for the last week: high winds and unusually cool temperatures. Not only that, but over the weekend, I'd gotten an email from a birder I know in northwestern Iowa who thought he spotted a Gyrfalcon flying over his farm fields. My hope was that the bird, if indeed present, might wander across the state line, giving me a Minnesota record for a summer sighting.

It wouldn't be the first time I'd driven half-way across the state hoping that a bird might ignore its accepted species range and show up somewhere it wasn't expected. Two years ago, there was practically a traffic jam of birders all the way from the Twin Cities and Duluth to Little Spirit Lake in Jackson County, every one of them praying that a Brown Pelican that had been sighted on the Iowa side of the border would just fly a teeny bit north so everyone could get it on their Minnesota state lists.

If I'd been thinking ahead, I probably could have set up a concession stand at the lake shore where everyone was waiting and made a bundle on snacks and drinks. As it was, I wasn't there long enough to launch an entrepreneurial career, since within ten minutes of my arrival on the shore, the pelican obligingly flew a pass over the border, making it a first state record of that particular species in Minnesota.

Score another one for Bob White.

My hope for a quick score this morning was rapidly fading, however.

Luce and I had already spent three hours scouring the land and sky around Red Rock Prairie, a piece of land owned by the Nature Conservancy. After seeing a Swainson's Hawk, a Grasshopper Sparrow, an American Kestrel, an Upland Sandpiper, and a couple of Horned Larks, we'd decided to swing west and take a look around the Jeffers Petroglyphs site, which is not only a huge tract of native and restored prairie, but also a state historic site.

Make that a prehistoric site.

Prehistoric because its big attraction is an exposed ridge of Sioux quartzite that's marked with more than two thousand ancient rock carvings dating back at least as far as five thousand years. Historians think that some of the carvings might be records of vision quests that early Native Americans experienced at the site. I know that even today, many of the Native Americans who live in and around the state believe it's a sacred place of worship and continue to hold religious ceremonies there. What's really cool is the way the park management balances public and private usage of the site—visitors are reminded to be respectful at all times—and when the site is needed for ceremonies, it's closed to the general public. It's one of those rare examples where multiple cultural and natural needs peacefully co-exist.

Thankfully.

I mean, really, you take one look at that ocean of prairie all around you, and you can't help but be awed by the natural magnificence of the place. No wonder the original inhabitants of the area deemed it holy. Throw in a multitude of grassland birds, and, for a birder like me, it's more than sacred—it's a piece of heaven itself on earth.

Maybe that was why I didn't mind the drive this morning. Seeing the Gyrfalcon would be absolutely great, but worst case, I got a gorgeous morning of birding with Luce. As long as I didn't stumble over any nasty pheasants lying in wait to attack me, I'd be happy.

What I didn't count on, though, was being ambushed by a hawk.

Especially one by the name of Lily.

Lily White-Thunderhawk, to be exact.

My sister, who also now happened to be the wife of my best friend, Alan, who, according to my nearly hysterical sister, now happened to be missing.

"I need you to get out here, Bobby," Lily demanded. "Now!"

I looked up at the hot August sun and wondered if I was hallucinating.

Mere moments ago, my only concern was spotting a Gyrfalcon that had been misled by Mother Nature into straying far from its seasonal home. My head had been filled with the mundane details of reporting a state record: getting a photo if possible, calling up a few other birders to come out and confirm the sighting, posting it on the mou-net listserve to alert the rest of the state community to the bird's presence.

My sister telling me that her new husband had disappeared hadn't quite figured in any of that at all.

Hello. My name is Bob White, and I suffer from delusions.

Okay, so maybe it wouldn't be the best way to introduce myself at the back-to-school faculty meetings I'd be attending at Savage High School in a few weeks. Even if they are delusional, high school counselors are supposed to keep that to themselves.

Lily's urgent voice in my ear was not a product of my imagination, however. Even though she was calling from Arizona, I could hear the growing panic in her voice as clearly as if she were standing next to me. Although, if she'd been standing next to me, she would probably have been kicking me in the shins at the same time just to drive home her point. Lily's really endearing that way.

"He was supposed to meet me back at the hotel for dinner when he finished his workshop for the day," she was saying, a definite teary edge to her voice. "But he didn't show up. He didn't show up all night! This was supposed to be part honeymoon for us, and now he's missing! What am I going to do now?"

"Go to Disneyland?"

"Bobby!"

"Okay, okay. Bad joke," I apologized. "Let's take this from the top. You and Alan fly out to Flagstaff so Alan can teach workshops for the Native American Young Leaders Conference at Northern Arizona University. You're there five days, and now he's disappeared."

"I know that! I'm the one who just told you that!"

Obviously, Lily was not responding well to my counselor-trained calming technique. She was practically screeching over the phone connection.

"I need you to get out here!" she repeated, then lowered her voice a decibel or two. "I'm afraid something's wrong. Alan's been . . . odd. I need you to help me, Bobby."

"What do you mean by odd?"

Since I'd known Alan for fifteen years, and that included his wild man days in college, I was fully aware that what my sister might consider "odd" behavior was actually nothing out of the ordinary for my best friend. This was Alan we were talking about, after all—the big, bad basketball player who made it his personal goal to nip the backside of every coed on campus. I wondered if he'd shared his old nickname —ABA—with Lily yet.

ABA, as in Ass-Bite Alan.

"Is he gnashing his teeth a lot?" I ventured.

Silence.

"Lily?"

"This has nothing to do with his teeth, Bobby. Why would you ask about his teeth?"

Okay, that answered that question. Alan had obviously not opted for full disclosure to his blushing bride.

"He's preoccupied," my sister said, "and it's not about his teaching at the conference, either. When I talk about . . . some things . . . he gets that deer-in-the-headlights look. Just a week ago, when we talked about . . . some things . . . he was fine."

"What things?"

Another moment of hesitation.

"Children. We both want to start a family, but all of a sudden, he's . . . it's like he's paralyzed. Every time I bring it up, he says he needs some space right now." She sniffed back some tears. "And now, I don't know where he is."

Great. I'd just been recruited as a marriage counselor, as well as a bounty hunter. It was time to draw the line: if Lily even hinted at needing a sex therapist, I was going to wing my phone into the prairie.

I looked back over my shoulder towards the carved rocks of the petroglyphs, where Luce was crouched on the ground, studying the ancient markings. I'd promised her we'd spend the last weeks of my summer break birding and planning our wedding, but now it sounded like I was going to be making a change in that agenda. For all the bickering Lily and I did, she was my favorite sister—albeit my only one—and this is the truth: blood is thicker than water, even if sometimes, in my relationship with Lily, it feels more like sludge. No matter how I cut it, if my sister needed me in Flagstaff, I was going to be on the next plane out of Minneapolis.

At the moment, however, that presented a bit of a problem.

Jeffers was three hours away from the Twin Cities airport. Luce and I had headed west in the wee hours of the morning in order to catch sunrise at Red Rock. Driving to the petroglyphs had added another fifteen minutes of road time, which meant it would be afternoon before we got back to the outer ring of the metropolitan suburbs. Too bad we didn't have that transporter thing figured out yet that you see in old *Star Trek* episodes. A quick zap to the airport would sure save some time.

Beam me up, Scotty.

Aye, aye, Mr. White.

I glanced at the ancient rock face that stretched out behind me. No transporters there, though there were plenty of primitive sketches of buffalo, turtles, men, and the rare thunderbird. As I replayed the cell phone conversation with Lily in my head, one particular petroglyph caught my eye—a hand print. Near it, a small sign explained it was the sign of a rock man—a medicine man who disappeared into the spiritual world by a secret passage through the rock; when the shaman returned, he sealed the passage closed with his hand, leaving his print behind.

Almost as good as a transporter, I thought. Just pop in and out of the rock when you needed to get away. No one could follow. No one knew where you were. Instant privacy and loads of personal space.

I thought again about Lily and Alan. Their sudden romance had taken everyone by surprise back in May, but that surprise was nothing compared to the announcement of their engagement three weeks later. Since then, they'd been practically glued to each other, with any former concepts they may have held of "personal space" as extinct as the dodo. In fact, the only time I'd seen Alan without Lily at his side since May was when she dispatched him to bring me back from a birding weekend in June in Fillmore County. Even then, he'd been in regular communication with her by cell phone, and I'd wondered if my long time buddy was beginning to chafe a bit under my sister's short leash.

Throw in a dash of the "children" discussion, and I could almost feel the deer-in-the-headlights response myself.

Maybe Alan had just felt the need for a little get-away in Flagstaff, and, like a rock man, had found a secret spot for a bit of privacy and space. If that were the case, he should be popping back up into Newlywed Land any minute now to whisk his bride back into married bliss. He had assured me, after all, that he was crazy in love with Lily and wanted nothing more than a lifetime at her side.

Of course, that was before the wedding day.

Now that the honeymoon, or rather, part-honeymoon, was almost over, was Alan having second thoughts about marrying my sister, deciding to call a time-out for himself?

If that was the case, I didn't want to know, especially since, somewhere in the back of my mind, I'd jammed a lid down on this nasty little fear that my sister and my best friend had made a mistake by rushing into marriage.

Now, after finishing my conversation with Lily, that nasty little fear was back, pushing against the lid to be let out, big-time.

"Okay, Hawk," I said to Alan, wherever he was, "what the hell is going on, and where are you?"

"I'm right here, Bobby."

I almost dropped the phone. I hadn't heard Luce walking up behind me.

"Are you all right?" she asked.

I turned to look at her standing next to me. She was dressed like a Norwegian goddess attending summer camp. Her waist-length blonde hair was braided in a thick rope down her back, a red bandana circled her head, and her T-shirt and cargo shorts left long expanses of her arms and legs bare to the sun. Of course, her skin tanned a glowing gold, while my redheaded genes always left me with a burnt edge, even after a summer of outdoor activity. She lifted her hand to my face and stroked her long fingers along the stubble on my jaw, reminding me I'd skipped a shave this morning in favor of an earlier start out to Red Rock.

"You don't look so good," she said.

"I don't feel so good," I answered. I realized I had a headache. It had started with the cell call, and it was getting worse by the minute from Lily's words and my fears banging into each other inside my head.

"That was Lily," I told Luce. "She says Alan's missing."

"Missing?" Her fingers dropped away from my face. "What do you mean, missing?"

"Lily says Alan didn't come back to the hotel last night after the seminar ended. He hasn't called or anything. She doesn't know where he is, and she says he's been acting odd the last couple of days."

Luce shook her head. "That doesn't sound like Alan, Bobby. He wouldn't take off and not tell Lily where he was going. They just got married. You practically have to get a crowbar to pry them apart. Are you sure you heard her right?"

"I'm sure."

I pulled off my baseball cap and with the inside of my wrist, swiped at the sweat that had accumulated on my forehead beneath my plastered-down hair. It was only 8:30 in the morning and I was already dripping from the heat. The sun was hot, and the earth was baking with it. In the distance, the air shimmered, and I could almost believe I could be hallucinating out here on a high ridge over the prairie. Unfortunately, the cell phone in my hand was real.

Very real.

And Lily had definitely called me.

Alan was missing.

Something was really wrong.

"Something is really wrong," Luce said, echoing my thoughts.

I glanced at her, narrowing my eyes against the glare of the sun. She seemed to have this knack of knowing exactly what I was thinking, and it prickled the back of my neck when she did it. She said she just knew me that well. I thought she had some psychic thing going on, but refused to admit it.

Besides, I was the one who was supposed to be the sensitive, intuitive type, not her. I was the one with a master's degree in counseling and years of experience working with high school students and their parents, reading minds, influencing behavior, eating donuts in the faculty lounge, and generally attempting to manipulate the lives of others.

Luce was a chef. A really great chef, to be sure, but a chef, all the same.

Maybe she was a psychic chef.

"Exactly what did Lily tell you, Bobby?"

I closed my eyes and blew out a long breath. I might not be hallucinating, but I sure was having trouble staying focused on Lily and Alan. The more I tried to process what Lily had said, the more I felt myself rejecting it. I loved Lily, but I loved Alan too. I didn't want to believe he'd run out on her. But based on what she'd told me, I didn't know how I could avoid that possibility.

What I had to repeat to Luce wasn't exactly reassuring, either.

"Lily said that Alan was being odd," I said. "Like he wasn't being the same person he is here in Minnesota. Like he was changing his mind about things they'd already talked about."

I had no desire to be any more specific than that. If Lily wanted to confide in Luce about the children issue, she could do that, but I wasn't going to be the one to share it. We counselors were really big on confidentiality. It was in our contracts. It was part of our code of ethics. I had it tattooed on my left bicep.

Just kidding.

About the bicep.

Besides, if I told Luce something that Lily didn't want her to know, I could be sure of getting a vicious knee-kicking the next time I saw my sister.

"You know Lily," I reminded Luce. "She's not exactly the most non-confrontational person on the face of the planet. Maybe she argued with Alan, and he got angry. Alan's a pussycat with Lily, but I've seen him lose his temper enough times over the years, that I sure wouldn't want to wave a red flag in front of him. Maybe he just needed some space. On his honeymoon," I added. It sounded lame even to me.

"Bobby," Luce said. "I know what you're thinking, but you're wrong."

The psychic thing again. This time, the prickle on my neck turned into a tingle that went down my spine.

"Alan did not dump your sister."

Luce unscrewed the cap of her water bottle and took a long swig. "Alan loves Lily. He couldn't wait to marry her. He would not walk out on her."

I gave her a hard look.

"How can you be so sure?"

"How can you doubt him?" She stared back at me just as hard. "Has the sun fried your brain? He's your best friend. You've known him for how many years?"

"Fifteen," I muttered.

Damn. Luce was right, I wasn't thinking clearly. I'd known Alan for almost half of my life—and his—from our college roommate days, through his radical activist phase to his doctoral studies in political science to his final landing at Savage High School. I knew Alan better than anyone, and while he might still do utterly stupid, impulsive things at times—ABA, remember?—he had a soul of integrity and compassion that I'd trust with my life.

Just like I trusted him with Lily's life . . . and love.

Which had to mean he wasn't hiding out from Lily in a lovers' quarrel. Or punishing her for being . . . well, for being Lily. Painfully honest, tactless, overbearing Lily.

But I sure didn't like the only possibility that left: Alan was in trouble.

Big trouble.

I put my hat back on, took Luce's water bottle and finished it off. I handed the empty bottle to her.

"This is really not good," I said.

Luce looked at the bottle in her hand. "It's just a little warm, Bobby. We forgot the cooler."

"No, I mean Alan and Lily, not the water."

"Oh. Right."

The heat was getting to Luce, too, I thought.

"So what is Lily doing?" Luce asked. "Did she call the police? The university? The hospital?"

"She tried all three," I told her, repeating what Lily had told me after she demanded my help. "No Alan at the hospital. The university referred her to the police. The police say they can't do anything for twenty-four hours, because Alan's an adult and can't be considered a missing person before then. They told Lily just to wait it out, which of course really ticked her off, since one of Lily's lesser-endearing qualities is her impatience. She's convinced Alan's not willingly missing. She—"

"See?" Luce interrupted. "Lily's not doubting Alan, either."

"Okay," I said, raising my hands in surrender "I'm a lousy best friend and a pessimist. I admit it. I owe Alan an apology . . . and I'll give it to him . . . as soon as I find him, that is."

At my feet, the mark of the shaman caught my attention again. In and out of the rock at will—a pretty neat trick, I'd say.

Alan was no shaman, though. He was a social studies teacher at Savage High School, for crying out loud. He couldn't have just disappeared like a rock man into the earth. Alan had to have left a trail.

And I was going to find it.

"I've never been to Flagstaff," Luce said. "I've heard it's got mountain air, cool mornings, pine forests." She paused. "Arizona birds."

I hooked my hand around the back of her neck and pulled her over for a kiss. That's one of the benefits of having a fiancée who was as tall as I was—I didn't get a sore neck from bending over to kiss her.

Lucky me.

I kissed her some more.

Really lucky me.

"Does this mean I get to go with you to Flagstaff to find Alan?" Luce asked when I finished kissing her.

"Do I get a choice?"

"Of course not," she laughed. "I'll do whatever I want."

"I knew that," I said. "Really, I knew that."

She started to punch me on the arm, but instead, her hand landed in a soft grip on my forearm.

"I'm worried about Lily, Bobby. I can't even imagine how she must be feeling right now to have Alan missing. She needs someone, and I want to help."

That made two of us.

I took one last look across the acres of tallgrass prairie, big bluestem and Indian grass spreading away over the rolling hills, the last remnants of the great prairie that once covered 400,000 square miles of the North American continent. What had that been like five thousand years ago, when the ancient artists were up here, leaving their marks in the rock? An endless sea of grasses, massive buffalo herds, bands of people moving across the land, maybe species of birds I could only dream about.

All disappeared.

Like Alan.

No, not like Alan.

I mentally smacked myself.

Alan wasn't gone, he was just . . . not currently available. When you're not available, it's because you're busy. Alan had things to do. They were taking longer than he had anticipated. There was a perfectly good reason he was . . . unavailable.

Although, sometimes, you're unavailable because you don't want to be . . . available.

Damn, again. That nasty little fear in the back of my mind wasn't going to give up without a fight. I kicked it back into a mental box, slammed the lid on it and turned to Luce.

"Let's go," I said. "My Gyrfalcon will have to wait for another day. We've got a plane to catch."

Chapter Two

Oh God oh God oh God.

I was going to die.

The plane bucked, slid sideways, and dropped like a rock before it jerked back up again. I was riding a runaway rollercoaster in the middle of the sky and I wouldn't even have the chance to try to find Alan or help Lily or bird around Flagstaff or marry Luce or anything else because this little propeller jet was going to crash in the pine trees and nothing would be left of me for anyone to even scrape up with a spoon.

I was going to die. At least Luce was with me.

We could die together.

I closed my eyes and waited.

"What a ride," Luce breathed next to me.

I was still alive. Maybe I had a couple of minutes yet.

I opened my eyes and turned to face her.

"I love you," I told her, just as the plane skidded again. I braced my body against the back of the seat. I could feel my stomach churning.

"I love you, too. Ow!"

I glanced at Luce's lap. Her seatback tray had shaken loose and slammed across her knees.

"Sorry about that, folks," the pilot's voice called over the intercom. "We always get a little roughed up, flying into Flagstaff this time of the day. The air currents coming off the San Francisco Peaks collide with the currents coming up from the Colorado Plateau, and we get a little turbulence."

A little turbulence? I'd made permanent indentations on the arm rest where my fingers had been locked in what I figured was my death grip. If that was a little, I hoped I never experienced a lot.

If I even lived that long.

"You really don't like flying, do you?" Luce commented.

Thank you, Queen of the Obvious. I didn't say it out loud because I was nauseous, shaky, and breathing too rapidly to speak. Luce, on the other hand, looked exhilarated.

"You know, Bobby, I just don't understand why you hate flying. You love speed. You drive like a bat out of hell every chance you get. Flying is speed. It's just in the air, not on the ground. Besides which," she continued, "you're a birder. Birders are connoisseurs of flight—it's one of the pure pleasures of birding to watch a bird in flight."

I couldn't agree with her more. At the moment, however, I couldn't agree with anything. It was taking all my concentration to keep my stomach out of my throat.

"I picked up a brochure about the Flagstaff Arboretum when we changed planes in Phoenix," she said. "They've got free flight and on-the-fist demonstrations with native raptors every Saturday morning this month. Maybe we can get out there tomorrow to see it."

I felt the plane's wheels bump on the runway and took a long, deep breath of relief. I was going to live, after all. The plane shuddered all over as the brakes took hold and barely seconds later, we were parked in front of the smallest commercial terminal I'd ever seen, surrounded by a dense forest of very tall, very straight, Ponderosa pines.

I looked over at Luce as she unbuckled her seat belt. "You were trying to distract me on the way down, weren't you?"

"Yes," she admitted. "I know you hate flying, and I have to say, that was probably the scariest five minutes in the air I've ever experienced."

She grabbed her knapsack from under the seat in front of her. "Next time, I vote we rent a car and drive from Phoenix."

"You got that right," I told her. "And you're also right about birds in flight. Even after all these years I've spent birding, there's still something about seeing a Bald Eagle soaring through the sky that rocks my world."

I felt my stomach finally sink back into its anatomically correct location.

"In a good way," I added, "unlike the rocking I got on this flight."

I stood up to follow Luce down the tiny aisle, but immediately ducked my head since the ceiling of the plane cabin wasn't even as tall as I was. Memo to me: the next time I get on a plane that is sized for six-year-olds, I'm getting right back off.

"We definitely should try the Arboretum tomorrow," I agreed. "I'm just really hoping that by the time we get to Lily's hotel, Alan will be sitting there with her, waiting for us."

"With a really good explanation," Luce added.

"Yeah. A really, really good explanation."

We walked down the five or so steps to the tarmac, where I resisted the urge to fall on my knees and kiss the concrete. Another ten steps and we were in the terminal, grabbing our bags when they slid out onto the baggage conveyor belt. Twenty steps more took us outside to the curb where two taxis idled.

"Not exactly a bustling metropolis," I commented.

"Or people know better than to fly in," Luce noted.

"The Inn at Northern Arizona University," I told the driver of the nearest cab, opening the back door for Luce. "Where are all the cabs?" I asked the woman behind the wheel. "Is it a slow day?"

The driver, whom I guessed was in her late fifties, laughed.

"Honey, it's always like this. This is Flagstaff. Nobody flies into Flag twice."

Score another one for my psychic fiancée.

"So I'm guessing this is your first visit here," the woman said, wheeling the car away from the curb. "Welcome to Flag, located on historic Route 66, the 'Main Street of America.' County seat of Coconino County, the second largest county in the United States. Gateway to the Grand Canyon and the Arizona Snowbowl. Home of Northern Arizona University and the Lowell Observatory, where the planet Pluto was discovered in 1930. Neighbor to Sunset Crater, Walnut Canyon, and the red rocks of Sedona. Tourism and transportation center of northern Arizona."

She caught my eye in her rearview mirror. "Do you want me to give you the free tour on the way to campus?"

I wanted her to shut up. Now that we were here in Flagstaff, I needed to figure out what I was going to say to Lily, and what I was going to do about finding Alan.

"Sure," Luce answered her.

I groaned in silence.

"I'm Patty. Been living here in Flag since '68. I was a flower child back then. Came to Flag with my boyfriend. Thought we'd start a commune, but it didn't work out. The commune, not my boyfriend."

She checked her side mirrors and signaled to take the exit to downtown Flagstaff.

"I've got grandkids now. I've seen this town grow up. Over there," she said, tilting her graying head towards the west, "that's where you catch the road out to the Arboretum. Nice trails and one of the largest collections of high country wildflowers in the country. I think they've got some birds of prey programs you can go to on Saturday mornings—you know, like eagles and owls and hawks. Raptors. That's what they call them."

"Sounds good," Luce said, cutting me off before I could assure Patty that I knew what birds of prey were called.

"Now straight ahead, we've got the tourist strip. Hotel after hotel after hotel. And this is the road you take into the Historic District, or up to Lowell Observatory on top of Mars Hill there . . . "

I tuned Patty out as we crawled along in the bumper-to-bumper traffic heading north towards the Grand Canyon. These hotels had a goldmine here, I realized, catering to the millions of visitors that trekked through Flagstaff on their way to the canyon. Without a doubt, tourism was a major industry in this town, and I would bet my last nickel that the city government liked it that way. What city council wouldn't? Judging from the volume of traffic, money was pouring into the town right along with the visitors, giving Flagstaff the best of both worlds—a healthy economy fueled by other people's money, without having to sacrifice the natural environment that made it such an attractive town in the first place.

Not too bad for a one-time whistle stop on the American frontier.

Patty turned right, crossed several lines of railroad tracks by the old depot and slowed down to let a gaggle of college kids dressed for soccer wander across the street. At the rear of their group, I spotted several young men dressed in the full regalia of Native American fancy dancers, their chests covered with elaborate beaded and fringed aprons and their heads crowned with enormous feathered headdresses.

"Is there a powwow going on?" I asked Patty.

"Not that I know of," she replied. "But I think there's a young leaders' conference going on campus, so maybe they brought in some fancy dancers to do a demonstration. You ever seen them dance?"

I had. Every year at Savage High School we had "Diversity Day" to recognize the different cultural groups our students came from. Part of the day included an assembly that featured dancing. I'd seen Native American hoop dancers, fancy dancers, and drummers perform right in our auditorium. Watching the dancers weave through their steps was amazing enough, but the best part was seeing how the kids reacted with both interest and new pride in their own cultural heritages.

"Yes, I have," I told her, admiring the last of the eagle-feather-adorned costumes of the passing crowd. The jangling of beads and bells from the ornate outfits made a soft musical accompaniment to the young men's movements. "I imagine those dancers must work up quite a sweat under all that clothing."

"Here comes Mother Nature's cool-off," Patty said, just as the first big, fat raindrops hit the taxi's windshield.

The rain poured, though the young men didn't seem fazed a bit. I doubted they could even feel the rain through their colorful layers of fabric and feathers. Moments later, the rain was gone, and the sun was back out, brilliant in a blue sky.

"Our typical afternoon rainstorm," Patty commented. "Just wait a couple minutes, and it's gone."

She turned into a small parking lot in front of a compact, one-story building. "Here you go. The Inn at NAU."

I paid our fare while Luce thanked Patty for her Flagstaff travelogue. We shouldered our duffels and walked into the inn's reception area, which consisted of a front desk and two upholstered wing chairs.

Behind the desk, a young woman dressed completely in black carefully reviewed the reservation I'd called in while waiting for our plane's departure in the Minneapolis airport. Her name tag said she was Elvira and that she was a student in the college's School of Hotel and Restaurant Management.

"I'm dyslexic, so I have to read things kind of slow," she explained. "I don't want to make a mistake and assign you to the wrong room. That could cost me points in this week's rotation, and I really want an A in this course."

I noted her blood-red lipstick and black-painted fingernails as she tapped away on her computer terminal. Her kohl-lined eyes and poofy jet-black hair completed the picture.

Unless I was mistaken, Elvira, Mistress of the Dark, was now a student at NAU and our check-in clerk. She was also Hostess of the Night according to the nameplate on the reception desk.

"Do you have in-room horror movies?" I asked.

I felt Luce's fingers pinch my side in reprimand.

Elvira was nonplussed.

Either that, or she didn't hear me. Maybe that was just as well. I didn't want the Mistress of the Dark holding a grudge against me when she knew exactly where I was staying that night. I made a mental note to double check the window locks, along with the door chain, when I went to bed.

Elvira tucked two magnetic keycards in a small folder and handed them to me.

"Welcome to the Inn, Mr. White," she said, her eyes locked on mine. "If you'd like to have dinner here in the restaurant tonight, reservations are recommended as we have limited seating. Tonight's special is Chilean sea bass in a tomato-leek glaze, and I'm sorry, but we don't have in-room horror movies."

"He's not always this obnoxious," Luce assured Elvira.

"That's okay," the Hostess of the Night replied. "I get it all the time. Actually, I think it's kind of funny. Maybe I'll open a restaurant some day and cater to horror movie fans. You know —do themed menus."

Beside me, I could sense Luce's chef instincts perking up at the mention of menus.

"I think we should go see our room," I announced before Luce could say another word. She and Elvira could plan gothic dinners tomorrow.

"Sorry about the horror-movie crack," I told Elvira. "It's been a long day. At one point, I even thought I was going to die."

She nodded knowingly.

"You flew in, didn't you?"

"Yup."

"I hear that a lot, too."

We turned away from the reception area and started down the hall to the guest rooms, only to run right into Lily coming out of her suite.

"You're here," she said, throwing herself against my body. "Thank you so much."

I put down my bag so I could wrap my arms around her. "You bet."

We stood like that for a minute or two. I could feel her shoulders heaving a little under my hug and I knew she was being brave, trying not to cry in front of me and Luce. Then Lily pulled away from me and gave Luce a hug too.

"Alan still hasn't shown up, I take it?"

"No." Lily's eyes looked puffy, but her voice was firm. "I'm going to kill him when I find him."

"Mrs. Thunderhawk?"

The three of us turned to see a boy standing in the hall. He looked to be about twelve years old.

"Yes?" Lily said.

"I'm Joe. I need to take you to my father. He said you'd be worried."

Lily and I exchanged a puzzled look. The boy was Native American, and from the look on Lily's face, she'd never seen him before.

"I think you must have mistaken me for someone else," Lily said. "My name is Lily White-Thunderhawk. I'm from Minnesota. I don't think I know your father."

The boy was silent just for a second, sliding his eyes quickly from Lily to Luce to me, then back to Lily again.

"Yes, you do," he insisted. "His name is Alan. Dr. Alan Thunderhawk."

For a moment or two, there was silence.

Complete, utter silence.

Lily stared hard at the boy.

"I don't think so," she challenged him.

Luce stepped forward. "What do you know about Alan?"

I continued to be speechless, as well as paralyzed.

Alan had a son?

Alan didn't have a son.

Did he?

"He's in the hospital," the boy explained, again looking from Lily to Luce to me. "He and my mom are there now. He told me to come here and find you and bring you to the hospital. He says to tell you he'll be all right."

He hesitated, apparently waiting for some kind of response before he said anything more.

"In the hospital? Alan's in the hospital?" Luce repeated.

"He's all right," Lily whispered, just as her knees gave way and she sagged against me. I wrapped my arm around her shoulders to hold her up.

"He's all right," she said again. "I knew there was something wrong. I knew it. But he's all right."

"His leg is broken," the boy said.

We all looked at him again.

"Will you come to the hospital?"

"You bet," I said, finally able to speak again. "Lead the way."

Lily was recovering, too.

"I'm going to kill him," she announced.

Chapter Three

We piled into Lily's rental car with me behind the wheel. Following Joe's directions, I crossed the railroad tracks and headed for the hospital. In the backseat, Lily began to grill the boy.

"What is going on? Why hasn't Alan called me himself? Who are you—I mean, really?"

"Lily, give him a break. He's just a kid," I said over my shoulder.

"He's the only person in this car who knows anything about Alan at this point," she shot back. "I want to know exactly what's going on, and he's the only one I can ask."

"He and my mom were at this place near Walnut Canyon and there was a rockslide," Joe piped up. "They got caught in it, and it banged up their cell phones, so they couldn't call anybody. I went looking for them, and when I found them, I had to hike back to the highway and hitch a ride back to town to get an ambulance."

"Walnut Canyon?" Lily said. "That's outside Flagstaff. When did this happen?"

"They went yesterday afternoon," Joe told her. "Right after the classes finished for the day. That's how I met Alan. I'm attending the Young Leaders Conference.

"Anyway, when my mom didn't get back before I went to bed, I figured she was working on a story. But this morning, she still wasn't back, so I was afraid something had happened, and the only place I knew to look was out near Walnut Canyon."

"Why there?" I asked, taking a glance at my rear-view mirror to see Joe's face.

"Because she's working on a big story out there, and that's what Alan was going to help her with," the boy explained. "That's what she said."

"Is your mom a writer or something?" I asked.

Joe met my eyes in the mirror.

"Yes. She's a reporter," he said proudly. "And she's working on a book."

Lily cut in.

"Why is Alan helping her?"

"Because she asked him to," he answered.

Lily didn't reply.

That was Alan, all right. He never turned anyone away who needed his help. And if that someone was the mother of his child . . .

I almost ran a stop light and hit the brakes hard.

"Sorry," I told everyone in the car as they bounced back against their seats. "I didn't see the light."

I was beginning to think there were a lot of things I wasn't seeing. Like Alan being a father all these years. Like what Lily was feeling right now. Like what the boy in the back seat must be thinking.

Waiting at the intersection, it struck me that Lily, Luce, and I weren't the only ones who'd had a bad day. The poor kid in the back seat was, well, just a kid—and his day must have been a nightmare.

First, he woke up in his home to find his mom missing, which had to be bad enough. Then he went looking for her—alone, from what I could gather from his story—somehow got himself out of town to Walnut Canyon, found her in a rockslide, summoned an ambulance, and was now in a car with a bunch of strangers. Other than tapping his fingers repeatedly against the window, however, he didn't seem especially upset. Certainly not frightened. It dawned on me that he hadn't said anything about his mother's condition at the hospital.

"Is your mom okay?" Luce gently asked Joe, taking the words right out of my mouth. She was doing it again, reading my mind.

"She'll be okay. Her ankle's twisted or something. It was really swollen when they put her in the ambulance. Alan's going to be okay, too," he added.

Something in his voice caught my attention when he said Alan's name. There was relief, certainly, but there was also something else—a note I'd heard in my office at work when kids talked about their parents . . . in a good way. Loyalty . . . quiet pride . . . a sense of belonging.

Joe was emotionally attached to Alan.

His dad.

Oh, man.

"How did you get out to Walnut Canyon, Joe?" Luce asked.

Clearly, she was the only adult in the car capable of conducting a conversation at the moment. My head was stuck on Alan having a son, and I couldn't even begin to imagine what Lily was thinking.

No, I take that back. I could imagine.

She was thinking about killing her husband.

I moved into the right lane as we approached the turn towards the hospital and took another glance at Joe in the rear-view mirror. This boy was not only unafraid of us strangers, I realized, but very resourceful. If the canyon was outside town, he had to have had a means of transportation, even if it was by his own foot. He certainly wasn't old enough to drive and he hadn't mentioned a bike or anyone going with him.

"I walked, hitched both ways," he answered Luce. "The ambulance dropped me off a couple blocks from the inn on its way back to the hospital."

"How old are you?" Luce asked, turning in the passenger seat next to me to take a good look at the boy.

"Almost thirteen."

"You shouldn't be hitchhiking," Luce told him. "It's not safe."

"I can do it," he said. "I'm careful. Besides, if I hadn't, my mom and Alan would still be stuck out there. I was the only one looking for them."

"You were the only one that you knew was looking for them," Lily corrected him.

I pulled into an emergency room parking slot and turned off the engine. Lily and Luce were already out of their side of the car, heading for the emergency entrance's big sliding glass doors.

"I'm not so sure about that," Joe muttered, slamming his own car door shut as we got out of the car. Lily and Luce were out of earshot, so they didn't catch his remark.

I, however, heard every word.

I put my hand on his slim shoulder and stopped him on our way in to the hospital. "Why do you say that, Joe?"

He looked up at me, his eyes big, brown and solemn.

"I think somebody made that rockslide happen to my mom and Alan."

It was so not what I wanted to hear.

To be honest, it was probably the last thing I wanted to hear.

Scratch that. The last thing I wanted to hear was that I was going to have to get back in a plane to leave Flagstaff. Compared to that terrifying possibility, Alan being targeted in a rockslide definitely came in second.

"Coming through! Move aside, please!"

I automatically stepped back, pulling Joe with me.

A very distraught young man, his arm supporting the back of a very pregnant young woman, rushed by me. I didn't think either of them could have been more than twenty years old.

Almost unconsciously, I began to calculate how old Alan was when Joe was born and came up with the number twenty-four. When Alan was twenty-four, he was working in Seattle as a community activist. I'd been doing fieldwork for the Department of Natural Resources in Minnesota, so we hadn't been in touch much for the better part of a year. Back then, Alan always had a girlfriend or two hanging around; it was only in the last five years or so that he'd pretty much given up on finding the right woman. Or at least, he had, until he ran into Lily in the grocery store last May and fell head over heels for my sister.

And now they were married.

And Alan had a son.

That nobody knew about.

Maybe I really was delusional.

Gee, I hoped so, because if this was real life, I had this awful feeling that it was only going to get worse. I could practically hear that nasty little fear in the back of my mind chortling with glee.

"Mr. White?"

The receptionist at the emergency room registration desk was waving at me, trying to get my attention. Joe and I walked over to her, and she directed us through the doors to the emergency suite. As soon as we were on the other side, a short, round nurse gathered Joe under her ample wing and scooted off with him to a curtained cubicle on the far side of the room.

"You must be Joe. Your mama will be so glad to see you," she chirped, her head bobbing with every word. "She's been so worried about you."

The woman must have been a Gambel's Quail in another life, I decided. Short, round, head-bobbing . . .

To my left, Luce stuck her own blonde head out of a curtained examining room.

"We're in here."

I pulled the drapes aside and stepped in next to her. Alan was sitting up, shirtless, with both legs stretched out in front of him on the bed. His left leg was covered by a sheet. His right leg was exposed from the thigh on down and he was sporting a big blue ice pack wrapped around his knee. Lily was in a chair next to the bed, holding on to Alan's right hand with both of her own. She didn't look especially happy, but at least she hadn't killed him yet.

"Hey, Bob," Alan said. "Thanks for coming."

I noticed the barely perceptible flick of his eyes towards Lily. It was an old signal from our college days: he had something to tell me, but not in front of present company.

"Anytime," I replied. I nodded toward his knee. "I take it we're not going to be shooting any hoops one-on-one tonight."

Alan started to smile, but stopped abruptly as a spasm of pain washed over him. Lily's hands clenched in response to Alan's tightened grip on her fingers. He took a deep breath and let it out.

"It's dislocated, or at least it was," he said. "The doctor rolled it back into place. Although I think it hurt less before he fixed it."

Alan winced as he shifted his shoulders against the top of the bed. I noticed that he had some scrapes on his cheek and an ugly bruise across the left side of his chest.

"I used to be tougher than this," he complained.

"You used to play on a basketball court, not in a rockslide, Alan." Joe's suspicion came back to me, and I felt my own composure beginning to slip. "What the hell is—"

"Would you come with me, Bobby?"

Luce was pulling me back through the curtains, then steering me towards the nurses' station.

"I think Lily and Alan need a little time alone, right now. You can beat him up later. Although from the looks of him, I think he's hurting enough."

She was right about that. Judging from what I'd just seen in his exam room, Alan was definitely feeling it.

I wondered how much damage his knee had taken, since dislocations almost always included ligament tears and sometimes bone breaks. Best case, Alan was going to be in some kind of knee brace and on crutches for a while. Worst case, he'd be back in the hospital in a few weeks for surgery after the swelling was gone and probably facing chronic knee pain for the rest of his life.

I glanced back at the drawn curtains hiding my sister and her husband. This was not an auspicious beginning for their marriage.

Then again, it could be worse.

Alan could have a son Lily didn't know about. Or, rather, a son she hadn't known about.

Until the last hour.

"Did he say anything?" I asked Luce, sitting with her on a bench by the nurses' station.

"About what?"

"Anything. You name it. His knee, the rockslide, Lily. Joe."

"Well, apparently he did leave a message for Lily last night," she reported, "saying he was running very late and that he'd be back to the inn by midnight, but obviously she didn't get the message. Granted, that still would have had her worried when he didn't show, but at least she wouldn't have spent the night thinking he was angry with her."

I thought about how I'd feel if Luce and I had argued, and then she didn't show up when I expected her. Of course I'd assume she was angry. A call explaining otherwise would be a major relief.

But Lily hadn't even had a phone call to console her through the night. No wonder she had been on the edge of hysteria when she called me this morning. No wonder it had shaken me so badly to hear my sister, Ms. Totally In-Control, so close to losing it.

"They have to take X-rays yet," Luce was saying, "so it might be a while before he's released. Do you want to go get some dinner?"

I had no idea what time it was. Somewhere between dawn in Minnesota and late afternoon in Flagstaff, I'd lost track. Now that Alan had reappeared in mostly one piece, my anxiety level had dropped dramatically, only to be replaced by a growling stomach. I stood up and saw Joe waving to me from across the room.

Joe.

Alan's son.

Really?

And then I felt more than a little sheepish. In the midst of my concerns for Lily and Alan, I'd temporarily forgotten Joe's situation. He was, after all, just a kid, albeit a clearly independent and self-reliant one.

Like Alan had been.

Exactly like Alan had been, actually.

I waved back at the boy.

"Hold on a minute, Luce. Let me talk to Joe, first."

I left Luce on the bench and crossed the space to Joe.

Was he Alan's son? If he was, why didn't we all know about him before now?

Alan wouldn't have hidden the existence of a child from me, I was sure of that. Alan loved kids—it was one of the reasons he was such an excellent teacher and why he'd ended up at Savage High School when he could have had his pick of better-paying jobs in a dozen other places. And parental responsibility—or the lack thereof—was one of his personal hot buttons. If there was anything that Alan couldn't abide, it was parents who abandoned children, physically or emotionally. So there was no way that Alan would have left a child behind him somewhere in his past.

And then it hit me.

The only way Alan would have left a child was if Alan hadn't known he had one.

Oh, man.

"Mr. White, my mom wants to meet you," Joe said when I reached him.

Oh, boy.

I put on the face I use all the time at school when I meet my students' parents for the first time: friendly but reserved, attentive, polite. As I followed Joe into another draped cubicle, I tried to focus on the boy, and not on the fact that I was about to meet Alan's former lover, a woman who had, some thirteen years ago, apparently neglected to tell Alan he was going to be a father.

Chapter Four

"You must be Bob White. I'm pleased to meet you. I'm Julie Burrows."

Joe's mother held out her hand to shake mine. She was sitting on the edge of an examining table with her left foot propped up on a chair, her ankle wrapped. Behind her, a pair of crutches leaned against the table. As I shook her hand, I also noticed that Julie Burrows wasn't, as I had assumed, Native American. Beneath the abrasions on her cheek and arms, her skin had the same pale tone of my own. Her wide-set eyes were green, and her short, spiky hair was rust-colored. From what I could see, the only family resemblance she shared with Joe was her high, sharp cheekbones. Kind of like mine and Lily's . . . and Alan's.

Julie laughed. "Yeah, I know. I don't look like I would be Joe's mom."

I opened my mouth to deny it, but instead, I covered it with a smile and said, "I guess you've gotten that reaction before."

"Only a couple hundred times," she replied. "Thanks for bringing Joe to the hospital. He'd already hitched more than enough for one day."

She slid a stern look in her son's direction.

"Hey, if I hadn't, you and Alan would still be sitting out there in a pile of rocks," Joe defended himself.

"I know. And I'm very grateful. But I don't want you to take those kinds of chances, Joe." Julie turned her attention back to me. "I'm afraid risk-taking runs in the family."

I tried to keep my face blank. Was she referring to Alan and thirteen years ago?

"I'm an investigative reporter," she explained.

"Oh," I said, trying to keep focused on the present conversation and not on all the questions I wanted to ask her, the primary one being the question of Alan's paternal status. "I didn't know."

"Then I obviously know a lot more about you than you do about me," Julie observed. "Alan thinks the world of you, you know. He always has."

"Ms. Burrows?"

Nurse Quail energetically pulled the cubicle's curtains back to each side. "You can go, now. The doctor signed the discharge forms, and we've already reviewed your instructions for that sprained ankle. Let's just get you into this wheelchair, and we'll get you out of here. Do you have a ride home?"

She expertly eased Julie into the wheelchair, then handed the crutches to Joe.

"I can take you home," I offered to Julie. "I owe Joe for bringing us here."

Julie glanced at Joe, then back at me.

"Are you sure? I don't want to impose."

"Not at all. I'd be happy to," I assured her. I took the handles of the wheelchair from the nurse and started pushing Julie across the room to where Luce was still waiting on the bench by the nurses' station.

"It looks like Alan will be here a while yet, and Luce and I need to get out for some supper," I told her. "You can point out a good spot for us. Would you like to join us?"

And maybe, that way, I could get some answers. My list of questions was growing by the minute, and it wasn't just about Julie's relationship with Alan, which, really, wasn't any of my business, though it was gnawing a hole in me anyway. How could he have hooked up with a woman who wouldn't even let him know she was having his baby?

What had happened in Walnut Canyon, however, was a different matter, especially since it had resulted in a serious injury to my best friend—an injury that Joe had implied wasn't accidental. If Julie and Alan were attracting trouble, I wanted to know about it. And if they were, I sure didn't want Lily falling into a line of fire by association. Alan might be my best friend, but Lily was still my sister.

That old sludge blood, you know.

"That's very generous of you, Bob, but I just want to go home," Julie was saying. "Although, if we could swing by a fast food drive-through, that would be great. That way, I could at least get Joe fed for the day."

I stopped the chair in front of Luce and introduced her to Julie.

"You've got quite a guy, there," Luce said to Julie, nodding towards Joe, who, at the moment, was trying to slip into Alan's examining room across the hallway. "He's the hero of the day."

Julie smiled in agreement. "He sure is. But don't tell him that, or else he'll be even more of a handful than he already is."

"Is he Alan's?" Luce asked.

All the air in my lungs was immediately sucked out by an invisible vacuum. Leave it to Luce to ask the question I couldn't—or didn't want to—bring myself to ask.

"No," Julie said, watching her son as he disappeared into the curtains surrounding Alan. "He's not. But somedays I almost wish he were."

Tension flooded out of me so fast, I thought I was going to pass out.

Not very manly, I know, but it's not every day a strange kid walks up to you and says he's the child of your best friend. Especially when your best friend just married your sister and you'd already beaten back these nasty little doubts nagging at you that the marriage was going to be the biggest mistake known to humankind.

"He told us that Alan was his father," Luce pressed.

For a moment or two, Julie didn't say anything.

"That's a problem, isn't it?"

Well, yeah. The boy thought he had a dad who wasn't his dad and to whom he was already attached, and, like every son, wanted to please, hoping his "dad" would stick around and be the dad he always wanted, but that "dad" was married and lived on the far side of the next time zone.

Yeah, that could be a problem.

Then, like a tiny jolt of counselor insight, I felt my gut tighten, a clear signal to me that Julie's response was holding something back—something important—but before I could pursue it, Joe popped back out of the curtains.

"I told Alan and Lily we were going home and that you guys would be back in a while to pick them up. Alan said to bring him back some onion rings. They're his favorite, you know." He grinned. "I said you'd bring him a double order, and he said he felt better already, knowing I was on it."

The kid was practically beaming.

Good job, Alan. Make the kid like you even more.

I went to get the car.

A minute or two later, I pulled Lily's rental around to the front of the emergency entrance, and Luce helped Julie into the back seat. Joe hopped in beside his mom and Luce climbed in next to me. We stopped at a drive-through window to pick up meals for Julie and Joe, then Julie directed me through an older section of town of maze-like streets to her bungalow at the foot of Mars Hill. The roads were narrow and lined with old pines and oaks. if I hadn't had Julie giving me the directions, I never would have found her house. Except for the steep road that took visitors up the hill to the Lowell Observatory, the streets in the neighborhood were empty.

"I was beginning to think there wasn't a single block in this town that wasn't overrun with tourists," Luce remarked as I turned into the driveway that ended in a carport beside the back door. "But this is like a little hidden pocket of small town America."

"It really is," Julie agreed. "I love living in Flagstaff, but some days, I wish all the tourist attractions would just shut down for a day or two and let us just live here in peace and quiet and obscurity. It's a little better in the winter, but then we get the skiers and snowmobilers. I can't complain too much, though. Tourism is the lifeblood of this community. Without it, Flag might still be just a remote stop on an old railroad line. Picturesque, yes. But profitable? No. As it is, tourism is the hen that keeps on laying the golden eggs, and lots of folks around here like it that way. "

"Are you from here?" I asked.

"Not originally. I was born in Kansas. I came west when I was a kid, liked it and stayed. I've lived in Flag, California, and Seattle."

"That's where you met Alan, right? In Seattle?"

I was trying to fix a time frame on her relationship with Alan. For some reason—namely, that little jolt of insight I'd experienced—her denial of Alan's fatherhood had rung a bit hollow. On top of that, she hadn't exactly confirmed that denial in the next breath when she avoided a direct answer to Luce's comment that Joe had told us Alan was his father. Besides, I'd done the math, and though I was no numbers whiz, I could certainly add up to nine: Joe was conceived sometime while Alan was in Seattle.

One of the Burrows was lying, but I didn't know which one, and I wasn't going to confront Julie about it in front of her son.

I had the distinct impression, though, that Julie knew what I was fishing for.

"Yes, I knew Alan in Seattle," she replied. "We were very good friends."

She turned to Joe.

"Why don't you go open the door for us and take our dinner in?"

Joe got out of the car and carried the food sacks into the house, while I helped Julie out of the backseat. Luce grabbed the crutches out of the trunk and handed them to Julie.

"You know, Bob, if you want to talk about my relationship with Alan, we can do that," Julie suggested. "But not with Joe around, okay?"

I could feel a little burn on my cheeks. There was a reason my own high school counselor had never recommended I pursue a career in acting: I was lousy at it. Even when I tried to be casual, like I'd just attempted with the Seattle comment, I was as transparent as glass. It had taken me years of practice to learn to mask my own feelings with my repertoire of counselor faces, but even then, if I wasn't concentrating really hard, I slipped up occasionally.

Like I'd just done with Julie.

And not only had I let my own feelings take over, but I was way out of line as well, questioning her with Joe right there, and I certainly knew better than to do that.

After all, I was a not-highly-paid school counselor, a trained professional who was discrete, sensitive and insightful. But ever since Lily's panicked phone call this morning, I'd felt like my discrete, sensitive, and insightful traits had left the building. Flown the coop.

Disappeared.

With Alan.

And the only thing I was suddenly capable of doing was flying by the seat of my pants.

And that seat was already beginning to feel pretty thin. If I was going to help Lily . . . and Alan . . . I needed to start thinking clearly and acting appropriately. I was a good problem-solver. I was an adult. Alan and Julie's past wasn't my affair.

Sorry. Bad choice of words.

Alan and Julie's past wasn't my concern. My concern was to get Alan and Lily home to Minnesota, where they could go back to being goo-goo-eyed newlyweds and stay away from rockslides, especially suspicious ones.

Crap.

Knowing Alan, "suspicious" was going to be a major problem for him. And if it was a problem for him, then it would be a problem for Lily.

Which meant it would be a problem for me.

And then I wouldn't be able to load the two of them on the scary airplane and send them back home.

Because if there was a chance his accident wasn't really an accident at all, there was no way Alan was going to walk—or limp—

away from a fight, especially if it had to do with protecting someone he cared about.

Or in Julie's case, had cared about at one time.

Yeah, I'd say "mother of my child" probably fit the "care about" category pretty well.

"I'm sorry, Julie," I apologized. "Forgive me. Your relationship with Alan is none of my business. But there is something I really do need to ask you."

I caught a warning look from Luce, who was walking on Julie's other side as we made it slowly up to the house. She obviously figured I'd made enough of a fool of myself for one day. Luce was big into quotas.

I ignored her.

"Earlier," I said, "when we got to the hospital, Joe...well . . . he indicated he thought your accident wasn't."

Julie stopped a few feet from her back door.

"Wasn't what?"

I looked deeply into her green eyes, willing her to answer me honestly. It dawned on me that she was only an inch or two taller than Lily. In fact, now that I thought about it, there were several ways she resembled my sister—the hair color, the skin tone, the cheek bones, the body frame. A crazy idea popped into my head: had Lily reminded Alan of Julie?

With an effort, I pulled my attention back to the question at hand. I didn't want any innuendos or trick answers to this one.

I wanted the truth.

"An accident," I told her. "Joe thinks your accident wasn't an accident. Why would he think that, Julie?"

Julie's gaze dropped to the ground. She clenched her jaws.

Double crap!

My trusty gut was going into override.

"I'm not going to like this answer, am I?" I asked her.

"Maybe you two better come in," she said.

I knew it. I was definitely not going to like this answer.

I thought about grabbing Luce and running back to the car, but I figured I wouldn't make it a block before my fiancée pulled the key out of the ignition and demanded what in the world I thought I was doing. Answers to our questions were the one commodity that seemed to be in short supply tonight, and running away wasn't going to change that, or make the answers I did get any more agreeable.

I held the door open for Joe's mom and waved Luce in after her. Somewhere in the neighborhood, I heard some Mourning Doves cooing.

It almost sounded like they were saying "Doom, doom, doom."

Thanks, guys. I really needed that.

We followed Julie through the kitchen, where Joe was devouring his hamburgers, to a cramped office at the end of a short hall. The three of us barely fit into the room around a large wooden table that Julie used as her desk. It was covered with notebooks, scraps of paper, a laptop, printer, fax machine, and a pile of books. On one wall, a map of Arizona was marked up with dates, arrows and question marks. A collection of photographs and news clippings was tacked up beside it. The room's only window was patched across its bottom half with duct tape.

"A long time ago, I knew this guy," Julie began. "I was fifteen, and he was this almost mythic hero to me. His name was Ron Walking Eagle and he traveled around Arizona, talking about the spiritual heritage of the tribes that live here. He was a member of the Yavapai band, himself, and he was demanding protection for native sacred sites and restoration of their property —stuff like that."

She shuffled some papers around on her desk, though it didn't appear that she was looking for anything in particular.

"I heard him talk in Prescott," she continued, "at a rally for Indian rights and . . . I don't know . . . I just sort of became an activist groupie, I guess. Anyway, I ended up here in Flagstaff with him, and he was fighting tooth and nail to stop this local bigwig from turning a part of his property into a public preserve. Ron said it belonged to the native peoples, that it was an ancient place of worship, and he took this guy to court, and . . . "

Julie dragged in a long breath of air, then let it out slowly. "He disappeared."

"Who disappeared?" I asked. "The bigwig or Ron?"

"Ron."

"Is this the book you're working on?" I asked. "Joe said you were writing a book."

"Yeah, it is," Julie replied. "Except my book is going to have a surprise ending that only one other person knows. Ron Walking Eagle didn't just disappear. He was killed."

Somehow, I knew she was going to say that.

Intuition?

Mind-reading?

Were Luce's psychic skills rubbing off on me?

Maybe it was the word "MURDERED" that was scrawled near Walnut Canyon's dot on the map.

I looked at the photographs on the wall. Two were of a smiling man standing in front of a wall of rock. In a third picture, he had his arm draped over the shoulders of a young girl, her face lit up with hero-worship. I assumed the man was Walking Eagle, but when I took a closer look at the girl, I could almost have sworn it was my sister Lily.

"It's you, isn't it?" I asked Julie, pointing to the photo.

She nodded.

"So you think," I said, "or at least, Joe does—that what happened to you and Alan was somehow connected to this murder that took place almost twenty years ago."

"Yes."

I picked up a book from the desk. It was titled *The Politics of Preservation* by Charles Corwin. I'd never heard of it. I wasn't planning to read it, either. I just needed something concrete to hold on to as I took a minute or two to mentally process everything Julie had just told us.

"And why have you come to this conclusion?" I asked, replacing the book amid the clutter on the desk.

Julie leaned the crutches against the wall and sat down in her chair.

"Because ever since I started asking questions around town about the preserve land dispute, things have been happening to me that don't usually happen. Things like this broken window in here."

She pointed to the taped window frame. "Things like my tires getting slashed. Hate mail in my mailbox."

"Hate mail?"

"You've told the police, right?" Luce asked.

Julie nodded. "But it doesn't seem to be helping. I have no idea who's behind the incidents, or when something will happen or where. All I know is that the more I dig for information, the more I'm getting threatened. Which, of course, tells me I'm definitely on the right track. And now this."

She nodded at the crutches.

"I've been climbing rocks and poking around that preserve for weeks, but this is the first time I've even had a few rocks slipping under my foot, let alone a whole rock slide that just happened to come down at me from the crest of a hill."

"I take it rockslides aren't common at this preserve?"

Julie shook her head, a small sound of disgust coming from her lips.

"Not one of that size. Believe me, if rockslides were a problem, the park rangers wouldn't think twice about closing the Ridge to the public. That's the name of the preserve, by the way: the Ridge."

She tilted her chin upwards in a mannerism that distinctly reminded me of my sister.

"There's nothing like a fatality in a local park to put a dent into an economy that lives and breathes tourism," she pointed out. "Use it or lose it."

Geez, she even sounded like Lily.

"So you're thinking somebody was already up there and gave the rocks a little encouragement," I said, deliberately ignoring her eerie resemblance to my sibling for the moment. I glanced in the hall to make sure Joe was still in the kitchen. I didn't think he needed to hear this right now.

"Yes, I do."

"Then you have got to get the police involved in this, Julie," Luce urged her. "Let them investigate. You get out. You're obviously putting yourself at risk here, and if you're at risk, then what about Joe? Who's going to keep him safe? He's just a kid. He needs his mom."

"I'm fully aware of that." Julie's voice went icy. "I'm a single mom, remember? I'm all Joe's got. Believe me, I totally know that."

Luce tried to backpedal.

"I'm sorry, I shouldn't—"

Julie held up her hand to stop her.

"Don't. You're concerned for Joe. I appreciate that. I really do," she said. "But I have to be the mom Joe needs and deserves. And Joe needs and deserves a mom who stands up for her convictions, who keeps her promises, no matter how hard that gets."

Her gaze fell across the mess on her desk.

"And Joe's mom needs that, too," she added.

Julie Burrows could have been one of the parents I met in my office at work. As a high school counselor, I didn't just advise students—parents were part of the package. They came in all sizes and types: single, divorced, married, widowed, angry, hurting, confused, inept, overbearing, charming, clueless, abusive, scared. Julie, I sensed, fell into one of my favorite categories, though: parents who parent by being the best role model they could be. The only flaw with that style was that sometimes, the parents were asking too much . . . of themselves.

"You're going to keep on with this investigation, aren't you?" I asked her.

"Yes, I am."

She spread her hands over the papers on her desk.

"I have to tell this story," she said. "Ron was a friend of mine— the only friend I had when I needed one. I won't let him down. Even if we can't find his murderer, I can at least tell the truth about him."

"I still don't get why the police aren't involved," Luce said.

"Because without a body, there's no proof of a crime," Julie answered. "Ron disappeared. No one filed a complaint. He just wasn't around anymore. That's why Alan and I were out at the Ridge. I was trying to find the last place Ron was seen, a cleft in the rocks that he believed was a sacred sanctuary. All I've got is a witness who saw Ron and another man enter the rocks. The other man came out. Ron didn't. Unfortunately, at the time, the witness was a runaway trying to stay clear of police. Not exactly a believable and trustworthy witness."

"And what about this witness now?" I asked. "Where is he?"

I felt a twinge of hope that this could all be wrapped up without much more ado. Julie could find her witness, write her story, and spend the next ten years on the book authors' speaking circuit. I could go birding early tomorrow morning at the local arboretum, get a few Arizona birds, put Alan, Lily, Luce, and myself back on a plane—although I didn't want to think too hard about that part—and go home.

Then I thought about Joe.

Okay, maybe I'd just put Luce and myself on a plane and go home. If there were some unfinished business here involving Joe, Julie, and Alan, then he and Lily could book their own flight home.

After my sister killed him.

Julie was gazing out the broken window.

"The witness?" she echoed.

Her eyes swung up to meet mine.

"You're looking at her."

Chapter Five

FROM EVERY ANGLE, IT HAD BEEN AN unbelievably lousy day, but the night was breathtakingly beautiful.

I was sitting in the courtyard patio at the Inn, looking up at a million stars. No wonder they'd built an astronomical observatory in Flagstaff. The high altitude made the atmosphere almost transparent, and the city generated minimal light pollution to dilute the stars' brightness. Even without a telescope, I could see cloudy collections of stars that hung together in distant galaxies. The immensity of the distances involved made me feel small and insignificant. At the same time, however, it was somehow soothing to think the chaos of the day was just a tiny ripple in the cosmos.

Although I could have done without this particular ripple, that was for sure.

"Hey, Bob."

It was the rippler himself.

"Mind if I join you?"

"You idiot."

"Whew," Alan said. "I was afraid you might be mad at me."

He hobbled carefully over the stone patio to take a seat next to me at the wrought-iron table.

"You're pretty good on those crutches," I told him.

"Like riding a bike. Once you learn how, you never forget."

He leaned the crutches against the edge of the table.

"Not one of my favorite skills to have to remember, however. I spent more than enough weeks on crutches in the course of my high school and collegiate basketball career."

We sat in silence for a moment or two. Alan shifted in his chair and winced.

"Can I get you anything?"

"You mean besides a brain transplant?" he replied. "Because the one I've got sure seems to be dysfunctional. I can't believe how stupid I've been for the last twenty-four hours."

"That makes two of us. At least."

"Yeah, I am in deep guano with Lily," Alan confessed. "Not that she doesn't have good reason. I have massively screwed up here."

"Look, Alan, I don't want to offer advice," I said.

"But you will, right? I mean, that would be good, Bob, because, in case you haven't noticed, I am really in need of advice. I don't seem to be doing too well on my own right now."

That was an understatement. Not only was he banged up, on crutches, and in trouble with his new wife, my sister, but he might have a son he hadn't known about.

Oh, and somebody may have tried to kill him last night.

In comparison, it made my day look a whole lot better.

Except for the plane ride into Flagstaff. Nothing was ever going to make that experience look better.

"Okay," I said. "Advice. Gee, where do I start?"

"Your choice," Alan sighed. "Have at it."

My first thought was for Lily. I'd never heard my sister closer to hysteria than when she had called me this morning.

"Before you do anything else," I suggested, "you better grovel in front of Lily and beg her to forgive you. Do it a lot. Do it repeatedly. And never, never fail to show up when she's expecting you, especially if you've had an argument. I can't believe you didn't call her last night — even if you were upset about the idea of starting a fam . . . "

Wait a minute. Of course Alan hadn't wanted to talk with Lily about kids all of a sudden. He'd just learned he had a son, or at least, that he might have fathered one.

Or not.

I expect that little revelation would give any guy the deer-in-the-headlights look. Heck, forget the deer. I'd think it would be more like watching a freight train coming right at you while you're stalled on the tracks.

Total train wreck.

Happy part-honeymoon.

"Alan," I said, "no matter what else was going on with you and Lily, or you and Julie, for that matter, you still should have told Lily that you were going out to that preserve near Walnut Canyon and might be late for dinner. At least that way, she wouldn't have imagined the worst. Although," I added, "I guess that wouldn't have made any difference since you didn't show up after dinner either."

I realized I didn't have any good advice for the situation after all, so I changed my tactics.

I went for guilt.

"She was a wreck, Alan. You can't do that to her."

"I know," he said, remorse clearly etched on the sharp planes of his face. "I know that now. I'm still pretty new at this, you know."

I opened my mouth, but he held up his hands to stop me from saying anything.

"I'm not trying to make excuses, Bob. I know I screwed up. I've already laid my heart at your sister's feet and asked her to stomp on it till she's satisfied."

"Did she?"

Alan grinned.

"Oh yeah," he replied. "She's a good stomper. Lucky for me, I was already wounded and in the hospital at the time, so she let me off easy. Although I think she scared the nurses a little. When Lily went to get coffee, one of them slipped me that card that you see in emergency waiting rooms—the one that asks if you're in an abusive relationship. I told her Lily was harmless, but I'm not sure she believed me."

He patted the immobilizer wrapped around his knee.

"With a little luck, by the time this comes off, Lily will have gotten over the worst of her mad. Then I figure it's just a matter of getting primo season tickets for the Wild, and I'll be out of the doghouse."

Alan definitely had Lily's number, thankfully. Before he'd burst into her life, only two things had thrilled my sister: a profitable bottom line for her landscaping business and a Minnesota Wild hockey game. Maybe there was hope for their marriage after all. If she hadn't booted him out after a day like today, she must have figured Alan was worth the trouble.

Then again, my sister was nothing if not tenacious in pursuing what she wanted. My dad used to say that Lily was a bulldog in disguise—that once she got her teeth in something, you couldn't shake her loose. I wondered if Alan had teeth marks on his neck, but decided not to ask.

There really was something such as too much information.

"And I did leave a message for Lily before I left for the Ridge," Alan pointed out. "I called the desk clerk at the inn and asked her to personally deliver it to our room. I may be impulsive, but I'm not totally irresponsible."

"But Lily told me she didn't have any messages from you," I reminded him, then remembered checking into the inn earlier today.

Elvira was dyslexic.

If she'd been Hostess of the Night last night, there was a better than good chance that Alan's message had probably ended up under someone else's door.

So much for Elvira's A in the course. I wondered if she'd consider switching her major to . . . oh, I don't know . . . film presentation?

I looked up again at the sparkling night sky.

"What else can we talk about that hasn't gone as planned?" I mused aloud. "Or maybe what wasn't planned at all. I know. Let's talk about Joe."

"Yeah, let's," Alan enthusiastically agreed, totally missing the sarcasm in my tone. "He's a great kid. He's smart, capable, and way too responsible for a twelve-year-old boy."

He followed my gaze upwards at the stars.

"Is he my son? He could be. The timing's right. Joe's definitely part Native American. Julie and I spent some time together in Seattle, but it was never a serious affair. Not for either of us," he maintained. "But I don't know for a fact that I'm his dad."

"That's what I figured."

Alan turned to face me.

"Thanks. I knew that you, of all people, would know how I feel about kids and their parents. How many times have we sat in your office and complained about parents of students who are clueless? How many times have I wanted to slug dead-beat dads? If I'd ever had a child —a child I knew about," he pointedly added, "wild horses couldn't drag me away from it."

That's also what I had figured . . . after I'd had a moment to think it through. I didn't, however, tell Alan it took me even that long. Having him sitting next to me, feeling like the world was going to right itself again eventually, I was ashamed to think I'd entertained a single doubt about him.

Or his feelings for Lily.

As Luce had reminded me more than once today, I knew Alan better than anyone.

So why had I doubted him? Why had that doubt about Alan and Lily's marriage resurfaced this morning out at Jeffers? I was going to be taking the plunge into matrimony myself in less than a month, so the last thing I needed was to be looking for warning signs in someone else's marriage.

A shooting star shot across the heavens.

Nice timing, if I believed in omens.

Which I didn't.

The only thing I wished upon that star was that Luce had been out here with me to see it.

Less than a month, I reflected.

I was getting married. To Luce.

We could watch shooting stars together for the rest of our lives.

"Wow," I whispered.

"Why are you surprised?" Alan asked. "We've had this conversation before, plenty of times, in fact."

I dragged my thoughts back from my starry-eyed anticipation of my upcoming nuptials and returned my attention to the man who was blazing his way to matrimonial bliss ahead of me.

Although blazing was probably, at the moment, overstating the case. Based on his banged-up knee and how it got that way, not to mention his bride's threats to kill him, I'd say Alan's trajectory into wedded nirvana was more like an uphill hobble.

"I'm sorry. What were we talking about?" I asked Alan.

"We were talking about Joe."

"Right. I knew that," I said. "By the way, Julie told us you're not his father."

"That's what she told me, too."

"You don't believe it."

"I don't know what to believe."

"Joe says you are."

It was Alan's turn to get lost in space. He sat silently, his eyes fixed on the night sky.

"Why would he say that?" he finally said. "Because it's true? Or because he wants it to be true?"

He let out another big sigh and shifted in his chair.

"He's twelve years old and never met his dad. He's not stupid, Bob. He knows when Julie and I were in Seattle. He can count," he said.

Me and Joe, I thought. Counters unite.

"Even if Julie told him I'm not his father, why wouldn't he wonder? Look at the two of us—we have more than enough physical resemblance to be related." He studied his knee brace. "If I were in his shoes, I know I'd wonder. The fact that he thinks it's possible . . . maybe that means that Julie's never told him who his father is. And why hasn't she done that?"

I thought about the interactions I'd witnessed earlier between Julie and her son.

Both of them seemed well-attuned to each other, and when Luce had expressed her concern for Joe's safety, Julie had all but bared the fangs of a mother tiger in reply. The woman was protective of her child, and I had no doubt that their bond was the organizing principle in her life. I'd seen the same dynamics taking shape in my office with pregnant students—once the decision was made to keep the baby, it seemed to jumpstart the teenaged mother's sense of responsibility. Years later, those same moms would come back to visit me, in between working a job and going to college, to tell me how their kids meant the world to them. Those young women never said the juggling was easy, but they did say it was worth it.

I saw that same conviction in Julie Burrow's face every time she looked at her son. Joe might have been all the family she had, but he was all the family she needed.

"Maybe, because that way, no one else can claim Joe," I quietly observed. "He's all Julie's. Alan, when Luce asked Julie point-blank if you were Joe's father, she denied it. But she also said she wished you were. I got the feeling there was something she wasn't saying."

"Hindsight? Could Joe be my son, and she's regretting never telling me?" Alan combed his hand through his long dark hair and winced, then leveled his gaze at me.

"We both know there's a world of difference between biologically fathering a child and fathering a child day in and day out. So are you thinking that maybe I am his genetic progenitor, but when she says I'm not his father, she's using the term non-genetically?"

Alan shook his head.

"I don't know, Bob. That's splitting pretty fine hairs if you ask me. Maybe she's just wishing things were different . . . that Joe really was my son, biologically or otherwise. Given her current situation, I can see where she might be concerned about Joe's welfare and his vulnerability—especially if she's feeling a threat to her personal safety."

"Speaking of which," I interrupted him, "how deep in this . . . project . . . of Julie's are you? Or, more to the point, why are you in it at all?"

Alan shifted in his chair and winced again. He didn't say anything.

I waited.

And waited.

It's one of those counseling tricks—you wait long enough, and counselees can't stand it, so they have to talk. Like a staring contest. The first one to blink loses.

Unfortunately, I knew that Alan was really good at this game. Over the years, I've learned that he could make me wait for hours before he'd start talking. It was that damn competitive streak of his. The Hawk loved to win.

I blinked. "Do you think you could get around to it sometime tonight, Alan?"

"I'm just trying to decide where to start," he said.

I waited some more.

"Okay," he said. "I'm ready. She asked."

I waited again.

He didn't say anything.

"That's it? 'She asked?' You've got to give me more than that, Alan. Come on. Try. Try real hard."

He settled his gaze on my face.

"Bob, she needs help. This could be her big break, her big story, and right now, she has no one else she can trust to not steal the story. She's done her homework, she's so close to putting it all together, and she just needed someone to help her locate the cave. I didn't think it would be a big deal to go out and find it. I certainly didn't expect to end up injured."

"You mean attacked."

Alan shook his head.

"We don't know that for a fact. Julie has always had a flair for the dramatic, Bob. It makes better copy. When you climb around rock faces, slides can be part of the package."

"What about the broken window, the slashed tires, the hate-mail?"

For a moment, the night stopped breathing.

"What?" Alan could barely get the word out.

"The stuff that's been going on with Julie," I told him.

Stuff she apparently hadn't mentioned, judging from Alan's reaction.

"Tell me you're joking," he said, his voice dangerously low.

"Sorry."

Alan's temper flared and he raised his hand to slap the table, but instead, he lowered it slowly to the wrought-iron top, a long sigh of frustration accompanying his gesture.

"Damn," he said. "I'm starting to see a really disturbing pattern here."

He looked me in the eye.

"That woman only tells you what she wants you to hear. Control. Julie to a T. So what else has she not told me? Or rather, admitted?"

I didn't have to be psychic to guess where this train of thought was headed.

Joe.

I also had the feeling that Joe was a big part of the reason Alan had agreed to help Julie in the first place.

"You don't want to let him down, do you?" I guessed. "Whether or not you're his father."

Alan drummed his fingers on the top of the table and avoided looking at me.

"Can everyone read my mind tonight?" he asked. "First Lily, and now you."

"Yes, Alan, everyone can read your mind," I agreed with him. "Your head is just a big glass case, and we can all see right through it. Let me read what it says right now: *I am a sucker for responsibility, just like my wife.*"

Even as I said it, I realized it was true, and I couldn't believe I hadn't recognized this similarity in them before now.

Alan and Lily were both gluttons for responsibility.

For Lily, it was her business that she had built from the ground up. Until Alan came into her life, Lily lived and breathed Lily's Landscaping. The fact that she willingly left the shop in the hands of her employees while she accompanied Alan to Flagstaff had shocked everyone in the family. For the first time in her life, Lily was handing over responsibility. Not a lot, but it was a start. And if Lily recognized that same sense of duty in Alan, then she'd have to cut him some slack for today's fiasco, knowing it was a result—at least partially—of his own obsession with responsibility.

Took one to know one, right? I suddenly felt a whole lot better about their tying the matrimonial knot. Alan and Lily had each other's numbers, big-time.

Besides, if she was still speaking to him tonight after everything that had happened today, this marriage had a better than fighting chance. And Lily—as far as I knew—had never been one to back down from a fight.

Just like Alan.

My new brother-in-law rubbed his hand across the immobilizer secured around his knee.

"This changes things," he said. "If Julie's investigation is putting her at risk, she needs the police in on it."

"She won't do it," I said.

I repeated to him the conversation Luce and I had had with Julie at her house while he was still in the emergency room.

"She says she doesn't want to wreck the credibility she's worked so hard for all these years as a journalist by exposing her past. She's convinced the police won't give her the time of day, let alone help her dig up a body, if she says she was a witness who just now wants to report a crime that happened twenty years ago," I explained. "And she seems to think that she can keep Joe out of the whole thing."

"She's a fool, then."

He pointed to his damaged knee.

"This is the risk I took and didn't even know it. If she's right about someone starting that rockslide, then the risk was even greater. Someone's willing to hurt her, maybe worse. If the window and mail are part of this, whoever it is knows where she lives, and if she thinks that means Joe is safe, she's crazy."

Alan pushed himself to his feet and grabbed his crutches.

"I'm calling her right now. She's got to stop."

He was halfway across the patio before he reconsidered. He stopped where he was and turned around to face me.

"This isn't going to work, is it? Even if she tells me she's finished with it, how can I be sure she's telling me the truth?"

"I don't know, Alan," I said. "Her batting average for honesty isn't looking too good right now."

He leaned heavily on his crutches, staring at the flagstone beneath his feet. The moonless night was quiet and the air cool. Under any other circumstances, I would be enjoying the Arizona evening, looking forward to a morning of birding the next day. But I knew what Alan was thinking about, because I was turning the same thing over in my own mind.

Who was going to keep Joe safe while his mother dug up a murder?

The answer was obvious: the man who wondered if Joe was his son.

Alan.

"In your professional opinion, Bob, do you think that Julie might be using me?"

Alan's question was slowly, carefully phrased.

"Could she be deliberately letting me ponder the possibility that I might be Joe's father, despite her denial, to ensure that he has someone to look after him in case she . . . isn't around?"

I rubbed my hand over my chin. The morning's stubble had thickened. Was it only this morning that I was standing in the open prairie at Red Rock and Jeffers?

"Anything's possible, Alan."

Especially since I'd had the same suspicion myself.

"That's what I'm afraid of, Bob."

He straightened up then and took a deep breath.

"But I'm not willing to bet that I'm right, and call her on it by just walking away. Besides, whether I'm right or wrong, Joe is still the one without a safety net. Mine or not, I can't abandon a kid in trouble, Bob."

I had a feeling that was exactly what Julie was hoping. Whatever else she did or didn't know about Alan Thunderhawk, she had him pegged when it came to responsibility.

"So what are you going to do?"

"Try to find out who's stalking Julie, for one thing. She has some ideas who it might be, and I can help her run down her leads."

He looked down at his wrapped knee.

"Okay, maybe not run, exactly. But two of us can work faster than she can alone. Then maybe she can get some protection for both herself and Joe and get the police involved. The second thing is to locate Walking Eagle's body. She thought we just about had the right spot yesterday before the rockslide."

"Julie said something about a cleft in the rock," I said.

"That's right. That's where we were heading. I didn't think she should go alone so late in the day, so I went with her. Not that it helped."

"You couldn't know there was going to be a slide," I reminded him.

"No, I couldn't. And we don't know for a fact that it was set off by someone, either. But it's beginning to sound like a real possibility. If that's the case, it sure would have been nice if Julie had told me about the harassment before we went to the Ridge," he said. "Maybe I would have taken some precautions. Maybe I wouldn't have gone."

"You know what they say about hindsight."

"Yeah, I know." Alan studied his injured leg. "It's twenty-twenty. I'm not going to make that mistake twice, Bob. Now I'm forewarned. And I need you to do something for me."

I knew it. I didn't think he'd limped out for the night air.

"I want Lily out of here," Alan said. "I want her safe at home. I'm not taking any chances with her, Bob. Tomorrow afternoon, when you and Luce get on the plane, I want you to take Lily with you."

"Take me where?"

Alan and I both turned to the patio entrance. Lily was already moving toward Alan, shaking her head.

"You don't get this, do you?" she asked him. "In for a dime, in for a dollar. I'm not going anywhere, sweetie."

"Yes, you are," Alan said. "I want you out of the line of fire. I'm—"

"Hopeless. You are hopeless, Thunderhawk."

Lily planted her hands on his back, trying to shove him towards the nearest chair on the patio.

"You keep thinking you're protecting me by locking me out of your problems. Surprise, cowboy. Your problems are my problems. I embrace your problems. I love your problems."

Lily jammed her shoulder against Alan's six-foot frame and pushed.

"Stubborn little thing, isn't she?" Alan commented.

"Buddy, you don't know the half of it. Yet," I added.

Alan gave up resisting her and swung back to my table. Lily pulled up another chair and sat next to Alan.

"In case you haven't noticed, you're also fairly helpless right now," she pointed out to him. "The last thing I'm going to do is leave you on your own after today's mess. Whatever has to be done, I'm doing it with you."

"Bob, can't you—"

"No, I can't."

If Alan thought I was going to run interference for him with Lily, he did need a brain transplant. But I wasn't quite ready to fly the coop, either.

"You know," I said, "I'd hate to think I'd come all this way and didn't take advantage of some excellent birding. I think Luce and I should stick around for a few days, see what's flying and work on our Arizona bird lists."

And maybe play some back-up to Alan and Lily's efforts with Julie, but I didn't say that part out loud.

I got up from my chair and headed toward the inn's courtyard door.

"Besides, I can't say I'm looking forward to getting back on that airplane too soon. If flying into Flag is any indication of what flying out of Flag is going to be like, I'm more than willing to delay the pleasure. I'll leave the flying around here to the birds, at least for a couple days."

Alan nodded. "Yeah, I thought that flight in was pretty rough, too. I figured this trip could only get better at that point."

He glanced at Lily, then at me.

"Guess I was wrong."

Chapter Six

"In that pine, about thirty feet up."

I had my binoculars trained on the gray-breasted bird that perched near the end of a branch. I'd heard a bird call a piping note from the stand of trees and focused my attention on the pine, trying to locate the bird. Now that I had it in my sights, it was an easy identification. Its notched tail and distinctive white eye ring could only belong to a Townsend's Solitaire, a thrush that occasionally showed up in Minnesota but was native to the western United States.

Beside me, Luce caught it in her binos.

"I see it," she said. "I can just make out those little dashes of rust color on the wings. I guess it does sort of look like a short-billed mockingbird. Although, in this light, its back almost looks silver."

It was before seven in the morning, yet the sun was already blindingly bright in the Arboretum at Flagstaff. It had taken me a few moments to be sure I'd even seen the bird amidst the tree needles, since the sun reflected off the bird's feathers at just the right angle to make it barely visible. Unlike the bright blue Stellar's Jay, which we'd been finding around every bend in the trail out from the Visitor's Center, the Solitaire presented a challenge for birders. Not only did it lack the Jay's attention-getting color, but one had to be listening very carefully to catch its single-note call. The fact that I'd been able to separate the Solitaire's call from the raucous noise of the Jay was more a result of luck than skill, since I had little experience with Arizona birds.

Then again, birders only develop skills through practice, and luck was always a birder's best friend.

Based on what we'd seen in the last thirty minutes, luck was definitely in residence at the Arboretum this morning, along with a fine assortment of Arizona birds.

We'd seen two dark morph Red-tailed Hawks, numerous Dark-eyed Juncos, a Spotted Towhee, a Sage Thrasher, a Bullock's Oriole, Mountain Bluebirds, and a Black-headed Grosbeak. Ahead of us, the nature trail opened into a clearing bounded on one side by a grove of tall aspens—a good habitat for Western Tanagers. Sure enough, near the tops of the trees, two of them were flitting through the leaves, catching insect breakfasts and showing off their brilliant red heads. I watched them fly, their yellow bodies darting in and out of the branches. It was like being in a postcard: blue skies, mountains for a dramatic backdrop, shimmery aspen, and colorful birds.

Wish you were here.

Except that was the reason we had come here in the first place—because Lily wished we were there.

Because Alan wasn't.

Now Alan was there again, and so were we, and it looked like that was not going to change in the next day or so, because Lily and Alan were planning to go on a scavenger hunt—a scavenger hunt for the person harassing Julie Burrows.

Oh, and did I mention the other scavenger hunt they were planning? The one to find a twenty-year-old corpse?

Never let it be said that my sister and her husband didn't know how to have fun.

So much fun it could—possibly—kill you.

And Luce and I were probably going to tag along for the ride.

"Look!" Luce said, pointing at a blur skittering across the large clearing that opened out from the aspens.

I watched the blur suddenly hover like a tiny helicopter, then dive through the grasses for a morning snack.

"American Kestrel."

"Yup," Luce said. "Those blue wings and the mustache give it away every time. It's sort of weird to think we saw the same bird yesterday morning half-way across the country. Well, not the same individual, but the same species. We could start a new birding list, Bobby. 'Birds that follow us around the country.'"

"While we bail out Alan," I added. "I bet no one else has a list like that. Gee, I wish I didn't have a list like that."

I watched the little raptor return to the sky and resume its hunt.

"This should be good territory for kestrels," I reminded Luce. "They like updrafts to help them hover when they hunt, and with the San Francisco Peaks just outside of town here, I bet they get a steady stream of wind."

I remembered yesterday's descent into Flagstaff.

"Good for kestrels. Not good for me."

Luce laughed. "When we go home, we'll drive to Phoenix to catch a plane. Okay?"

I reached out and snagged her into my arms.

"I knew there was a reason I wanted to marry you. You always know exactly how to make me happy, and nothing will make me happier than not getting on a plane in Flagstaff."

I kissed her loudly and then released her.

Above us, the sharp little falcon hovered and dove two more times. American Kestrels were the most common falcon in North America. Sometimes people called it a Sparrow Hawk, because in cooler climes, it often took sparrow-sized birds as prey. Here in the open country around Flagstaff, I expected it fed mostly on insects and rodents.

"I wonder when the raptor handlers get here," Luce said.

We'd checked the day's schedule at the Arboretum's Visitor's Center when we arrived. The raptor demonstration was slated for mid-morning. But a moment later, another falcon sliced through the air. This one, however, was huge and almost pure white.

"A Gyrfalcon," Luce breathed.

It was, indeed. Broad-winged and broad-chested, the Gyr was an avian muscle missile with a four-foot wingspan, and the bird we'd just seen streak over us was unbelievably fast for its size. In fact, in level flight, the Gyrfalcon was the fastest bird, beating out even the smaller Peregrine Falcon, which topped two hundred miles per hour when it made those rocketlike dives called stoops. Yet it was not only the Gyr's speed that endeared it to countless kings in the Middle Ages for the sport of hunting; the big falcon's stamina and strength allowed it to literally chase its prey into fatal exhaustion, at which point it swooped in for the kill with its powerful feet and bill to finish off the victim.

So if you were a rabbit, you'd probably not enjoy looking up and seeing a Gyrfalcon coming your way.

I, on the other hand, enjoyed it immensely.

The last time I'd seen a Gyrfalcon, it had been near the Minnesota-Canadian border in March, which made sense considering that this particular falcon made its home in the tundra regions of the arctic and subarctic. That was also why spotting the bird yesterday in southern Minnesota would have given me a state record. Seeing it today in an Arizona sky, far from its icy range in the north, could only mean one thing.

Like us, the Gyr was a visitor, and not a native.

"I think the raptors have landed, Luce."

We followed the trail back to the Visitor's Center. Two vans were parked in front. They both had *Blue Sky Raptors* emblazoned across the side panels. A muscular young man was lifting a hooded cage out of the back of one of the vans. Behind him, an older woman with short brown hair was holding heavy leather gloves and a metal bucket.

"Who's hiding behind Door Number One?" I asked, nodding toward the cage.

The woman smiled. "That's Britta," she said, "our Harris Hawk."

She spoke briefly to the young man, directing him to take the cage around the side of the building. Then she turned back to me.

"Are you here for the show? Because if you are, I'm afraid you've got a little wait ahead of you. We don't start till ten o'clock. We just thought it was such a beautiful morning, that we'd come out early and work with the birds for a while before the demonstration."

"We came out for early birding," Luce told her. "We're visiting from Minnesota."

"I'm Suzie McDaniels," the handler said, putting down the bucket and gloves to shake our hands. "I run *Blue Sky*."

"Bob White and Luce Nilsson," I told her. "Do you mind if we watch you work with the birds?"

"Not at all," she said. "Are you very familiar with raptors?"

"We've seen a few," I said.

I caught Luce rolling her eyes at me.

"Actually, we've seen a lot," I amended. "I've been birding since I was a kid, and I've got a special place in my heart for Bald Eagles. But we just saw a Gyrfalcon fly by. A real beauty. I assume he's yours?"

"Not really mine," Suzie said. "But one of the Blue Sky Raptors, yes. I do rehab with the birds that we receive and help train them for our demos. Khan, the Gyr you saw, belongs to Bill Warner, one of our docents. Of course, Khan isn't a native bird, but we still include him in our program just so people can see him. He's just so impressive."

"So you work with mostly local birds," Luce noted.

Suzie pulled a small cooler out of the van and set it on the ground next to the metal bucket.

"We do," she agreed, "though we field a lot of calls about all kinds of wildlife. Last week, we had a woman call us who was upset because she kept putting a baby squirrel back up in its nest, but the mother kept pushing it back out."

"So she called you?"

"She did," Suzie said. "We occasionally run commercials on the local radio stations to encourage people to care properly for wildlife, and I guess she figured if anyone could help her out with the baby squirrel, it would be us."

"What happened?" I asked.

"We told her to bring the baby in, and we'd check it over to see what the problem was," Suzie said. "So she did, and we found out the problem right away."

I could see she was trying not to laugh.

"It wasn't a baby squirrel. It was a baby bunny."

"You have got to be kidding," Luce said, laughing. "She couldn't tell a bunny from a squirrel?"

"You'd be amazed how little some people know about wildlife," Suzie said. "In our ads, we tell them to call before they do anything in hopes we can prevent them from making a mistake when they think they're doing the right thing."

"Like with thinking a Killdeer parent is injured when it flops around on the ground away from its nest," I said. "I've heard from rehab folks back home that it's a common misperception. The parent looks incapacitated, so out of concern for the babies, someone takes them home to be sure they get care."

"Oh, yeah," Suzie said. "We've had those calls. People don't realize the adult Killdeer is faking injury to lead the person away from the nest, and instead, they go to 'rescue' the babies. It's one of the reasons wildlife rehabilitation programs are so important for communities—they provide a lot of education about the natural world. It's a shame to think we've become so disconnected from our natural environment that someone could do harm when they think they're doing good, but it happens all the time, I'm afraid."

"I'm going to post pictures of bunnies and baby squirrels on my Facebook page," Luce laughed, "and point out the differences. Consider it my small contribution to wildlife education."

"Every bit helps," Suzie said.

I pointed to the cooler.

"You need help with that?"

"Sure," Suzie said. "I'll show you where we're going."

I picked up the cooler and followed her lead.

"You sound like you've been doing this for a while," I commented.

"That's because I have been doing it for a while," Suzie replied. "Twenty years, as a matter of fact, come December. I started Blue Sky with two eaglets after their parents were killed by a poacher dealing in the illegal feather trade. These days, we rehabilitate probably fifteen to twenty birds a year to release back into the wild, but we've got twelve birds on staff that work in our community education programs."

"I heard that the clinic at the Raptor Center at the University of Minnesota treats 700 raptors a year," I recalled.

"No doubt," Suzie said. "They've got a world-class facility. I know they train veterinarians from around the world in avian medicine and surgery. We're just a tiny outfit here in Flagstaff, but we keep plenty busy with the raptors we get."

We rounded the side of the Visitor Center and headed toward a high country prairie restoration area. Open and level, the meadow gave the birds lots of room to maneuver without crowding each other. As we approached, a Barn Owl swept silently over our heads, homing in on the meaty tidbit held aloft in its handler's fingers. Some ten yards away, we saw the Gyr, sitting majestically on the leather-clad fist of a stocky, elderly man. Completing the crew was another woman and the muscular young man we'd seen unloading the hawk. Nearby were three more covered cages, in addition to Britta's.

Luce followed Suzie to take a look at the other birds, while I walked over to the Gyr and its handler.

"Beautiful bird," I said, stopping a couple of yards away from the man.

"You can come closer. He won't bite. Actually, he won't move at all unless I tell him to."

With a slight twist of his wrist, he released the bird and it went flying across the meadow.

The man extended his hand. "I'm Bill Warner."

"Bob White."

"Are you a falconer?"

I shook my head.

"A birder. I live in Minnesota. I'm just in town for a visit. Thought I'd try to add some Arizona birds to my life list while I'm here."

"Well, this is a great place to do that," Warner said. "Not only does the Arboretum here attract a wide variety of species, but we've got a whole host of other habitats all within a couple hours' drive. Go just thirty minutes south to Lower Oak Creek and you get the riparian birds. Go a little further and you get a freshwater marsh at Tavasci. Twenty minutes north, you're in the mountains. Go east and you've got desert. You name it, you can find it around Flagstaff."

I smiled at his enthusiasm. "You sound like a travel brochure."

"I am!" he laughed. "I'm Flag's Number One Fan."

He lifted his fist and the white falcon landed, flapping its wings as it settled its talons on the tough leather glove.

"I better be, since I've spent my life promoting this town and building it up," he said. "I was the Chamber of Commerce director for fifteen years, and before that, I practically bankrolled this town as the CEO and owner of Flagstaff Savings. I've even got a building downtown named after me."

A little alarm began beeping in my head.

Here we go again, I thought. A total stranger was revving up to tell me his life story.

My "fight or flight" response began to kick in, but, as usual, I squelched it, reminding myself that some people just need to talk, and if I could offer a sympathetic ear, then I was doing a good thing.

Whether that made me a sucker or just a nice guy, I hadn't figured out yet. All I knew was that in my line of work, listening was important.

Besides, I got paid for it.

Most of the time.

Today, however, I was off the clock. But I still couldn't make myself walk away even though I could see another life story coming straight at me.

Not that I was surprised, since this seems to happen to me on a regular basis. I swore that I had a "tell me your life story" sign invisibly tattooed on my forehead which became a flashing beacon for everyone I met. Even Julie Burrows, secretive as she was, had shared with me more personal information than anybody had a right to expect on a first meeting.

Or a second.

Or third.

Seriously, I'd been considering getting a tattoo of my own to complement the invisible one, only this time, it was going to read, "Shut up. I don't care."

"'Course, now, I'm retired from the business end of Flag," Warner was explaining.

I'd apparently missed the first part of his monologue.

Thank goodness. I was on vacation, sort of, and I could only take so much of doing a good thing.

"I decided it was time to devote my energies to something more permanent," he said. "Something that's going to last a whole lot longer than me. Give back to the community sort of thing."

He swept his free hand in a wide arc, encompassing the meadow, mountains and sky.

"This. This is going to be my legacy," he announced. "I'm on every conservation, preservation, and nature-loving board there is in Flag. Thanks to Khan. When Khan's owner dumped him, I contacted Blue Sky Raptors to get him rehabbed. Before I knew it, I was hooked on both the birds and the program. One thing led to another, and all of a sudden, I've got a new career in my retirement. My son says it's senility. I like to think of it as a change of heart. Either way, when I see something that needs to happen, I just do what it takes."

He pointed to the Blue Sky logo on his denim shirt.

"I'm one of the regulars, now. Do demos almost every week."

He pulled what looked like a pellet from a small pouch that hung off his belt and fed it to Khan. Then he winked at me.

"But don't think for a minute that I'm out of touch with what's going on in Flag. No sir. Nothing happens in this town that I don't know about."

I didn't doubt it. He seemed to be a fountain of information and proud of it. If the Flagstaff tourist bureau didn't have a live feed on this guy, they were missing out.

"What happened to Khan?" I asked, hoping to hear less about Bill Warner's love affair with Flagstaff and more about his bird.

"He took a bullet in his wing," he told me. "His owner had him flying in a competition over at the preserve near here, and someone took a shot at him. At Khan, not his owner," he clarified.

He stroked a finger down Khan's snowy breast.

"Our guess was that the shooter thought Khan was an eagle, because we still have some problems around here on occasion with people trying to collect eagle feathers for illegal trade. Any idiot can see Khan's a falcon, not an eagle, but no one ever said that poachers were known for their smarts."

"Suzie mentioned that to me," I said. "The feather trade."

"Did she tell you that she used to be involved in it? In a good way, I mean," he added. "She was an undercover cop for the U.S. Fish and Wildlife Service. That's how she ended up in Flag. She was chasing down some poaching ring, but she never cracked it."

Khan gave me a bright-eyed stare.

"What? Do I look like brunch?" I asked the falcon.

Warner laughed. "Anyway, Khan's former owner didn't want a falcon that couldn't compete, so he dumped him."

Warner tilted his wrist again, and Khan sailed away. The raptor flew low over the grasses, then rose slightly before diving down for a catch.

"Did you meet my grandson?" Warner asked. "He's over there with the eagle."

I turned to look back to where Luce was still talking with Suzie. Close by, the young man who'd carried Britta's cage was now holding an immature Golden Eagle on his gloved hand.

"Now that's a killing machine," Warner said.

"The eagle, not my grandson," he told me. "When that baby is all grown up, it could take down a full-size deer if it wanted to. It's an avian apex predator, you know. Not even a big boy like Khan can claim that title."

Actually, I had a soft spot for that particular group of birds, ever since that Bald Eagle was the first bird to make it onto my life list when I was just a little kid. Like any apex predator, the avian ones sat at the top of their respective food chains, which meant that an adult of the species had no natural enemies that would consider it lunch.

In the natural world, that was a handy spot to hold, since it meant you can sleep at night without suddenly finding yourself clenched between somebody else's jaws. Humans were apex predators, too, though I was happy to say I did most of my hunting for meals in the grocery store or in my refrigerator instead of out in the wild. Worst case, I could always pick up some fast food at a local drive-through.

When Golden Eagles thought of fast food, though, they were thinking of plucking a mouse out of a field at about 200 miles per hour, which was almost as fast as the Peregrine Falcon's dive.

Except that a Peregrine Falcon was a much smaller divebomber to be heading your way than a Golden Eagle. I had friends at the National Eagle Center in Wabasha, Minnesota, who said that a diving Golden Eagle could sound like a low-flying airplane coming straight at you. If I were the mouse, I think I'd be dead of a panic attack long before the eagle's talons hit.

Small consolation.

"Unfortunately, Golden Eagles are beginning to see some population losses here in the west," Warner said, clearly oblivious to my wandering attention. "My grandson loves those birds, and he's making it his personal mission to insure that the eagles we do have get all the help they need to thrive again."

Aware that I should make some kind of response, I latched onto his last remark about his grandson.

"You sound pretty proud of him," I noted.

"I am, and I've got reason to be," he replied. "Not only is he standing up for something he believes in, but he's a good man, too.

He'd like to join the Fish and Wildlife Service himself and track down poachers. I don't know if I can see him disguising himself the way Suzie did for undercover work, though—she said she pretended to be a gang member's girlfriend once—but you never know."

Khan was back, settling onto his owner's fist. With one hand, Warner hooded the big falcon and started toward his grandson.

"You know, Bob, when you get as old as I am—eighty-one next month—you spend a fair amount of time remembering the past. You think about the mistakes you made. You think about the good things you did. And you realize that even though those things happened a long time ago, they're still alive in some way today, for better or worse. They still have an effect on what's happening right now."

"You sound like one of my ecology professors from undergrad," I commented. "Do you lecture at the university here?"

"Heck, no. I just lecture on the wing, like this," he said, tossing me another wink. "It's a whole lot more satisfying than sitting in a classroom, that's for sure. And out here, I can say whatever I want. I can brag about my grandson and all the ways he's just like me. I can talk about the lessons of the past and how we can make the future better, even if I'm not going to be around to see it. Today is what we've got, Bob, and we need to make the most of it for tomorrow."

Warner stopped walking and started laughing.

"Maybe I am senile," he said. "Here I am, doing philosophy on the prairie. You must think I'm an old fool."

I assured him I didn't.

The truth was, I wasn't thinking about him at all.

I was thinking about Alan.

About past events that played into the present.

About Julie.

About Joe.

About a murder twenty years ago that was now the reason I was in Flagstaff today.

Warner slipped Khan into one of the covered cages, then introduced me to his grandson, Gil.

"Where did this beauty come from?" I asked, nodding at the eagle on Gil's arm.

"We found him abandoned in the nest," the younger Warner said. "Our assumption is that someone shot or trapped the parents. Suzie and I had been monitoring the site as part of a study we're doing on local eagle population breeding, and then one day, the parents didn't return. There's still some illegal hunting around here, and eagles are mighty big targets, unfortunately. The Zunis used to keep Golden Eagles for their religious ceremonies—did you know that? They'd go out and trap them and take them back home. We don't have a Zuni community around here, so I doubt that was what happened to this bird's parents, but you never know. Blue Sky took custody of the eaglet, and we've been caring for him ever since."

He stroked the bird's golden wings.

"But we're getting ready to release him into the wild. Time for Walking Eagle to fly home."

Walking Eagle.

Wasn't that the same name as Julie's friend?

The one she was trying to . . . locate?

Ron Walking Eagle. That was the name. I was sure of it.

And Gil Warner had a bird with that name.

I was speechless. No, I was thought-less.

It couldn't be.

Could it?

Yes, I told myself, it was true: I was thought-less. There couldn't possibly be a connection here with Julie's missing murder victim from twenty years ago. Gil's Walking Eagle was a bird. Julie's Walking Eagle was a corpse.

And I was a walking idiot.

"Why is he called Walking Eagle?" Luce asked. She obviously was not experiencing the brain cell short-circuit I was.

Gil lifted his arm.

"Fly, baby," he commanded the eagle.

The eagle spread his enormous golden wings and . . . hopped down to the ground.

"That's why," the young man said. "He'd rather walk than fly. We've been having a heck of a time getting him to take to the air. We don't know why, but it probably has something to do with his imprinting on us, his handlers, instead of on other birds. I usually have to model the behavior for him before he gets the motivation to go airborne."

Luce looked from the grounded eagle to Gil.

"How do you do that?"

"I run a lot," Gil explained, a smile spreading across his sun-browned face. "Flap my arms. Look like a crazy man. But it seems to help. We've got him doing some short flights now."

"We had him flying around the Ridge a little bit yesterday," the elder Warner added. "There are some good elevations there for launching him. He seems to be getting the feel for riding thermals, too, so we're hopeful he's real close to being ready for release back into the wild."

"The Ridge?" I asked.

My brain had finally come back on line.

"It's a public preserve just south of Flagstaff, near Walnut Canyon National Monument," Warner said. "The Ridge is primarily high plateau meadow with pine forest, but it's got some cliffs and caves. Walnut Canyon, on the other hand, has a four-hundred-foot-deep canyon, with cliff dwellings that were inhabited by the Sinagua Indians some eight hundred years ago. Sixty million years ago—"

"I've heard about it," I interrupted, remembering Warner's earlier claim to fame: he was Flag's Number One Fan and a former director of the Chamber of Commerce. No doubt he could tell me everything and more about Walnut Canyon, but at the moment, the canyon's ancient history wasn't nearly as intriguing for me as the most recent past of the preserve nearby.

Recent, as in yesterday.

Since the elderly fellow had also said that nothing happened in Flagstaff that he didn't know about, I decided to give him a pop quiz.

"I heard that there was a rockslide at the Ridge yesterday."

Both Warner and his grandson turned their attention to me.

"I heard that too," Warner replied. He shook his head. "Very unusual. The few cliff trails there are well-marked and well-maintained. My guess is that some curious tourists went off-trail and found some loose footing."

"It doesn't surprise me," Gil said. "I've walked just about every inch of the Ridge, and there are lots of places that I think could get tricky if you didn't have a guide. Late in the day, you get shadows in the rock faces, and they can really mess up your depth perception. A fall down those cliffs would be pretty scary, unless you've got wings."

He made a soft rumbling noise in his throat, and Walking Eagle leapt back up onto his keeper's wrist.

"You should go to the Ridge with us," Warner said, inviting Luce and me. He turned to Gil. "Aren't we planning on doing some flying lessons there this afternoon?"

Gil nodded. "That's the plan, Granddad."

"I can't promise, but there's a chance we might see a wild eagle or two out there," Warner offered. "And I saw on our local bird postings that a Scott's Oriole was spotted in Walnut Canyon yesterday. Maybe it'll swing by the Ridge."

I glanced at Luce, swearing that I could almost hear her thoughts. We could see the Ridge. Maybe see some eagles. Score a Scott's Oriole, a bird neither of us had ever seen, a prize for our life lists.

Hunt for corpses.

Oh, boy.

"We're in," I told the two Warners. "Where do we meet?"

Chapter Seven

I parked Lily's rental car in a tiny space on the street around the corner from a little bistro called Brix in downtown historic Flagstaff. When Luce and I had left the hotel that morning to go out to the Arboretum, my sister had given me detailed directions to the restaurant, along with explicit instructions to be there at noon sharp for lunch. I checked my watch.

Eleven fifty-seven.

"If Lily's happy, everyone's happy," I told Luce, pulling her down the sidewalk after me.

"So I guess that explains why nobody was happy last night," she said. "I don't know if I've ever seen Lily more upset than when we got back to the hotel."

I held open the bistro's door for her, and a wave of cool air washed out over me. After our morning in the sun at the Arboretum, the coolness was a welcome reprieve from the August heat of northwestern Arizona.

"Yeah," I said. "I guess finding out that your spouse almost got himself killed while he was out searching in a cliff for a dead body with a former lover would do that to you."

Luce punched me playfully in the shoulder as she passed through the doorway.

"You're so sensitive, Bobby. I love the way you sugarcoat things. No wonder Lily likes to kick you."

I followed her into the restaurant and spotted Lily and Alan at a round table near the front window.

They weren't alone.

Julie was sitting next to Alan, with an older fellow on her other side. I pulled out a seat for Luce beside Lily, while Alan made introductions.

"Bob and Luce, this is Charles Corwin. He's an adjunct professor at NAU, and he's teaching at the conference with me."

We did a round of hellos and hand-shaking and sat down.

"Perhaps more to the point, Charles has been helping me with my research," Julie said.

That's why his name sounded vaguely familiar to me, I realized. I'd picked up his book at Julie's house last night.

"You're a political science professor?" I asked the man.

He pushed his heavy glasses a notch higher on his Roman nose, his completely bald head shining with the light pouring in through the bistro's big window.

"Actually, no," Corwin said. "I teach journalism. It's my second career. I was an editor in Phoenix until I retired two years ago. The newspaper business just isn't what it used to be when I was a young, hungry reporter determined to expose graft and corruption, and become a legend in my own time. These days, by the time you see anything in print, it's not even yesterday's news—it's virtually history."

"What he's not telling you, though, is that he's one of the most talented investigative journalists in the state," Julie said. "And he thoroughly researched the battle between Ron Walking Eagle and the local council about the designation of the Ridge as a public preserve. It's a case study in his book, *The Politics of Preservation*."

Corwin brushed Julie's compliment aside.

"Thank you, but you give me too much credit," he told her. "Every reporter knows he's only as good as his sources."

Out of the corner of my eye, I noticed Alan shifting his weight in his chair and wincing.

"How's the leg today, Hawk?" I asked.

"Banged up. I'm not registering for any marathons, that's for sure. This afternoon is my last seminar, though, so I think I'll survive."

He put his arm around Lily and pulled her close.

"And then I plan to spend the evening with my icepack."

Lily threw him a deadly look, and Alan laughed.

"An icepack on my knee, sweetheart," he told her.

"You know, Lily, you may have missed your chance last night, after all. You probably should have killed him then," Julie suggested, smiling at my sister.

Lily smiled back.

"I'm not worried. I'm sure he'll give me many, many opportunities in the years to come."

Interesting.

Sometime between last night and lunch, Lily and Julie had become buddies.

I guess I had expected some kind of rivalry, seeing as Alan was the thing they had in common, but from the tone of their repartee, it sounded more like they'd joined forces. Hopefully, they were working together with Alan, and not against him, but that remained to be seen. I, myself, had learned long ago not to underestimate my sister's skill at scheming. Recalling Alan's comments last night about Julie's control issues, I shuddered to think what the two women might put Alan through if they put their minds to it.

Watching them interact, I marveled again at how alike my sister and Julie were. Not only did their personalities seem eerily similar, but sitting here at the table, they could almost pass for sisters, their auburn heads and shared facial features making the physical resemblance impossible to ignore. For a moment, I wondered what it would have been like to have grown up with two older sisters. Would one of them have sheltered me from the other, or would I just have twice as many bruised knees?

Judging from the way they were talking about Alan, I guessed the latter.

I was suddenly really glad I was sitting across the table from both Lily and Julie, well out of either's kicking range.

We all ordered lunch, although the waiter had to practically tear the menu from Luce's hand as she tried to memorize the ingredients listed in each entrée. The restaurant had a reputation for creative cooking with local organic foods, and I could see Luce beginning to salivate over the recipes she was already concocting in her head to try out in her kitchen back home. Realizing that she was going to be mentally absent from the table conversation for the next few minutes or so, I turned to the professor seated beside me.

"I haven't read your book," I said to Corwin as we waited for the waiter to return with our drinks. "But I'm guessing that you've provided Julie with some ideas about who in town might not appreciate her reviving the story about Ron Walking Eagle?"

He nodded as he dug in his jacket pocket and then raised a small inhaler to his lips and took a quick hit of the medication.

"Asthma," he explained. "The high altitude in Flagstaff always gives me a hard time."

He returned the inhaler to his pocket and pulled his jacket lapels closer over his chest, as if to ward off some of the restaurant's air-conditioned coolness.

I, on the other hand, was luxuriating in the respite from the late morning's heat. I'd noticed that the clouds were building over the San Francisco Peaks just beyond Flagstaff before we'd entered the restaurant, so I was hoping that the daily thunderstorm would make its appearance before Luce and I drove out to the Ridge. Birding in the rain was no fun, no matter where you were, and I'd heard from today's student concierge—Elvira had, unsurprisingly, disappeared before dawn—at the inn this morning that the daily rain could be a gully-washer.

"Yes, I've been able to help her out a bit," the professor replied. "She's got marvelous instincts for a reporter, and she's certainly tenacious. I have to say, she reminds me of myself when I was just starting out, when I thought good journalism could change the world, right wrongs, and all that blissful naiveté."

For a moment or two, his eyes seemed to lose focus, as if he were pondering other thoughts before he continued.

"If she can prove that Walking Eagle was murdered," he resumed, "then she's going to do more than rewrite an old story here in Flagstaff. I predict she'll be able to write her own ticket in the field of investigative journalism, which would be a wonderful thing for both her and her son."

His use of the word "if" caught my attention.

"I take it you don't believe that Walking Eagle was killed?"

"That's not what I said, Mr. White," he pointed out. "I said if she can *prove* he was murdered, not *if* he was murdered. Besides, what I believe is immaterial in this case. What counts are the facts that Julie can produce and the way in which they are presented."

I narrowed my eyes in mock suspicion. "Are you a lawyer?"

Corwin chuckled. "No. I'm just older and wiser and a lot more cynical than I used to be."

He tipped his head in Julie's direction.

"Unlike Julie. Julie wants the truth, no matter how it's represented. Or who it might damage."

"And that's why someone's targeting her," I said. "Her research is threatening to someone. Why would that be, professor?"

He smiled, the blue veins of his temples standing out in contrast to his white skin. I had the impression he was pleased with my interest in Julie's project.

"Because despite its big spaces, parts of Arizona are still very much like any small town in that gossip flies and reputations suffer," he said, "and pride is both a sin and a virtue, depending on whose eyes are looking at it. You get someone new in town poking around in old wounds, and those wounds reopen. When Ron Walking Eagle accused the city leaders of prioritizing tourism over cultural sensitivity to the local Native Americans, he split the town in two, and some of those bad feelings take a lot longer than twenty years to heal."

He pulled a small bottle of pills from his pocket and tapped two out into his palm. He caught me watching him as he tossed them into his mouth and took a drink from his water glass.

"Headaches," he told me. "Too much staring at fine print for the last thirty years. It's an occupational hazard."

Occupational hazards, I understood. Mine had to do with people indiscriminately pouring out their life stories to me, or teenage drama queens setting up court in my cramped little office at the high school.

"In fact, there are some strong parallels between the old Ridge dispute and the current Snowbowl controversy that's been going on for close to nine years now," the professor said.

"The Snowbowl?"

"It's the ski area just outside of town, Bobby," Luce explained, momentarily distracted from her culinary daydream. "Our cabdriver mentioned it yesterday when she drove us to the inn. What's the controversy about?" she asked Corwin.

"Money and religion, basically," he replied. "The Snowbowl sits in the San Francisco Peaks, one of the four sacred mountains for Navajos. Since the area doesn't always get enough snow for good skiing, the resort owners want to make snow, but the original plan called for treated wastewater to be used, which the Navajo Nation contends will both desecrate their sacred lands and potentially cause irreversible environmental damage."

"And this has been going on for how long?" I asked.

"Nine years," the professor repeated. "Between the lawsuits, injunctions and appeals, there were some twenty different groups involved, last I counted. That includes the Sierra Club, the Center for Biological Diversity, and six Native American tribes. I considered using it as an example of how difficult it can be to manage public lands for multiple users, but decided it would take a book of its own to work through that whole mess."

I thought about standing on the quartzite at Jeffers, surrounded by natural beauty and the ancient records of sacred experiences etched in stone, both of them protected and enjoyed by millions of visitors.

"They could take a page from Minnesota's book," I suggested. "The Jeffers Petroglyphs site accommodates both religious tradition and public use."

Corwin shrugged. "I'm not saying it can't be done. It's just almost impossible. And in the Snowbowl case, as often happens in these kinds of disputes, it leaves a lot of people unhappy."

"Which is just what happened with the Ridge dispute," Julie said, joining the conversation. "The reason that Ron Walking Eagle was able to ruffle so many feathers was because he deliberately structured his opposition to the preserve as an issue of Native American religious rights. Everyone agreed that the preserve was a good idea, but he didn't want it available for public use. He wanted it designated as land sacred for the tribes in the area. When the judge finally ruled in favor of the preserve's owner, there were some very angry people in Flag, and not all of them were Native Americans, either."

"What do you mean?" Luce asked.

"It's the same deal as with the Snowbowl dispute: multiple interest groups. A lot of environmental advocates live in Flagstaff," Julie explained, "and back then, they felt the Ridge would be better served by being reserved to Indian usage, but the court didn't see it their way. They felt like they didn't have a voice in the decision and that ticked them off."

"But the land is still a preserve, right?" I asked. "So, what's the problem?"

"It's political, Mr. White," Corwin said. "When you have multiple interest groups all with a different stake in a decision, somebody has to lose. You're from Minnesota, right?"

I nodded.

"Are you telling me that your state's Department of Natural Resources has never made a decision that didn't sting some special interest groups? That everybody agrees with everything they decide?"

Ouch. I was still nursing the lumps I took a year ago when I opposed the DNR's sudden sanctioning of Sandhill Crane hunting. As a fervent proponent of restoring bird populations across the state, I couldn't believe that the DNR would legalize hunting the cranes without so much as a public hearing on the topic.

I wasn't the only one who was furious, either. Birding clubs and naturalists around the state were in an uproar, calling meetings and taking the DNR to task for cloaking its decision-making process in secrecy. Thankfully, no one actually came to blows over the matter—that I know of—but it certainly left a bitter taste in the mouths of most of the members of the Minnesota Ornithologists' Union, myself included.

"I see your point," I agreed.

"Throw in some political hot buttons, like the rights of Native Americans, or bad press for struggling local economies, and you've got a volatile brew," Corwin continued. "It only takes one firebrand to start a brushfire, but the burn marks it leaves can scar a whole lot of people."

"Such as?"

"In this particular case, anyone in Flagstaff who opposed the public use of the land," the professor said, "like the supporters of Walking Eagle and some environmental advocates. A few of them called for boycotts of local tour operators who planned trips to the proposed preserve, which only served to fuel the controversy. Then, it wasn't a big leap for people to start worrying about losing tourist dollars, which could be fatal to a town like Flag that depends on that income stream. By the time Walking Eagle disappeared, he had a good portion of the city up in arms about the preserve."

"It wasn't good for local morale," Luce noted.

"Or for local business," Corwin said. "And money trumps morale, every time."

Julie laid her hand on Corwin's arm and nodded at the restaurant's entrance. Her eyes caught mine and she lowered her voice.

"The man who just walked in—he's my number two suspect for the harassing I've been getting. And he's heading our way."

A moment later, I could feel the man's presence almost directly behind my chair, and not just because everyone at the table was looking at a point above and beyond my right shoulder. The distinct smell of whiskey assaulted my nose, and I turned slightly in my chair to take a look at the newcomer.

"Professor Corwin," the man said, his voice a few decibels above a normal conversational tone. "You're back in town. I take it that one round of embarrassing my father with your book research wasn't enough for you?"

He flicked a glance at Julie, then aimed his comments back at Corwin.

"And do I have you to thank for letting that viper," he pointed at Julie, "loose in town?"

Across the table from me, Alan leaned forward on his elbows and locked his gaze on the inebriated man.

"I don't know what your story is, but you owe an apology to the lady and the professor, mister."

"Who are you?" The man turned his attention to Alan and narrowed his eyes. "Oh, wait a minute. You're that Indian she's got helping her out with her . . . research."

He slurred the last word and made quotation marks in the air with his fingers, obviously insinuating what he thought of Julie's project.

Alan started to rise up out of his seat, bad knee or not, the temper hot in his eyes.

Cripes.

All I wanted was a little lunch, and Alan was primed for a barroom brawl.

I stood up and stepped in front of the guy.

"How about we take a little walk?" I asked him and motioned with my open hand towards the bar on the other side of the brick-lined room. Before he could say a word, I wrapped my arm around his shoulder, turned him in the opposite direction and began steering him away from our table.

It seemed to take a second or two for it to sink in that he was not in control of his forward motion, and when he did realize it, he planted his feet on the polished wood-plank floor and shrugged off my hold.

"Who are you?" he asked, his voice hitting a note somewhere between angry and confused. Judging from the lines in his tanned face, I guessed he was in his fifties. Based on the reaction of recognition from the bartender as we approached, I also assumed the guy was a regular customer at the restaurant.

"Bob White," I told him. "Who are you?"

"I'm Wilson Warner," he said. "What are you doing with those people? They're troublemakers, and we don't need their kind in Flagstaff."

So much for that warm western hospitality that all the other residents of the Gateway to the Grand Canyon seemed to possess in such overwhelming abundance. Mr. Warner here seemed pretty determined to keep the frontier closed and strangers out.

Warner?

"I just met a couple of Warners this morning out at the Arboretum," I told him. "An older gentleman and his grandson. They were handling raptors with the Blue Sky group. Really nice people. Relations of yours?"

Warner focused his bleary eyes on mine, his answer thick with resentment.

"My father and my son. Two peas in a pod. They love those birds. Khan and Walking Eagle." He laughed bitterly. "I couldn't believe it when Gil named that eagle. If he only knew."

"Knew what?"

Warner scrubbed his hand over his face, his eyes closing as his fingers and thumb massaged his temples.

"Look," he said, his eyes still shut, "I'm sorry about . . . your friends."

He dropped his hand from his face and looked me in the eye. "You know that old saying 'let sleeping dogs lie'?"

I nodded. "Yes."

He tipped his head in the direction of our lunch table. "Tell her that."

"Why?"

He looked towards our table, then back to me.

"Because my father went through enough grief when Walking Eagle took him to court about the Ridge."

Then he slipped off the stool and walked out of the restaurant.

Imagine that.

Bill Warner, Flag's Number One Fan, was the man who had owned the Ridge and turned it into a public preserve.

A man, who, according to his son, had suffered greatly for his act of generosity, and apparently wouldn't appreciate Julie's continued investigation into that piece of his life. After my brief encounter with Wilson, I could see why Julie had put him near the top of her list of harassment suspects—the man seemed to be harboring both anger and resentment, not to mention an alcohol-abuse issue, and he clearly wasn't enamored of Julie's project. As soon as I returned to the table, I would be sure to pass along his advice to her.

Wilson Warner, however, hadn't advised *me* to let those sleepy dogs catch a few more winks. Who knew? With a little luck and smooth conversation, maybe I'd find a Scott's Oriole *and* some pertinent information for Julie when I joined Bill Warner for some birding this afternoon.

Ms. Burrows could let the sleeping dogs lie, but I was going to try to kill two birds with one stone.

Ouch.

I sent up a silent plea to all my feathered friends to forgive me for using that old cliché.

But if the shoe fits . . .

I shook my head. I'd heard that Flagstaff's high altitude affected people in different ways, but I hadn't expected to get a case of the clichés.

Then again, I couldn't have predicted how any of this trip was turning out.

Flagstaff, I was discovering, was just full of surprises.

Chapter Eight

When I returned to our table, Alan was still steaming about the younger Warner's words while Julie and Luce carried on a rather animated conversation. Apparently, as soon as Luce had learned the identity of the stranger, she'd shared our morning's adventure with everyone, including our invitation from the elder Warner to join them at the Ridge this afternoon.

"Do you know how long I have been trying to talk to that man?" Julie asked, though she clearly didn't expect us to know the answer.

"Three months, two days, and forty-seven minutes?" I said, taking up the challenge.

I figured that somebody at the table should be polite enough to offer a reply.

Beneath the table, Luce swatted my thigh, and I captured her hand with mine. I gave it a squeeze and threw her a quick smile.

Julie barely paused.

"Ever since Charles published his book last year, I have been hitting my head against the wall of Warner's longtime secretary who is now virtually stone-deaf, his charming son Wilson whom you just had the pleasure of meeting, and the family lawyer, all of whom guard Bill Warner's privacy like he's the head of an international cartel or something."

"Maybe he is," I suggested. "He seems to consider Flagstaff his personal kingdom. Maybe it's only the tip of the iceberg, and he actually owns the western half of the United States. For all we know, he's got the president in his pocket, and a line of senators waiting for his commands."

Next to me, Corwin burst out laughing.

"You've definitely met Bill Warner," he said. "That's exactly the kind of man he fancies himself to be: a power broker extraordinaire. The truth, though, is a little less glamorous."

He took off his glasses for a minute to clean the lenses with his napkin. After replacing them on his nose, he continued.

"Bill Warner made his fortune here in Flagstaff with banking and then by supporting the tourist trade, but I think the extent of his influence ends at the county line. The only time he was in disfavor with the community was during the Ridge dispute. Walking Eagle made him look like a greedy capitalist who cared nothing for the local tribes or a cultural legacy."

"Funny you should use that word," I told the professor. "Just this morning, Bill Warner was telling me about the legacy he wanted to leave, and it was all about conservation and preservation. He sounded pretty passionate about it."

"I'm sure he is," Julie said, then added with emphasis, "*now*. But Charles's book and my research, which includes the court records of the land dispute, show that Bill Warner's interests twenty years ago were at the opposite end of the spectrum. The local bank president didn't want anything to do with reserving land anywhere for the exclusive use of Native Americans. In fact, he downright hated Ron Walking Eagle and everything he stood for."

Our conversation came to an abrupt halt as our waiter arrived with our lunch plates. I caught a whiff of the three-onion tart with oxtail ragout that Luce and I had ordered, and my mouth automatically began watering. Weakened by its aroma, I finally let go of Luce's hand that I'd kept prisoner on my thigh, and she gave me a farewell swat in retribution.

Speaking of retribution . . . I rolled over in my head what Julie had just said about the friendly elderly gentleman we'd met at the Arboretum. I picked up my fork and pointed it in her direction.

"Are you saying that you think Bill Warner murdered Ron Walking Eagle?"

Julie took a sip of her iced tea.

"I think it's possible, yes, given the intense dislike the two men demonstrated for each other during the dispute."

"Dislike is a long way from murder," Alan reminded her, "not to mention the question of whether there was, indeed, a murder committed."

Julie leaned back in her chair and leveled a stern look at him.

"Are we going to go around this particular bush again? I've told you the reasons behind my suspicions, and I thought you agreed with me that they were more than plausible."

"Yes, but—" Alan began to protest, but Julie cut him off.

"Alan, there's something else I haven't told you," she said.

A hush fell over the table as everyone's eyes locked on Julie's.

Oh, great.

Now what?

She was Ron's daughter?

Ron's child bride?

His long-lost sister?

"Someone was after Ron," Julie said. "He told me he was afraid he was going to be arrested or killed. He knew that someone was following his movements because other people told him about it."

"Why would he be arrested?" I asked. "Or killed?"

"I don't know!" Julie's voice was filled with weary frustration. "But he was afraid for his life. Maybe he thought the Warners would drum up some reason to arrest him so he couldn't fight them in court anymore. I remember that Bill Warner barely said a word to the press about the case, and whenever he was on the television news, his lawyer would only say 'no comment.' The people who sided with Ron said awful things about Warner, and it just got so ugly."

Corwin nodded in sympathy.

"Even when I was researching my book all those years later, the Warners were very defensive, and it was like pulling teeth to assemble the research I was looking for," he told the rest of us. "As you may have noticed, Wilson wasn't happy to see me when he showed up here a while ago."

"And that's really why you think Julie's on the right track, professor?" Alan asked. "Because Ron felt threatened?"

"Yes," Corwin said. "I think there's more to the story here than has already been told. Ron felt he was in danger for some reason. Think about it, Alan. You're a history teacher. You know how violence can unexpectedly erupt in civil conflict. Radical activists like Ron Walking Eagle don't simply disappear. And even if they do, it's only for a short time, while they retool and regroup. Then they pop up somewhere else to fight for another cause. But Ron has never resurfaced anywhere."

Sort of like the rock man at Jeffers Petroglyphs, I realized.

Need a break? Pop in and out of your private sanctuary when it suits you. Come back refreshed and recharged to face a new day. The more I thought about it, the better it sounded. After all, wasn't that the reason we had a summer break from school? Wasn't that why I loved to go birding? Even people without a counseling degree knew that getting away from the daily grind once in a while is an important strategy for maintaining mental health and functioning at peak effectiveness.

Unless the getting away was permanent and involuntary.

As in death.

Then the functioning part was pretty much off the table, I'd say.

I took a bite of the tart, and my taste buds broke out in an alleluia chorus. Whoever would have imagined that a pile of onions could be transformed into a melt-in-your-mouth delicacy?

"Maybe someone paid him off," Lily said between bites of her own lunch, "to disappear. Money can be very persuasive, you know. Some problems just go away if you throw enough money at them."

My sister, poster girl for rampant materialism.

"That's true," Alan agreed. "And Warner was the bank president back then, wasn't he, Julie? Who's to say he didn't cut a deal with Walking Eagle to . . . walk? Without a body, you can construct as many scenarios as you want, but you don't have a case for the police."

"And the rock slide yesterday?" Julie challenged him. "You think that was mere chance?"

Alan shifted in his seat. "Pretty coincidental, I'll grant you that."

Corwin shook his head. "I'm with Julie. There's an untold story here, and I believe she's the one to uncover it."

"Thank you, Charles," Julie said.

She turned to Alan. "I totally understand if you don't want to pursue this any further with me. I appreciate the help you've given. But for my sake, and for my son's, I need to see this through to its end. I'm the only parent he's got, and he deserves a parent who honors her commitments."

Even from across the table, I swear I could feel Alan's conflicted feelings beating him up. Julie was challenging him, and she was cheating by pulling Joe into it. Alan had admitted to me he didn't trust Julie to tell him the truth, but he couldn't be sure that she wasn't being honest with him, either. As a result, she had a sure-fire way to mess with his mind, and so far, he hadn't figured out a way to avoid it. Alan needed help, I decided, and it was spelled P-A-T-E-R-N-I-T-Y T-E-S-T.

"We're not leaving Flagstaff until you find the body," Lily announced. "We're your friends, and that's what friends do: they help."

I struggled to pick my jaw off the floor.

Did my sister just say what I thought I heard her say?

Lily was coming to Julie's rescue?

My sister, who has all the social skills of a starving piranha, was defending a woman who might, or might not, have given birth to her new husband's previously unknown illegitimate child?

That did it for me. There was no question in my mind: either I had a mind-scrambling attack of altitude sickness, or I was experiencing the longest hallucination in human history, and, in reality, I was still standing in the prairie grasses in southwestern Minnesota, suffering from sunstroke.

Man, was this going to be a great story to tell at faculty back-to-school workshops.

"In fact," Lily continued, "Bobby and Luce can take another look at that Ridge spot where you and Alan got caught in the rock slide, since they're going out there after lunch. Right?"

My sister pinned me to the chair with that don't-argue-with-me look I knew well from my childhood.

"Absolutely," Luce told her. "And I'll pump Bill Warner for information."

"Wait a minute," I objected. No way was I going to let Luce grill a kindly old grandfather about a twenty-year-old land dispute.

Especially since I'd already decided I was going to do it.

"That would be great!" Julie enthused. "He won't be on his guard with a couple of visiting birders. I'll give you some loaded questions to ask."

"Perfect," Luce replied.

"But," I tried to interrupt, but the women were off and verbally running, planning the afternoon's slate of stealth sleuthing. I turned to the professor, who was taking another hit from his inhaler.

"We still need a body," I told him.

"Yes, you do," he agreed. His eyes bounced from Luce to Lily to Julie. "But with this kind of determination, I'm convinced you're going to find one."

Oh, boy. Just what I wanted to hear—confirmation of our group insanity.

Then, for the first time in my life, I actually began to hope I would indeed find a dead body while I was birding.

An old dead body.

Because if it was a new dead body, I was afraid the odds were good that it just might belong to one of us.

A cell phone chirped, and Julie pulled hers out of her purse. She checked the caller ID, then apologized to Luce and Lily, saying she needed to take the call. A minute later, she dropped the phone back into her bag, her face several shades paler than her already fair complexion.

"That was the conference office at the university," she said. "Joe didn't show up for his noon session."

She skimmed all of our faces, fear growing in her eyes. "No one can find him. He's missing."

Chapter Nine

Lily, Julie, and Luce hustled up the stairs to the second floor office housing the headquarters for the Native American Young Leaders Conference on the Northern Arizona State campus, while I rode up in the elevator with Alan.

"This sucks," I said.

"What? Getting stuck with the gimp while the able-bodied women forge on ahead?"

I rolled my eyes at Alan.

"No, you numbskull. I'm talking about Joe. He's missing, remember?"

Alan poked at my leg with his crutch.

"Of course I remember. I may be lame, but I'm not suffering from short-term memory impairment," he said. "And I'm not overreacting, like everyone else is doing."

"Overreacting? He's a twelve-year-old kid," I pointed out, "and he's not where he's supposed to be, and nobody can find him. Not to mention that his mother has received hate mail and been targeted for vandalism. I think Joe's being missing is a legitimate cause for concern, Alan."

Alan shook his head in disagreement.

"He's an almost thirteen-year-old boy," he corrected me, "and he's an Indian. He's dealing with a lot of stress in his life, and sneaking off for some quiet time is perfectly normal. Believe me, I know. I was an almost thirteen-year-old Indian kid once myself."

He had a point. If anyone would know how an Indian kid thought, it would be Alan. Heck, there were a lot of days that despite his doctoral degree, my best friend still acted like he was an adolescent.

"All right," I conceded. "You have the mind of an almost thirteen-year-old."

He poked me in the leg again with the tip of his crutch.

"Thanks for the vote of confidence, Counselor," he replied.

"Anytime."

"But I'm not just talking about his mom's problems right now, either," Alan continued. "Joe is like every Indian kid—he's trying to find where he fits between two different cultures with two different sets of expectations. That's why he's here at the conference: we're trying to give all these talented kids the tools they need to thrive. Unfortunately, the American educational system champions the idea that the norm is conformity, and these kids are keenly aware that they don't match the norms that white society has established."

He shifted on his crutches.

"Native American kids are different, Bob, and they know it, but they get mixed messages about how to deal with that difference."

Without even trying, I could think of a dozen good examples of what Alan was talking about. Since Savage High School sat near the borders of the Shakopee Mdewakanton Sioux Community just south of the Twin Cities, we had a good-sized population of students from the reservation. As a result, we had a lot of support programs in place for them that not only aimed to motivate their academic achievement, but also gave them opportunities to share their cultural traditions with the rest of the non-Indian student body. Our Diversity Day was one of those events.

Unfortunately, on too many other days, their preference not to attract undue attention to themselves—a cultural trait—resulted in poor academic performance and lackluster school attendance. Even with all the encouragement our kids got from involved adults on the reservation, it was still the exception to the rule when we got even a handful of Native American students who stayed in school long enough to qualify for walking in our graduation ceremonies.

"Sometimes the pressure comes from home," Alan was saying, "because the kids' parents are afraid their children will get sucked into the white culture and lose their Indian identity. Then the kids act out with hostility or indifference at school. Or sometimes the pressure is from their own peers."

The elevator doors opened and Alan hobbled forward.

"I remember plenty of times I got razzed in high school by my buddies because I actually liked school and wanted to get a college degree. They didn't see the point. But I knew who I was, who I wanted to become, and how to get there."

He paused a moment.

"Thanks to my father."

From down the hall, we could hear familiar voices coming from an open doorway.

"I've been keeping an eye on Joe this week, Bob," Alan assured me. "He wants to succeed, and he knows it's going to cost him some of his buddies. Julie may not know it, but Joe's been teased pretty mercilessly in classes this week because he's so bright. My guess is that he just needed a time-out today, and that he's going to show up in the next session this afternoon. My session," he added.

We approached the noisy doorway.

"So you're not worried about somebody grabbing Joe to get at Julie?" I pressed. "Even after your 'accident' two days ago?"

Alan shook his head.

"I agree the timing is pretty weird for that rock slide, but the fact is, we were off the designated trails. You have to take responsibility for risk when you do that in a wild preserve."

"Sounds like a stupid risk when you're talking about cliffs with big drop-offs, Alan," I pointed out.

"Yeah, well, you're right. You know me, Bob. I have to learn things for myself the hard way."

That was an understatement. He'd married my sister.

We walked into the conference headquarters and saw the three women clustered near a desk. I could hear the clucking from the doorway.

Joe was with them.

"Was I right, or was I right?" Alan asked.

"You were right. This time," I clarified. "Don't let it go to your head, though."

Luce detached herself from the little crowd to join me and Alan.

"He told Julie that he skipped the session this morning because he missed it yesterday while he was tracking her down at the Ridge," my lovely fiancée informed us. "He didn't want to show up unprepared, so he decided to not show up at all."

"And not let Julie know," I filled in.

"He's assuming responsibility for his actions," Alan said, "but he doesn't know how to negotiate that with his mother, yet, so the easy route is to just not tell."

"Hey, I'm the counselor here." I gave Alan a stern glance. "Back off. Joe's just assuming responsibility for his actions, but he doesn't know how to negotiate that with his mother, yet."

Luce laughed and Alan rolled his eyes.

"Okay, Counselor, why don't you spend a little one-on-one with Joe and see if you can give him some strategies for negotiating with his mother," Alan suggested. "I need to hobble on over to my office to prep for this afternoon, and Julie and Lily are heading to the courthouse to see if they can get copies of some documents about the Ridge."

"That sounds like a great idea, Alan," Luce said. She turned to me. "I need to go back to the Inn to make some recipe notes, so I'll meet you there at three o'clock to go out to the Ridge." She dropped a kiss on my cheek and left the office.

"Looks like I'm on duty," I told Alan. "Shoo those red-headed hens out of here, and I'll see what I can do with Joe."

I watched Alan break up the clutch and herd Julie and Lily out of the office. Joe's eyes caught mine, and the resemblance of the boy to Alan almost knocked me for a loop. He had that same determination in his eyes that I recognized from more than fifteen years of knowing Alan.

He could be Alan's son.

And my nephew.

Holy shit.

Chapter Ten

"SEE THAT ONE OVER THERE? That's a Broad-tailed Hummingbird," I told Joe. "It looks a lot like the Ruby-throated Hummingbirds we have in Minnesota. If you put the two of them in a room together, you'd have to compare the color on their flanks to be sure you identified them correctly. The Broad-tailed has orange or buff-colored flanks, while the Ruby-throated has grayish green."

I stole a glance at Joe's stoic face.

"Let me know if this gets too exciting for you," I added, hoping for at least a snort of derision in reply.

Joe and I were sitting on a bench outside one of the dorms on the west side of the NAU campus. The daily thunderstorm had just passed through, leaving the air fresh and pine-scented and us with only a brief drenching before we'd scurried under a building overhang for shelter.

Now the sun was back out, and the Flagstaff sky was its habitual brilliant blue again. After everyone had left me alone with Joe in the conference office, I'd invited him to take a walk with me around the campus, hoping that a casual stroll might induce him to open up to me. So far, he was doing a great imitation of Alan in non-communication mode—I was getting a lot of one-word answers and long silences.

"That's one of the things I really like about birding," I said, still trying to get more than an "okay" or "sure" from the kid. "All you need is a few clear field marks, and you can identify one bird out of the thousands that are out there."

"What, no halfbreeds?"

I didn't take my eyes off the hummer, which was a good thing, because I felt like the earth had just imploded beneath my feet, and I was absolutely certain that showing Joe how totally blown away I was by his very frank—not to say *revealing*—question would not necessarily inspire him with the confidence to confide in me further.

But, geez Louise.

Talk about a conversation starter.

Where will you take it from here, Mr. White?

Door Number One—Confront Anger.

Door Number Two—Explore Feelings about Mom . . . and Absent Dad?

Door Number Three—Dealing with Cultural Bias.

Door Number Four—never mind, you get the idea. With only three words, Joe had ripped open a Pandora's box of personal pain, and I needed to make some kind of response to him, or the lid on that box might slam shut so hard, nobody would ever get it open again.

And Joe would continue to suffer, confused and alone.

I watched the hummer zip away and turned to face the almost-teen sitting next to me on the bench.

"You can tell me whatever you want, Joe, and I promise I won't repeat a single word of it to anyone."

I looked him straight in his brown eyes.

"You're getting grief from the other kids at the conference, aren't you? And it's not about how smart you are, either, though that might be part of it, because from what I've seen, you've got a really good brain."

I noticed his jaw clenching, but pressed on.

"You're getting teased about your mom."

The sparkle of a tear appeared in the corner of his eyes, and he blinked it away. He might as well have reached into my chest and twisted my heart.

This kid was hurting.

"Talk to me," I told him. "You've been carrying this too long, Joe, and I want to help."

Silent tears ran down his face. His jaw continued to clench, then relax, then clench again.

I put my arm around him and pulled him against my side.

"Come on, Joe. It's just you and me, and I'm a sucker for tears. Even Alan lets me see him cry because he knows how much of a sap I am."

The noise that burst out of Joe was part cry and part laugh. I hugged him tighter, and he finally let go his resistance, crying until his shoulders shook with it. He bent his head into my chest and his hand clutched at my shirt as if he were holding onto a life preserver. Like the summer thunderstorm that had just pounded its way over the campus, Joe's misery was intense, and, mercifully, quickly exhausted. His sobs subsided, and he leaned away from me, aiming his attention at the flowering branch where the hummingbird had nectared.

"The other kids say I don't belong at the conference, because I'm not a full-blooded Indian like they are. They say halfbreeds are useless, that nothing good comes from someone like me."

"But you know that's a lie," I said. "They're just scared that they're not good enough, themselves. It's bullying, Joe. Kids bully other kids to make themselves feel superior. It doesn't matter if you're red, white, or blue. Alan's told me about the bullies he encountered when he was growing up, and he was living right there on a reservation. It takes a strong man to stand up to the people who try to prevent him from becoming who he really wants to be, Joe. And, by the way, that's true for every young person—life knocks you around sometimes to see what you're made of."

"The hate mail in my mom's mailbox—it wasn't for her."

He turned his head to catch my eye.

"It was for me. The second day of the conference, the guys who did it laughed about it at lunch."

And Joe had obviously not shared that information with his mother, since she assumed the mail was directed at her. I tried to remember the other incidents of harassment that Julie had mentioned.

"What about the tires, and the window?" I asked. "Did they do that, too?"

Joe shook his head. "They never said anything about it, so I don't know. I just didn't want to tell my mom about the mail because then she'd get all upset and come to the conference and want to get in the guys' faces."

He ran his hand through his chin-length black hair.

The gesture was Alan's.

"My mom's like that," Joe continued. "Confrontational. It doesn't exactly make me a lot of friends, if you know what I mean."

I nodded. "And you wanted to handle it yourself, right?"

"Yes. But then when the tires got slashed and the window busted, I was afraid to tell her that I hadn't told her about the letters, and then it was too late, anyway. She and the professor decided it was all because of the research they were working on. He told her that it was proof she was on the right track. And then she wasn't home the other morning, and I was really afraid something had happened to her, and . . . "

His voice trailed off, and I could see his throat working, trying not to cry again.

I pulled him against me one more time.

"You're just a kid, Joe," I reassured him. "A really smart, resourceful, talented kid, but still a kid. You're supposed to be afraid when your mom is missing. That's normal. But right now, for just a few more minutes, let's not worry about her. Let's figure out what you need to do when other kids tease you about having a white mom."

"About being a halfbreed," he said.

"About being a halfbreed," I repeated after him. "What do you think are your options?"

Joe studied the sidewalk in front of the bench. "I could ignore them. Or I could find out where they live and go break one of their windows."

He threw me a sly smile. "That's not one of the answers you want, is it?"

"Not especially," I admitted. "Although it's better than saying you could beat them up."

"I was going to say that next."

He smiled again.

"Just kidding."

I gave him a smile of my own. "Yeah, I figured that. Bottom line, Joe, is that it's really not about you, or where you come from, or who your parents are. It's about the other kids' self-image. I know that doesn't stop the bullying from happening, but if you can remind yourself that you're strong, and that you can walk away from the teasing, it might help you get through it."

I nudged him with my shoulder.

"At least until you get bigger than they are, and my guess is that you're going to start doing that in the next year or two. Funny how that works, you know. Bullies quit bugging you when they have to look up to look you in the eyes. Does any of this help?"

He shrugged. "I won't know till they bug me again, which will probably happen this afternoon."

"Why do you say that?"

"Because this is a small town, and all the other kids will have heard about my mom and Alan getting hurt at the Ridge while she was working on her book," he explained. "Her book about a half-breed who caused a lot of trouble here in Flagstaff for the other Indian families."

It took me a minute to realize what he was saying, and even then, I wasn't quite sure I was following him.

"Are you talking about Ron Walking Eagle?" I asked. "His parents weren't both Native Americans?"

Joe nodded, then stood up.

"That's what the other kids say their parents say. Mom doesn't believe it, though. She says those parents are still angry about how some of the whites treated them during the preserve mess, so Ron's an easy target to blame."

He pushed his hair back from the sides of his face.

"Mom never wants to deal with my being a halfbreed, you know. She thinks it shouldn't matter to anyone, and since she thinks that way, she just assumes everyone else acts that way. Which they don't," he noted.

He looked towards the south side of the campus, and pointed a finger in that direction.

"Did you know that Northern Arizona University is the only college campus in the United States to have graveyards on three of its sides? The first day we were here, we got a tour, and that's what they told us. They said the local joke is that people are dying to go to school here." He shrugged again. "It doesn't make me want to go here. They should talk about the really cool genetics research they do here, instead. That's what I want to do."

"Genetics, huh? Very cool," I said. "Maybe you should tell the admissions office: push bioscience and ixnay on the dying joke."

I had to agree with Joe—equating death with higher education wasn't the most optimistic recruiting strategy I'd ever heard. Granted, I'd met lots of zombies when I was in college, but I was pretty sure they slept in dorms at night (and day) and not in local cemeteries.

Although that did explain why Elvira, our very own Hostess of the Night, had chosen NAU as her collegiate option. She probably felt right at home surrounded by graveyards. I'd have to remember that the next time any of the living dead came to me for college suggestions.

Joe checked his watch.

"I need to get to the session, or they'll call Mom again."

"I'll walk back with you," I offered.

We left the dorm behind and headed back towards the conference classrooms.

"You're a pretty good guy, Mr. White," Joe said. "I can see why my dad likes you so much."

I winced a little at the "D" word, dreading that moment for Joe in the not-too-distant future when Alan would have to force Julie into full disclosure regarding her son's paternity. In my opinion, whatever reason his mom had had for keeping that information from Joe in the past had now been trumped by the complications that secret was causing other people in the present; in fairness to her son, Julie needed to tell him the truth. Contrary to what I'd just suggested to Joe, where you come from is a critical piece of personal identity, and though it should never limit what you can do, it can sure help you figure out where you're going.

If Joe was indeed Alan's son, I knew that Alan and Lily would do the right thing by him, whatever that might be.

If he wasn't a Thunderhawk, then Joe would have to reconfigure who he thought he was by incorporating the truth into his life. And I could only hope that he'd become a better man because of it.

Another hummingbird darted across our path in search of blooms.

"Not a Broad-tailed," Joe observed. "This one's got a black throat with a purple stripe beneath it."

"It's a Black-chinned Hummingbird," I said. "Very good, Joe. You looked for field marks to compare it to the Broad-tailed. You learn fast."

"That's what my mom says, too," he told me. "She says I get it from her, but sometimes, I'm not so sure. If she was a fast learner, you'd think she would have given up on this story of hers after getting nowhere with it for the last year."

We came to a stop in front of the building that housed Joe's afternoon session.

"Actually, I think she was ready to quit when she met Professor Corwin at the banquet the first night of the conference," he continued. "I guess he gave her some tips about the Ridge business that he'd discovered when he was working on his book a few years ago, and since then, she's more determined than ever to prove that Walking Eagle was killed."

I put my hand on his shoulder and gave it a squeeze. "Believe it or not, I think your mom is doing this as much for your sake as for the sake of her friend Ron. She wants to set a good example for you of perseverance, and loyalty, and I bet she wants to make you proud of her, too."

"I'm already proud of her," he assured me.

"I can see that, just like I can see how proud she is of you. You two are lucky to have each other, Joe."

He nodded. "Yeah, we are. I've got to go."

And with that, he turned towards the red stone block building's entrance and vanished inside.

I continued past the building in the general direction of the inn where Luce was waiting for me. In the distance, I could see the pine-covered slopes of the San Francisco Peaks, which soared more than twelve thousand feet into the air and provided Arizona with its sole alpine tundra region. In the opposite direction, I knew that the high desert plateau stretched to the state line with New Mexico, while towards the south lay a patchwork of canyons and fertile valleys. As Bill Warner had explained this morning, Flagstaff was a virtual crossroads of habitats, offering someone like me a goldmine of birding opportunities. In fact, if I'd arrived in Flagstaff under happier circumstances, I could easily see myself falling in love with the place, thanks to the wide diversity of bird species that could quickly lengthen my life list.

Yet, as Chatty Patty the cab driver had pointed out to us yesterday, Flagstaff's original claim to fame and history wasn't its birding paradise, but its role as a transportation hub. Late last night, I'd read a brochure in our room at the inn that claimed that seventy trains a day still passed through the town. Until the city forbade it a few years ago, shrill train whistles routinely sounded in the air. And while many folks had just been passing through Flagstaff, others stayed, and some became wealthy as commerce increased with the advent of the tourist trade. Families like the Warners snapped up big pieces of property in anticipation of rising real estate values and enjoyed a certain level of prestige in the town—Bill Warner did own the bank and had a building named for him, after all. He probably was, as the professor had suggested, the leading power broker in Flagstaff—or, at least, he was until he got hauled into court by a wandering Native American activist.

Yeah, that kind of a black eye would probably upset a guy like Bill Warner, Flag's Number One Fan.

Based on his behavior at lunch, I'd say it also upset his son Wilson twenty years after the fact. What was it he'd said about his own son Gil and the Golden Eagle he handled?

Oh, yeah.

"If Gil only knew about Walking Eagle."

What did that mean? Did Gil not know about the dispute over the Ridge? Was the grandson unaware that every time he mentioned his bird's name, he was reminding his grandfather of a public embarrassment?

Had his grandfather killed Ron Walking Eagle?

Try as I might, I couldn't picture Flag's Number One Fan as a killer. Given the situation of the court case, I could understand Julie's suspicions, but the fact of the matter was that she had only been a teenager at the time, and Alan had said she'd always had a flair for the dramatic. As for Ron Walking Eagle's hints to her that he might be in danger, there was no way to gauge their accuracy all this time later. For all anyone knew, he might have been on the lam for a speeding ticket.

Not that I would know anything about that. I was a law-abiding citizen. I'd paid every one of my speeding tickets so far.

I think.

However, if the court case had been as nasty as Julie and Corwin made it sound, then I could see where Wilson would just want to keep his mouth shut about his son's unfortunate choice of the eagle's name. If he had to explain to his son why the name was objectionable, it would result in dredging up a painful past, and Wilson clearly wanted to protect his father from that because he'd asked me to tell Julie to back off.

But did he want to protect his father so much that he'd go as far as harassing a journalist investigating the Ridge court case?

Maybe.

Maybe not.

Personally, I wondered if Wilson was capable of those kinds of overt, planned acts of aggression. I had run interference between him and Alan in the restaurant because the man didn't have the brains to see that my buddy was ready and willing to pound him into the polished wood floor. In my experience, Wilson's type of bravado was all hot air induced by alcohol; when push came to shove—once he sobered up—he'd turn tail and run away rather than slug it out . . . or slash a tire.

In other words, he was a coward, as well as a drunk.

So maybe Julie's slashed tires and broken window had nothing to do with the bad blood between Ron Walking Eagle and Bill Warner at all, and everything to do with her son's bullying classmates.

If that were the truth of the matter, then any search we undertook for a missing body was a wild goose chase, because if no one was panicking that Julie was close to finding a body and uncovering a murder, then that meant there was no murder to be uncovered.

And Ron Walking Eagle had simply slipped into a hole in the rocks and disappeared.

Like the rock men back at the Jeffers Petroglyphs site a thousand years ago.

Joe needed to come clean with his mom . . . for everyone's sake.

A small flock of Western Bluebirds flew into a clump of tall bushes near the footpath I was following. Aside from the males' blue throats and rusty upper backs, they looked like the Eastern Bluebirds I knew in Minnesota.

Really, what was the difference between one breed of bird and another?

A change of coloring, a different range.

What was the difference between a child with two Indian parents and a child with one Indian parent?

Different cultures, different expectations, perhaps.

To be honest, I really didn't know what the difference might be, or if one even existed.

So what if Ron Walking Eagle had been half-Native American? Like any activist worth his salt, he'd found something he believed in—in Ron's case, the religious rights of his people, or at least, half of his ancestors—and he'd championed that cause across the state. Until he got to Flagstaff, where he tangled with Bill Warner and then disappeared, his sudden absence noted only by a young runaway.

A teenaged Julie who idolized the activist who'd taken her under his wing.

As I played with that picture, though, I suddenly got the feeling that Julie Burrows wasn't telling the whole truth.

Again.

Why was I not surprised?

I'd just reached the doorway of the inn when my cell phone vibrated in my pocket. I took it out and saw Lily's name pop up on the caller ID.

"What's up?" I asked her.

"Bob, it's Julie. Your sister is fine, really. She's just a little shook up. She said I should call you, not Alan, since he's in class."

An awful little chill raced up my spine.

"Let me talk to Lily," I said, my throat gone as dry as the mountain-thin air of Flagstaff.

"She can't come to the phone right now," Julie told me. "They're taking X-rays."

X-rays.

A hospital.

"Swear to God, Julie, you better tell me exactly what happened in the next ten seconds or I'm going to—"

"She jumped out of the way of a car and hit her head on the curb when she landed," she interrupted me. "She has a minor concussion and a sprained wrist, and that's why the doctor wanted X-rays."

"Lily walked into the path of a car?"

I looked around for something to sit on before I ended up on my rear end on the sidewalk leading into the inn. My head wasn't feeling too secure on my shoulders at the moment.

Julie hesitated.

"What are you not telling me, Julie?" I demanded.

Damn. Now the woman was doing it to me, too. What did it take to get the whole truth from this woman?

And why didn't the inn have at least a patio chair out here in front to catch guests who've been informed that their sister had narrowly escaped being the victim of a hit-and-run accident? I was definitely going to write that suggestion on the room comment sheet before I checked out.

Assuming I didn't check out in the next second here and crack my head wide open on the freaking sidewalk.

"She didn't walk into the car, Bob," Julie finally confessed. "It came after her."

Chapter Eleven

OH YEAH, THAT WAS MUCH BETTER.

I was totally euphoric to have Julie tell me the whole truth.

In fact, I was so euphoric, I couldn't decide if I should throw up or just pass out.

I stretched my hand out to the sun-warmed stone of the inn's front doorframe to brace myself so I wouldn't keel over in the entryway. Heaven forbid that any of the College of Hospitality students got an F for their rotation at the inn because they failed to notice the dead man on their front step. The success of students was important to me. It was one of the reasons I always tried to teach my charges that honesty was the best policy, and that it was essential for success. When you were honest, you didn't have to hide anything. You didn't have to worry about someone coming after you with murder in his eye when he found out later that you weren't honest with him.

Instead, you could worry about him coming after you with murder in his eye right then, which was exactly how I felt about Julie Burrows.

"What do you mean, the car came after her?"

I enunciated each word clearly and slowly, hoping that adding more words to my question would lengthen the fuse of my temper, which was now running dangerously short.

Julie must have noticed the absence of my usual casual tone, however, because her own voice came over the phone connection soothingly calm and reassuring.

"We were crossing the street to the Coconino County courthouse, and a car accelerated out of a parking spot on the street directly at Lily," she explained. "I saw it first and yelled at her to move, and she jumped back, but she tripped and went down on her wrist, and then her head hit. I insisted we come over to the emergency room and have her checked out."

She paused and her voice went even softer.

"She's going to be fine, Bob. Believe me, I'm more than sick it happened to her, because I have no doubt that the driver meant to hit me."

I clenched my fist against the doorframe, my frustration and dread rising even as my temper fell back into the manageable range.

"Who was it, Julie?"

"The windows were tinted, so I can't be positive," she hedged, "but I'd bet my last dollar that it was Wilson Warner's Porsche. Not a lot of silver Porsches in this town, Bob."

Great. A drunk driver. A drunk driver with a grudge against Julie, and who undoubtedly hadn't noticed my sister's uncanny resemblance to her.

Not only had Lily moved into the line of fire of this maniac, but he'd almost killed her in broad daylight in front of the county courthouse.

"Please tell me you got the license plate," I begged her.

"Sorry."

"Then tell me you got it recorded live on your cell phone, and we can post it on the Internet along with a monetary reward to nail this idiot. The man is a walking—driving—time bomb."

"Bob, I'm sorry," she repeated.

"So am I!" I exploded. "I'm sorry any of us came to Flagstaff for any reason! If you thought it was the perfect opportunity to introduce Alan to the son he never knew he had, and, at the same time, get help in settling a debt you think you owe some wandering Native American activist who abandoned you without even saying goodbye, then you were wrong. I think your time would be much better spent, Julie, if you stopped trying to prove yourself to everyone, and instead, just listened to what your son really needs right now from you: your attention."

Silence.

On both ends of the connection.

I mentally smacked myself in the head. *Way to go, Counselor.* I'd always privately wondered if tact, respect, and trust were overrated in counseling practice, but I'd never field tested my theory. Now I had evidence—going directly on the attack really did stop the conversation cold. Kind of like what a Gyrfalcon diving in for the kill did for meaningful communication with the mouse destined for dinner.

Squ -

I needed to apologize, big-time.

"Julie, I—"

"I didn't ask you to come here, Bob," Julie cut me off. "I never asked for your help, and I'm certainly not asking for it now. Please, feel free to go back home to Minnesota anytime. Maybe there's somebody there who would appreciate your advice, because I don't. You don't know one thing about me, or about what Joe needs."

"You're wrong," I argued. "I do know one thing about you, the most important thing. You love your son so much you'd do anything for him, including putting yourself in harm's way. That's what you do when you're a family, Julie. And that's why I won't be leaving Flagstaff as long as my sister and Alan are in danger."

I rubbed my free hand across the back of my neck, trying to knead away some of the tension that had gathered there. Clearly, I had yet to discover the relaxing wonderland of Flagstaff touted by the tourist brochures, because rather than unwinding, my nerves were getting tighter by the minute.

I needed an escape.

I needed to bird.

"You don't know me, either, Julie," I pointed out to her, "but I will tell you one thing about me: my family and my friends can count on me. Always. Yes, I occasionally act like an idiot, but my intentions are good."

"So are mine, Bob."

I closed my eyes and said a little prayer of gratitude that she was still speaking to me. Maybe there was hope I could actually extract my big fat foot from my mouth.

"I know they are, Julie. And that's why I want to help you and Joe."

"I'm not asking you to."

"I'm offering. That's what friends do."

There was more silence on the line.

"Within the hour, I'll be walking the Ridge with Bill Warner, Julie," I reminded her. "If you could ask him one question, what would it be?"

I could hear her intake of breath at the other end of the connection. A moment passed while I waited for her response.

"I need to think this through," she said. "If I could ask Bill Warner one question and know I'd get an honest answer, I'd ask him if he killed Ron. But the problem there is the qualifier 'honest.' The man may be one of Flag's most respected senior citizens, but if he's responsible for Ron's 'disappearance' twenty years ago, the last thing he's going to do is say he had anything to do with it. So I need to make my question a good one that will give me what I'm looking for without tipping him off."

I stared at the sidewalk that was still solidly beneath my feet, despite the vertigo I had just experienced with the news of Lily's near-accident. According to Julie, my sister was alive and well, though given the events of the last few days, I didn't feel very secure in assuming that would remain the status quo, especially if Lily insisted in accompanying Julie on her investigative errands around Flagstaff. Clearly, only one thing was going to guarantee Lily's safety in this town, and that was for Julie to find out what really happened to Ron Walking Eagle. But what one question could Julie possibly come up with that could help her solve the mystery of Ron's disappearance, or, as she believed, his death?

"I've got it!" Julie's voice filled with certainty. "Ask Warner why he never made it public that the Ridge wasn't sacred Indian land after all."

"Wait a minute," I said. "I thought that was the whole reason Ron Walking Eagle took Bill Warner to court—he wanted the land returned to the tribes because it was sacred."

"That's what everyone thought, including me," she replied. "But when Charles was researching his book about the political aspects of preservation, he found some historical records claiming that the Ridge was never anything but ranch land. He didn't pursue it since it didn't impact his study of the actual court conflict. That's why

Lily and I were headed to the courthouse —to look up old property deeds and any archived material we could find about tribal property rights around Flagstaff."

In the distance, one of the seventy trains a day must have rumbled through town, because I swear I could feel the vibrations of its wheels on the tracks thrumming through the ground beneath my feet.

Either that, or the tectonic plates under northern Arizona were shifting, and we were on the threshold of one humdinger of an earthquake. Good thing I saw the Grand Canyon when I was a kid, huh? I had a feeling that any measurable earthquake would reduce Flagstaff's nearby number one tourist attraction into one big rockslide. Of course, Flagstaff itself probably wouldn't fare too well in a cataclysm like that, either—I could just imagine all those graves around the university opening up as the ground heaved and buckled.

Elvira might like it, but how would the admissions people work that little detail into the tour they gave prospective freshmen?

NAU, where not only are applicants dying to get in, but where the campus opens up to swallow you whole once you do.

Yeah, like that's going to result in a spike in admissions.

"And I believed him," Julie was saying. "Why wouldn't I? He'd done the same thing in other counties around Arizona."

The apocalypse faded before my eyes.

"Sorry, I missed that last part," I told Julie, tuning back into her voice over the phone connection. "Can you run it by me again?"

"I said that I was a teenager with a bad case of hero worship when Ron took me in," Julie repeated for me. "I was a runaway from a very dysfunctional—make that a totally unfunctional—household, and he treated me with kindness and respect, like the dad I never had. I believed every word that came out of his mouth, so of course I believed him when he said the reason he took Warner to court was to secure the rights to religious practice for the local tribal community. It never occurred to me he wasn't telling the truth."

I almost asked her how she liked being on the receiving end for a change, but I bit my tongue just in time.

"So now the question is why he lied about it, and why Warner didn't come clean about it," I summed up, instead. "If Ron had a false claim on the land, good old Bill should have been able to put a stop to the case before it even made it to court."

"Exactly! Get the answer to that," Julie speculated, "and it should lead us right to a motive for Ron's murder, if not to the murderer himself."

Something in her emphasis on the word "murderer" caught my attention, and I instantly recalled her comment in the restaurant at lunch that Wilson Warner was her number two suspect behind the harassment she'd experienced.

"You think Bill Warner is behind it all, don't you?" I asked her. "Ron's disappearance. Your slashed tires. The broken window."

I briefly wondered if she noticed I didn't mention the hate mail. Joe's withholding of that information was a bone that mother and son would have to pick over later, preferably after I'd made my return to Minnesota, since I had no desire to be the mediator of choice in that particular family meeting. I had no doubt that Julie wouldn't take it well when she found out that her son had confided in me, instead of her. Our truce was fragile enough as it was.

"Bill Warner is your number one suspect," I finished.

"Yes," Julie agreed. "Or at least he was, until a silver Porsche sent your sister scrambling for the sidewalk. Now I have a tie for the number one suspect slot. The more, the merrier, right?"

And maybe I needed to revisit my earlier evaluation of Wilson Warner's inability to do someone bodily harm.

In fact, if he had been the one behind the wheel of the Porsche that homed in on my sister, I needed to make myself a mental note: at the earliest opportunity, be sure to sucker-punch Wilson Warner.

I took a quick glance at my watch and calculated how long it would take Luce and me to drive out to the Ridge to meet the oldest and youngest Warners. Since the vibrations under my feet had ceased, I figured the end of the world wasn't imminent after all, and that the Grand Canyon would probably continue providing millions of visitors every year with spectacular views and awesome inspiration, along with a multitude of kitschy souvenir shot glasses and key rings.

"I need to get going," I told Julie. "I'll ask Warner your question. You keep my sister safe."

As I walked into the inn and down the hall to my room, I wondered if leaving Lily with Julie was a sign of intelligence—or stupidity—on my part. Julie was proving herself to be fearless in the face of adversity, while my sister didn't know the meaning of the word "fall back." Together, who knew what trouble they could get themselves into.

Okay, I know. "Fall back" is two words, not one. Still, Lily didn't know what that meant. Her whole life, she'd been a bulldog when it came to something she wanted. I learned at an early age to stay out of my big sister's way when she set her sights on something, whether it was winning her Brownie Troop award for selling the most boxes of Girl Scout cookies, or building her own landscaping company from the ground up.

Which got me to thinking: what exactly was Lily after?

Alan was safe, repentant, and planning to shower his bride with bribes to regain her good favor. He'd also promised her they'd return home to Minnesota as soon as Julie solved her mystery, thus ensuring both mother and son's safety. For her part, Lily had embraced Julie as a friend.

But as to my sister's relationship with Joe, I had no idea where it stood, nor did I know if she harbored suspicions about Alan's paternity, even though Julie had denied it. Granted, I was no expert in understanding the intricate twists and turns of the female personality, and it might be entirely possible that my sister was just being a really nice person to help out her husband's long-ago lover.

Not.

This was Lily, schemer extraordinaire, and if I knew nothing else about my sister, I knew there was always a lot more going on behind those gray eyes of hers than she ever let on. Without question, Lily had an ulterior motive for her enthusiastic participation in Julie's detective work.

I just had to figure out what it was.

Chapter Twelve

The Ridge was a lot more than a ridge.

As Luce and I approached the entrance to the preserve, the land around us changed from a relatively flat plateau to thick pine forests on rolling foothills. Though it didn't feature the dramatically deep gorge of the nearby national monument, the Ridge was dotted with limestone ledges and alcoves above its own small portion of the same Walnut Creek that had carved Walnut Canyon's breathtaking vistas. As a public preserve, the Ridge offered visitors a great spot to enjoy the natural charms of this part of Arizona's varied geographical zones; as a wildlife preserve, it was a birder's paradise that hosted several habitats in one spot. Even as I stepped out of the car, I could hear Canyon Wrens whistling and a Wild Turkey calling.

"Looks like we're the first ones here," Luce observed from the other side of the car. "This place is really something, isn't it? I can't think of anywhere else we'd find Canyon Wrens mixing with turkeys."

"It's all the different elevations," I pointed out. "The Ridge has canyon walls, plateau, pines, lots of vegetation, and water. It's almost like those charts you see in tourist centers or school books listing the different species of wildlife you find at different elevations, except instead of being spread out over a whole state like in Minnesota, they're all right here in one preserve."

The sound of an engine interrupted the chorus of the birds, and both Luce and I turned towards the SUV that had pulled into the graveled parking lot. A moment later, Bill Warner was lifting Khan's cage from the back of his vehicle.

"I couldn't resist bringing Kahn along," Warner explained. "It's much too nice a day to have to stay cooped up when we've got this whole preserve to play in. 'Course, every day is too nice a day to stay cooped up in northern Arizona. Glad you could make it, Bob, Luce." He set Khan's cage on the ground.

"Gil should be along any minute," he added. "He called to tell me he was having a late lunch with his dad, and then he'll swing by the house to pick up Walking Eagle."

Warner took two deep breaths of the pine-scented air and beamed at the preserve laid out before him.

"I love this land. I grew up out here. My dad used to say it was rotten for ranching, but great for rambling."

"We actually met your son when we were having lunch today," Luce told Warner.

I caught her eye and lifted my right eyebrow in silent admonishment. On the way here, we'd agreed to bird first and play detective second. Luce was jumping the gun.

Which instantly reminded me that, last I'd heard, Arizona allowed private individuals to carry firearms.

As in guns.

To be exact, rifles and shotguns could be carried without a permit, and a handgun could likewise be carried without a permit, as long as it was at least partially visible in a belt holster.

Well, gee, that sure made me feel safer. At least I'd see the gun before someone fired it at me.

But this was the Great American West, after all, right? Guns were part of the picture.

The frontier, filled with rugged land and tough men.

I didn't know about the women. Except for Chatty Patty and Elvira. Although I think Patty could probably talk you to death, and Elvira could just call up some ghouls if she needed a hand.

Or any other body parts.

I glanced again at Bill Warner.

He seemed to have all his body parts intact from what I could tell.

What I couldn't tell, however, was if he was packing a gun. For all I knew, Flag's Number One Fan was a gun-toting grandfather with an itchy trigger finger. If that were the case, I sure wouldn't want to be asking him any potentially upsetting questions in a remote preserve empty of any other witnesses or emergency medical personnel.

Call me paranoid, but I did a quick scan of Warner's clothing.

No gun butts in sight.

Luce, meanwhile, was continuing her conversation with Warner.

"Wilson seemed unhappy with a local journalist doing some research for a story here," she said.

Talk about understating the situation. From my perspective, Wilson had been stinking drunk and spoiling for a fight.

But Luce was a chef—she's got an inborn predilection to make anything palatable. Even drunks who publicly embarrass themselves.

Warner leaned back against his vehicle's rear bumper.

"Let me guess. Wilson was drunk and making a spectacle of himself. I swear, the boy's come unglued since that Julie Burrows has been trying to get an interview with me."

His eyes met mine for a moment, then returned to Luce's.

"If my son was being his usual inebriated loud-mouth self, then I'm guessing you all heard what that little gal is interested in." He waved his hands to include the Ridge. "She thinks that there was some cover-up twenty years ago when I donated this land to the county. From what I hear, she's got it in her head that the fellow who took me to court over the donation met with foul play."

The sound of another engine reached the parking lot just before a second car turned into the lot and came to a stop beside Warner's SUV. Gil Warner climbed out of the car and threw us all a brilliant smile.

"Hey, everybody. Sorry I'm late."

He immediately rounded the front of the car and wrestled a hooded cage out of the front seat. I think he said something else then, but I missed it because I was too occupied in staring at his sleek four-door sports car.

It's not every day you see a Golden Eagle arriving in a silver Porsche.

Chapter Thirteen

"Nice car," I finally managed to say.

Gil was grabbing some equipment from the four-door Porsche's back seat. He emerged with a bucket of tidbits for Walking Eagle, along with his thick leather gloves.

"Thanks," he replied. "But it's not mine. It belongs to my dad. I had to give him a lift home after lunch, so I'm stuck with the Porsche for the afternoon. Luckily, this new model has just enough space to fit in Walking Eagle's cage in the passenger seat."

"Yeah, I don't suppose they take that kind of space requirement into consideration when they design Porsches."

Could I sound any lamer? I was still so stunned to see a silver Porsche—Wilson Warner's silver Porsche—that I was having trouble moving past a vision of its front bumper barely missing my sister.

"Which way?" Luce's voice cut into my fog.

She was standing near the edge of the parking area, holding the handle of Gil's bucket in one hand while she shaded her eyes from the bright sunshine with her other palm. Cool and collected as always, Luce had apparently already processed the appearance of the Porsche and acted as though nothing more than an afternoon of helping rehab an eagle was on her mind. On the way to the preserve, I'd filled her in on Julie's news and Lily's condition, and I knew she'd been rattled. But here she was, chatting comfortably with the father and son of Lily's suspected attacker.

My fiancée had nerves of steel. She also had an inventive imagination. In fact, I bet she was concocting a recipe this very moment—one that included the vivisection of Wilson Warner.

And that was just for starters.

I mean appetizers.

I hustled across the gravel and packed-sand parking area to join Luce at the trailhead.

"We'll take this path," Gil said, leading the way into a stand of pines with Walking Eagle on his gloved fist. "It takes us up to a rise above one of the bigger ledges in the preserve. So far, it's Walking Eagle's favorite launch pad. I don't know if seeing the ledge—something solid— beneath him makes him feel more secure, or if he likes the thermals along the cliff face there, but it's the one place in the preserve where he seems to be developing his confidence and desire to fly."

Luce fell into step beside the young man, and I followed a little behind them with Gil's grandfather. A hooded Khan was perched on Warner's own gloved fist, and I had the opportunity to admire the white Gyrfalcon up close.

"Khan is a classic white-form Gyrfalcon," I commented to Warner. "I can't recall ever seeing a Gyr with such uniform white coloring. Even in the photos I've seen of birds from around the world, Gyrfalcons are usually mottled with brown or gray."

"Gyrs actually run the gamut from white to black," Warner said. "though there does seem to be some correlation between geographic populations and color morph, according to the experts. Bottom line is that Gyrfalcons can fly long distances, and there's apparently no taboo against trading genes with Gyrs from other populations. The result is uncontrolled hybridization among subpopulations and thus, a multitude of plumage variations."

He smiled and threw me a wink.

"I guess what happens in the Arctic, stays in the Arctic. Or not," he added. "I've even read where scientists have tried to track the development of different populations of Gyrfalcons using DNA sequencing, but the gene pools are so muddied, it's hopeless. People may care about bloodlines, but Gyrs don't."

His comment about bloodlines made me think about Joe for a moment. Too bad Joe's classmates weren't Gyrfalcons.

"Sounds like you've taken a real interest in Gyrs," I noted.

Warner nodded. "When you've got a beauty like Khan living with you, it's hard not to. Bloodlines were the reason Khan's former owner was so furious when Khan was injured. He was a Saudi fellow, and he'd paid a small fortune for Khan from a breeder who could trace Khan's lineage back five generations. That was important for this fellow, since he planned on entering Khan in falconry competitions, and captive breeding ensures a healthier bird. Wild Gyrfalcons typically die pretty fast once they're taken from the wild, you know," he added.

We skirted a stand of big Ponderosa pines. I noticed that the pines were getting sparser as we went up the trail.

"Their immune systems aren't designed for human environments, so they can't fight off disease," Warner continued. "That's why serious falconers want captive-bred birds, and not the Gyrfalcons that are illegally captured in Russia and smuggled into the Middle East."

"Like the ones that were discovered at the airport in December," I said.

"Exactly."

I remembered the article I'd read last winter about eight Gyrs that had been found hidden in two pieces of personal luggage during an airport security scan at Moscow's international airport. The birds, bound for the Middle East, where falconry was embedded in Arab culture, were clearly illegally taken from the Kamchatka Peninsula, the winter home and breeding ground of the endangered Gyrfalcons. After four weeks of rehabilitation, the birds were successfully returned to the wild. The article didn't say where the smuggler ended up, but I bet it wasn't the Ritz. The only other thing I remembered from the article was that wild Gyrfalcons sold for as much as $50,000 per bird, so I could only imagine how much Khan's former owner had paid for a pedigreed Gyr.

"A small fortune" was what Warner had said.

What a shame, I thought. It all came down to money. Once Khan couldn't compete for purses, his owner had no more use for him. Khan was a liability instead of an asset.

I took another look at the bird on Warner's fist as we walked up a slight rise, smiling to myself as I realized the soft murmuring I heard wasn't the wind in the pines, but Warner crooning a soft tune to his Gyrfalcon. Khan's hooded head was tipped in the direction of Warner's voice, obviously intent on the presence of his master. Khan may have descended from a wind-swept tundra clan, but he'd found a good home here in Flagstaff.

"This is the place," Warner said, coming to a halt in a boulder-strewn meadow. "We'll let Walking Eagle make a few flights before I'll give Khan a turn."

He pointed to the left where distant mountains held a trace of snow even in August. "Watch your step over there," he warned me, "it might look like the perfect spot for taking in the view, but there's a steep dropoff you won't see till you're right on top of it."

I looked at Luce and Gil, who must have stopped right on the lip of the same dropoff.

"You mean where they're standing?" I asked Warner.

"Right there," he agreed. "I can't even walk over there. I get some vertigo these days, and looking down that cliff just about does me in. Don't want to go pitching down the hill before it's my turn to go, you know."

He sat heavily on a flat boulder surrounded by wildflowers. I thought he looked a bit pale under his tan, then realized that the gradual uphill walk might have winded him. Granted, Khan probably didn't weigh more than three pounds, but even having that light load on his arm was likely more strain than Warner was used to.

"Are you okay?" I asked him, feeling a little hesitant about leaving him sitting alone on the boulder.

"I'm fine," he insisted. "This view always takes my breath away. Reminds me of being a young buck with my whole life ahead of me. Used to be you'd come out here and see all kinds of eagles flying, even Golden Eagles. They used to nest around the Ridge, but their numbers are way down now. You go on over to Gil and that lovely lady of yours. Maybe you can make that Walking Eagle a flier."

I turned to walk away, but suddenly remembered my promise to Julie. If Gil really didn't know about his eagle's namesake, I didn't want to introduce what might be a forbidden family topic within his earshot, so I figured the time was now or never to ask Warner about Julie's question.

I turned back around.

"About Julie Burrows," I said, "you're right. She does think there's more to the story than Ron Walking Eagle just walking away from your court case, never to be heard from again. She thinks he was murdered."

Warner held my gaze, his face devoid of any kind of reaction.

"Are you working with her, Bob? Is this all a set-up to talk to me since I won't give her an interview? You're pretty slick if that's what's going on. You had me fooled."

I shook my head.

"No set-up. Totally chance encounters, Bill. This morning when I met you, I had no idea who you were, or that you were somehow involved in the reason I came to Flagstaff. I'm a birder, plain and simple. I came out to Flag because my sister asked me for some help, and that turned into something that involves Julie . . . and you. But now my sister isn't safe, and I'm not going to let her get hurt."

Warner narrowed his eyes, his gaze intent on my face.

"What are you talking about, son?"

"Actually, I'm talking about your son," I replied. "Julie Burrows has been the target of vandalism and suspicious violence, and she thinks Wilson is behind it, trying to keep her away from you and from solving Ron Walking Eagle's disappearance. I had a call from her just before I headed out here to the Ridge. My sister, who could be Julie's double, was almost run down outside the county courthouse in Flagstaff. The car in question was a silver Porsche."

I waited for that information to register on his face before I asked the question that had been on my mind since I saw Gil drive up in his dad's car.

"So you tell me, Bill, how many silver Porsches are on the streets of Flag?"

Warner went another shade paler under his tan.

"And while we're at it, I have another question for you," I forged on. "If the Ridge wasn't sacred Indian land, why didn't you make that fact public, instead of letting Walking Eagle take you to court about your donation? Don't deny it," I cautioned him. "Julie's probably combing through every deed and land document in the county at this very moment."

So I was bluffing a tiny bit. I had no idea what Julie was doing at the moment. For all I knew, she and Lily were getting hot stone massages and drinking martinis in a Flagstaff spa.

Or maybe they were swapping tales about Alan's bad habits.

Maybe they were plotting revenge, and staking out Wilson Warner's home with a couple of bricks in their purses.

Geez, I hoped not. It wasn't going to help Julie's case if she got arrested for vandalizing the home of her vandalizer.

Then again, if she—and Lily—got tossed into jail, at least I wouldn't have to worry about them getting into trouble for a few hours. I imagined my sister handcuffed to cell bars.

Man, did that feel good.

Flag's Number One Fan scrubbed his hand over his face, then dropped his hand to his belt, where he popped open a small leather case I'd previously missed seeing.

I knew it! This was Arizona, after all . . . but before I could visualize a tiny gun in his hand, he reached into the case—more of a pouch, really—and pulled out a morsel for Khan. Feeding it to the bird, he refused to meet my eyes as he answered me.

"I had my reasons."

"Reasons good enough to allow a Native American activist to perpetrate a fraud?" I asked. "A fraud that, according to Julie, damaged your reputation in Flagstaff and divided the community into opposing camps?"

"I did what I had to do to protect my family," Warner claimed.

Well, I was trying to protect my family here, too, I reasoned. And that, for me, was definitely a reason good enough to drop all my tact and subtlety and just confront the man.

"What are you hiding, Bill? What else was going on with you and Ron Walking Eagle?"

"Try 'blackmail,' Bob," Warner said. "And by the way, I happen to know for a fact that Ron Walking Eagle was no Native American activist."

Joe's comments about the local gossip surrounding Ron's tribal ties came thundering back into my head.

"He wasn't a full-blooded Yavapai?" I asked.

Warner looked me in the eye, searching for something. Understanding? Pity? Sympathy?

"He wasn't even half Yavapai," he said. "Ron Walking Eagle didn't have a trace of Indian blood in him at all."

Damn.

Now Warner was doing the same thing Julie had done to me earlier when she'd told me the land wasn't sacred to anybody: changing the facts, or at least, the facts as we knew them. What was it with these Flagstaff people, anyway? Couldn't anyone get their facts straight? Did anyone in this whole town know how to tell the truth?

I heaved a sigh of frustration and gave Warner a baleful look.

"So why was he posing as an Indian to claim your land as sacred—"

And that's when Luce shouted.

I spun around to see her where she and Gil had been standing on the edge of the dropoff, but she was gone.

Gone.

Holy crap!

Chapter Fourteen

I raced across the meadow and caught Gil's muscled arm in my hand just in time to keep myself from going over the edge into space.

"Luce!" I yelled, looking down the steep side of the cliff, frantically sending a prayer skyward that she was alive, if not exactly well.

"Bob," she replied, looking up at me from where she was sitting on a small shale ledge that extended out about fifteen feet down the slope.

"Are you all right?" Hopefully, my heart would stop hammering in another moment or two so I could see clearly again. Crazy rushes of adrenaline will do that to you, I've discovered: obscure your vision, make your heart pound, your head spin, your stomach heave.

Really fun stuff.

"I'm fine," she said, brushing off dust and vegetation that she'd apparently collected on her impromptu slide to the ledge. "I lost my footing. Be careful," she warned me. "That's just about where I was standing when the earth slid out from under my feet."

"That was weird," Gil commented to me. "It was like she took off flying. Flapping her wings and everything."

It wasn't the first time someone had likened my fiancée to a bird. I did it all the time. Luce the Goose, I called her, though never out loud.

"I heard that," Luce called up from below us. "Thanks a lot, Gil. Not only am I now bruised, but I'm embarrassed."

"You'd make a great eagle, honey," I assured her. "You'd fit right in with all those apex predators."

Speaking of which, I looked around for Walking Eagle, but Gil's raptor was nowhere in sight.

"Hey," I said, "where's Walking Eagle?"

Gil was scanning the sky.

"I don't know. When Luce fell and shouted, it startled him, and he leapt off my fist. I assumed he jumped to the ground, but," he swept his hand around to include the meadow, "obviously not."

"He's here." Luce's voice came up the cliff again.

Gil and I both directed our attention to Luce, who was pointing to a shallow alcove on another, narrower, ledge situated midway between her ledge and the rim and about twenty feet from her right. The Golden Eagle was perched on a small stump that rose out of the rocks, his head turning abruptly from side to side as he eyed Luce and then Gil and me. Near him in another tangle of branches growing out of the cliff were the unmistakable traces of an abandoned eagle's nest.

"I never noticed that nest before," Gil said. He frowned for a minute, then snapped his fingers.

"That's it!" he turned to me to explain. "That alcove wasn't visible before now. I thought the rocks below us looked different than they usually do, but I assumed it was the angle of the sun and the shadows at this time of day. I think I told you this morning how some of these rock faces and clefts can be deceiving, depending on the light."

Gee, maybe the cliffs could form a club with Julie and Warner: Not What You Think, Inc., or perhaps Obfuscation Unlimited.

Obfuscation. I've always wanted to use that word in a sentence, but I was afraid no one would know what I meant. Now that I had a reason to use it, though, it only made things worse, because it proved just how messed up this whole Flag trip was.

"Hello? Remember me? Down here?"

I swung my attention back to Luce.

"I'm looking for a way to get you up here," I assured her. "That cliff behind you is pretty sheer, so I'm going to have to come at you from a diagonal, I think. If I can work my way to the pile of rocks just below me here, I think I can reach far enough to give you a hand up."

I caught Gil's eye.

"So you're saying the nest was hidden in broad daylight?"

"No," he replied. "There's been a rock slide since we were here two days ago. I think those boulders down there," he pointed to the rock jumble below the narrow ledge, "used to be up there."

His finger traced a line from below the ledge to above it.

"There must have been a thin wall of rocks between us and that nest, and it blocked our view from here."

"Maybe that's where the accident we heard about happened."

I looked over my shoulder at Warner, who had come up behind me. Khan was back on his fist, his hood now removed.

"You know, the one here at the Ridge," he explained. "The one involving Julie Burrows and some friend of hers."

"My brother-in-law," I corrected him.

"Pardon?"

I turned to face Bill Warner.

"My brother-in-law was the person with Julie in the accident. He's got a damaged knee thanks to it, and he's on crutches."

Warner looked at me in puzzlement.

"I thought you said your sister was the one in danger."

"She is! But she's married to my brother-in-law, who's an old friend of Julie's and happened to be climbing around out here with her two days ago when they got caught in a rockslide."

"Are you guys going to help me get back up there or not?"

Luce again. This time, however, I thought I detected a bit of pique in her usually sylvan tones.

I looked back over the rim at my fiancée.

"Yes. Just a minute."

I turned again to Warner.

"So what was Ron Walking Eagle blackmailing you with that was so awful that you went along with not only pretending he was a Native American, but that this land was sacred?"

"Blackmailing?" Gil asked.

"Get me up there!" Luce shouted.

I spun around and crouched on the edge of the dropoff. A few stones skittered out from beneath my feet and slid down the steep slope towards Luce.

"Do you mind? I'm going out on a ledge here with Warner," I told her, my own voice a little on the piqued side. "If I can crack this case for Julie—"

"*You're* going out on a ledge? I'm already on one, and if you don't get me off it in the next thirty seconds," she threatened, "I will tell everyone that you wear my lingerie."

"I don't wear your lingerie."

"I know that, and you know that, but do you want everyone else wondering? You've got fifteen seconds left, Bobby."

"I'm on it," I said, scanning the slope for a toehold within my leg's reach.

What was wrong with me, anyway? Luce was stuck on a rock shelf, and I was playing detective. Sure, my best friend was lame and my sister was shook up, but at least they weren't sitting out in space above a rocky abyss. A few less feet of that ledge's width and Luce might have fallen a lot further than fifteen feet. Gil had been right when he said some of the Ridge's paths could get tricky.

He hadn't mentioned they might be deadly.

I studied the drop down to Luce's ledge. I figured if I could step down into the cliff, I could make my way to the top of the rock pile that Gil said wasn't there two days ago. From there, I could lean over and stretch my arm far enough to grab Luce's hand and haul her up past the smooth boulders. Then she could find a toehold of her own in the rocks to help boost her all the way up to join me on the top of the rocky pile.

For crying out loud, what had Gil been thinking to let Luce stand so close to that crumbly edge of the rim? Anyone could have taken that fall. If he was as familiar with the Ridge as he claimed to be, he should have found a safer location to launch Walking Eagle. I couldn't imagine that providing visitors with a free fall experience would encourage their return.

Over to my right, about five feet down, I spotted a tiny outcrop of rock that looked like it was just the size of my foot, so I rolled over onto my belly and slipped my legs and lower body over the rim of the dropoff. Blindly, I searched the rock surface with the toe of my left boot until I felt it land on the outcrop, tested it for my weight, then slowly eased the rest of my body down the cliff face.

"To your right, Bob," Gil directed me. "There's a tiny cleft where you should be able to jam in your right toe."

So, Warner's grandson really did know the lay of this land, I mused as I followed his instructions. He even knew where a toehold was in this cliff.

Pretty specific knowledge, if you asked me.

Like, really specific.

Gil Warner had climbed down this cliff.

When, and why, would he have done that?

My boot found the crack, and I wedged my toe in tightly, using the bits of tough vegetation that somehow survived on the cliff as anchors for my hands. Thankfully, the slope wasn't as steep as it had appeared from above. Instead of feeling like I was a picture hanging vertically on a rock wall, I had the odd sensation of lying down while standing up. Beneath me, the rock slope was warm from the day's sun, and if I hadn't had an irate fiancée below me and an elderly possible murder suspect waiting above me in the meadow, I might have enjoyed rock-climbing with Gil.

Who clearly knew his way around the Ridge.

A weird thought popped into my head.

Maybe Gil knew more about that rockslide that injured Alan and Julie than he had let on.

Hadn't Warner mentioned that they'd been in the preserve the day of the rockslide?

Gil was strong, no doubt. Strong enough to start a slide?

Holy cow.

How many Warners were involved in this mess, anyway?

My foot slipped just a fraction of an inch, reminding me that I'd better pay attention now and play sleuth later. I refocused on the rock beneath me.

"Almost there," I told Luce.

I carefully stretched my left foot over and down to the top of the tall pile of rocks, then shifted my balance to bring the rest of my body above the pile. I dropped to my heels and reached down to grasp Luce's hand. I wrapped my fingers around her wrist, braced my body against the rock wall and pulled her part-way up the pile until she could find her own footing amidst the boulders.

"Got you," I told her. "You know, you're going to have to do better than that if you think you're going to get out of marrying me next month."

Luce wiped a strand of blond hair off her forehead and smiled. "Oh, darn. You saw through my ruse."

"I have the eye of an eagle," I assured her. "I see things that others can only imagine. Speaking of which, maybe I should take a look at some of your lingerie . . . "

She pointed her finger at the rim above us. I looked up to see the two Warners watching us.

"Let's get up there, first, Eagle-eye," she said. "We can talk about my lingerie later."

"Promise?"

"Climb, Bobby."

I began my traverse back up the slope when I felt a small rock hit my back. Looking up, I saw the big white Gyrfalcon staring down at me over the edge of the cliff. Tiny rocks were tumbling down where his talons bit into the bare earth. I ducked my head so I wouldn't get the grit in my eyes, and just as I did, I heard the flap of powerful wings taking to the air.

Almost instantaneously, another set of wings rustled to life off to my left.

I turned my head.

Walking Eagle soared off into the empty sky, just as Khan landed on the abandoned nest in the shallow alcove.

From the rim I could hear Gil cry in triumph, "Fly, baby!"

When I looked up again, more pebbles rained down on me. But this time, they weren't falling from between Khan's talons.

They were crumbling beneath Bill Warner's shoes.

Chapter Fifteen

THE OLD MAN BENT OVER AND extended his hand down to me. "Can I give you a lift?"

Three possible answers spun through my head.

Answer number one: "No, thanks."

The reason: the man suffered from vertigo, remember? It would be just my luck that he'd have an episode when I clasped his hand, and then we'd both be taking the express slide down.

Answer number two: "Hell no."

The reason: I'd decided that Julie was definitely on to something pretty incriminating about Bill Warner, and now that he knew I was involved in her investigation of him, it didn't take a big leap of my over-active imagination to see him letting my hand go as soon as I put my trust in him.

Answer number three: "I may be slow, but I'm not totally stupid."

The reason: see both of the above.

Before I could reply, though, Gil had moved his grandfather back from the precipice and taken his place, assuming the same posture, offering me his hand.

And then that weird thought I'd had about him and the rockslide turned into a full blown siren inside my head.

Gil had been here at the Ridge, here at the cliff, the day of the rockslide.

Gil should have known better than to bring Luce so close to the edge.

Gil drove up in a silver Porsche, and a silver Porsche had almost run down my sister in Flagstaff.

But Gil had only been a toddler when Ron Walking Eagle disappeared. What reason would he have to be involved in Julie's mystery? Judging from his father's comments at the restaurant, Gil wasn't even aware of the elder Warner's history with the activist, and his bird's name was just one of life's odd coincidences.

Along with his driving up in the Porsche.

And being here at the Ridge the same day of the rockslide.

Could I be any more pathetically paranoid?

I grasped the hand Gil offered, and he helped pull me up the final two feet. As soon as I scrambled back onto the rim, I turned around, and with Gil's help, we lifted Luce right off the slope and helped her walk up the last bit of the climb. I wrapped my arms around her and held her close.

But not until we'd moved a good ten feet back from the crumbly edge of the rim.

"I've decided rock-climbing is not on my list of hobbies I'd like to take up," she murmured. "There's too much empty air involved, if you know what I mean. I like air, really I do. But not when it's under my feet." She gave me a quick kiss on the cheek. "Thank you."

I smoothed her hair behind her ear.

"That must be why you always have both feet on the ground, then. My mom's been saying that about you for years, you know. 'She might be a dumb blond, Bob, but at least she has her feet on the ground.'"

Luce half-heartedly slugged me in the shoulder. "She does not say that."

"You're right. I lied," I confessed. "And you're welcome. I'm sorry I took so long to get you up here. I was . . . distracted."

She slugged me again, but this time there was more Luce-like force behind it.

"Ow."

"You think?" she said. "From what I could hear of the conversations up here while I was stuck out in space, imagining the ledge falling away and taking me with it, my well-being clearly rated behind the whereabouts of a certain Golden Eagle and the motives of a possible murder suspect."

Her accusing eyes reminded me of the fierce intensity of Khan's as he had glared down at me from the top of the cliff just moments ago.

Except that Luce's eyes are sky blue, not yellow like the Gyr's.

And when she looks at me, I feel all warm and happy inside. When a Gyr looks at you, it feels like you're being measured for a meal. A big meal, for sure, but raptors can really put it away when they want to.

If Luce, on the other hand, was thinking of having me for lunch, I'd consider it a privilege.

Lunch.

Wilson Warner's comment to me before he lurched out of the restaurant at noon popped up in my head.

"If Gil only knew," he'd said.

At the time, I'd assumed he meant that the youngest Warner was unaware of the details of his grandfather's public debacle twenty years ago, and that the reminder supplied by his eagle's name was a very sore spot for both Wilson and Bill. Yet when I'd asked Bill about it in front of Gil before I finally clambered down to Luce's rescue, the only part of my question that seemed to surprise Gil was the word "blackmailing." To the other details of the scandal, he didn't bat an eye.

Not to Ron Walking Eagle's name, not to the man's passing himself off as a Native American, and not even to the fact that the land wasn't sacred.

Which meant that Gil knew all about his grandfather's history with the activist, except for the big blackmail secret.

And if Wilson had said, "if Gil only knew,' then, by my superior deductive reasoning, I concluded that Wilson did, in fact, know something that Gil didn't.

Bill Warner wasn't holding the only key to Julie's mystery.

Wilson Warner had one, too.

I looked over Luce's shoulder and watched Khan soaring in the empty space beyond the precipice. A moment later, he circled back and with a few elegant beats of his powerful wings, the white raptor came to a stop over the raised fist of his owner. Settling onto Warner's gloved hand, Khan folded his wings against his body and threw me what I could only describe as a smug look.

"Show off," I muttered. "No fear of heights, or empty air, for you, obviously."

He flexed his big talons, and I saw something that looked like a small yellow tube drop from his feet to roll in the earth. Caked with soil, it must have stuck between Khan's toes when he'd landed in the old nest and only dislodged when he'd grasped his master's wrist. Even from where I stood some twenty feet away, the object looked oddly familiar, but I couldn't quite place it. I unwrapped myself from Luce and walked over to Warner and his bird, thinking I'd pick up the item and stick it into my pocket until I could remember why it looked familiar to me.

"Is your fiancée all right?" Warner asked as I approached.

I nodded.

"She's fine. She's just not finding endless vertical living space all that appealing at the moment."

Warner smiled. "I know how she feels. Just now, when I offered to help you up, I had a pretty bad bout of vertigo, I have to admit. I don't know what I was thinking, trying to help you up when I can't even tolerate being on a rim like that."

He fed Kahn a tidbit from the leather case at his belt.

"Good thing Gil was there. If you'd taken my hand, we probably would have both gone flying all the way to the bottom."

I didn't bother to tell him the same thought had occurred to me, along with a much less flattering scenario of his intent.

I bent over to retrieve the dusty yellow tube from the ground. It was plastic and jagged at one end, as though part of it had been broken off. Only about an inch in diameter, the two-inch long cylinder had grit and earth packed inside of it; wherever it had originally come from, it had clearly sat in the abandoned nest for a long time. I dropped it into my jeans pocket.

"Listen, Bob," Warner said. "If it's so important to you, I'll tell you about the blackmail. But not here. Not in front of Gil."

He darted his eyes in the direction of his grandson, who was sitting cross-legged on the edge of the cliff, apparently waiting for his eagle to return.

"If you and Luce still want to try to find that Scott's Oriole, I'll show you where it was reported," he offered. "Along the way, I'll fill in the sordid details."

"Deal," Luce said from behind me. Recovered from her fright, my fiancée was back in the game.

A game that, with any luck, was just about over.

Chapter Sixteen

We walked back across the rocky meadow to take a path that wound into a stand of pinyon pines. The sharp tang of the wood scented the air, and the afternoon sun filtered down through the upturned branches, warming the spaces beneath the trees. Here and there, I caught a quick look at a short-horned lizard or a gecko sunning itself on a rock before they heard our approach and scurried away. On a high branch of one tree, I spotted a flash of blue. Seeing as we were surrounded by pinyon trees, I expected to find a Pinyon Jay, but once I got a good look at the bird, it was clearly one of his cousins instead. Pinyon Jays had shorter tails and were steel-blue all over, whereas this bird had the long tail and white breast of the Mexican Jay.

I grabbed Luce's arm to bring her to a stop beside me and pointed up at the bird.

From our vantage point below, the jay's white belly formed a sharp contrast with the bluish-green of the surrounding needles, and the dark mask around his eyes was impossible to miss. He was tugging seeds off the branch, and Luce let out a little sigh of envy.

"You know how much those pinyon nuts he's wolfing down for free cost from my specialties supplier these days?"

I smiled. Not even being trapped on a mountain ledge was enough to make Luce forget her executive chef priorities.

"Don't worry," I assured her. "That jay up there is probably single-handedly responsible for starting at least a dozen more pinyon trees in this little grove, even as we speak. The way he's scattering seeds as he eats is going to result in plenty more pinyon nuts for your future culinary efforts."

"We used to call them Gray-breasted Jays when I was a boy," Warner commented. "Now we call them Mexican Jays. Same bird, different name. I guess it just goes to show you that, contrary to what some folks will tell you, the world's getting bigger all the time."

"How so?" Luce asked.

The Ridge's former owner sat down on a fallen log and laid his gloved fist on the rough bark beside him. Khan, hooded again, tilted his head to the side, listening to his master's voice.

"Well, some people say all our technology and fancy communications are making the world smaller. Personally, I think that's the glass half-empty approach." He pulled a morsel for Khan from his belt pocket and popped it into the bird's beak.

"I like to think that the world is getting larger—the glass half-full—because we keep adding to our store of knowledge, thanks to those same technologies. Look at the advances in molecular science and how that's impacted birding: based on DNA analyses, we've identified new subspecies of birds. That's the reason the American Ornithologists' Union changes bird names on occasion: we've got new birds to add to the inventory, so the names need to be more accurate. For instance, what we used to call the Scrub-Jay is now a family of three: the Florida, Island, and Western, depending on where you find them."

He pulled a handkerchief from a pants pocket and mopped his brow. I realized I'd forgotten to grab the water bottles from the car before we left the parking lot and was glad for the shade of the pinyons. Though we weren't out in the hot Arizona desert, it was still plenty warm at this higher elevation, and birders should know better than to hike without water. I made a mental note to be sure Luce and I rehydrated when we got back to the car.

"But in the case of the Mexican Jay," Warner continued, pointing to the bird high overhead, "he actually got his original name back. In 1983, the AOU officially reinstated the name Mexican Jay for the Gray-breasted Jay. My guess is that the AOU decided the original name was more descriptive based on the bird's range."

He tucked the handkerchief back in his pocket.

"Names are important, for birds and men. In fact, a name was exactly what Ron Walking Eagle was using to blackmail me twenty years ago."

My eyes locked on his.

"A name?"

"My name," Warner said.

"Your name," I said, slowly.

How does someone blackmail you using your own name?

I wondered if the heat was getting to the old man, and that instead of solving Julie's mystery, we were only getting more . . . obfuscated.

Although we did just see a Mexican Jay, and I still had hope for that Scott's Oriole. If I added that southwest specialty to my list, I certainly wouldn't call the day a waste.

Obfuscation, maybe, but not a waste.

"I don't get it," Luce said. "How can you be blackmailed with your own name? Are you actually someone else, and you've just been using the name of Warner all these years?"

The old man chuckled.

"Oh, no. I'm Bill Warner, clear and legal. You see, the deal was, so was Ron Walking Eagle."

Now, that made sense.

Not.

"I still don't get it," I said.

"I do," said Luce, staring at Warner. "Ron Walking Eagle was Bill Warner. Junior," she added. "Ron was your son."

Warner nodded. "Yes, ma'am, he was. Now if you want to find that oriole, go another hundred yards ahead. Look at the oaks on your left. I thought I just heard that boy singing."

And then he grabbed his throat, his eyes rolled up in his head, and he pitched forward off the log.

Crap. I hate it when that happens.

Chapter Seventeen

KHAN'S WHITE WINGS FLAPPED in confusion, his eyes blind to his master's collapse, while he tried to regain his balance on the gloved fist that was now lying on the rocky soil along with the rest of Warner. I leaned down and wrapped my arms around his prone body, lifting him off the ground as I administered the Heimlich maneuver at the same time—the man had, after all, given me the universal sign for choking: he'd grabbed his throat. Khan, meanwhile, still loosely attached to Warner's wrist, continued to flap his wings, hitting me in the face and blocking my vision.

"You got it!" Luce informed me from somewhere in front of us. All I could see was the back of Warner's head and white feathers. "Something just shot out of his mouth."

But I could feel through my hands on his body that the old man still wasn't breathing.

He needed air in his lungs.

Fending off a flurry of Khan's wingbeats, I laid Warner on the ground and took a breath.

I looked quickly at Luce.

"He means nothing to me," I assured her. "Really. Now go get Gil."

She took off at a sprint, and I grabbed Warner's jaw. I sealed my lips to his, pinched his nose shut and began mouth-to-mouth resuscitation.

Don't you die on me. Don't you die on me. Don't you die on me.

Julie's going to kill me if you die on me.

The words rolled through my head, and I kept up the drill. Good thing I'd taken that first aid refresher class that Katy the Trauma Queen, our school nurse, had offered to our faculty last spring.

"You need a refresher course," she'd badgered me in the staff lounge. "What are you going to do when you're chaperoning at prom and some student starts choking because he's stuffed so much food in his mouth and tried to sing rap at the same time to impress his date?"

"Never happen," I said.

"Last year. Minneapolis Market Square," she recited. "Dinner was lasagna and garlic toast. Ugly when it came back up. I may never eat Italian again. Or listen to rap, either."

Katy had even borrowed a responding dummy from the Savage police department for us to use in the class. At the time, I wasn't thrilled to be practicing my lip lock on an oversized doll, but now I was grateful I'd had the chance to perfect my technique, as Warner suddenly caught a breath and his lungs inflated.

Yes! I mentally pumped my fist in triumph. *Who's the man? Me! Bob White, mouth breather!*

Okay, maybe not the most flattering trait I could claim, but hey, a very valuable one in this case.

I helped Warner slowly sit up, while Khan seemed to finally settle down again on his master's fist.

"You were choking on something," I explained to him after he'd shaken his head and focused his eyes on me. "Take some more deep breaths."

He obliged, and I watched his chest rise and fall with the draughts of fresh air he took in.

"Better?" I asked.

"Much," he replied. "How long was I out?"

"Hours," I told him, and his eyes glazed over.

"Just kidding," I added hastily. I didn't need the guy to have a heart attack, too. Katy the Trauma Queen had said my CPR technique had about as much finesse as a kick in the head.

"I don't know if it was even a minute, to be honest with you," I told Warner. "I wasn't timing, just breathing. You feel okay?"

"I guess so," he said. "So I can't plead brain damage and conveniently forget all about what we were talking about before I choked on that beef jerky, huh?"

"Is that what it was?"

"Don't tell my doctor. He told me to lay off after the last time I ended up in the emergency room after a choking episode," he explained. "I figure an old man like me is entitled to a few vices, yet."

He stroked Khan's smooth white chest, his eyes growing a little watery as he watched his Gyr.

"Speaking of vices. Ron was the result of one of them. I met his mother when she passed through town on her way to California. It was 1960, and she was headed for San Francisco. One of the original flower children. Free spirit and free love. Pretty heady stuff for a high plateau boy like me."

I crouched on the ground in front of Warner.

"You don't have to tell me this stuff," I said. "I just needed to know why you let Ron blackmail you, because Julie thinks it will help her solve his disappearance."

"You mean his murder," he corrected me. "I know that's what she thinks, and believe me, I've lain awake many a night over the years wondering if that's the truth."

"You really don't know what happened to him, do you?"

He shook his head.

"I didn't even know he existed until the day he showed up at my office in the bank. It's Wilson's bank now, you know," he added.

"He doesn't personally handle anyone's money, does he?" I asked.

Having just met Wilson during one of his benders, he didn't exactly inspire financial confidence in me. To be frank, I wasn't confident he could cross the street, let alone handle a portfolio.

"Not any more. He just makes public appearances, mostly."

I started to roll my eyes.

"Usually they're not of the same type as you witnessed today in the restaurant," he said. "Thankfully."

He took a tidbit from his belt pouch and fed it to the bird while he resumed his story.

"So here's this full-grown man in my office, telling me he's my son, and that he wants his inheritance." Warner threw me a pointed look. "He'd heard about my plans to donate the Ridge, and he'd decided he wanted it for himself. If I gave it to him, he'd go away, leave my wife unenlightened about her husband's cheating past, and bury the scandal it would cause me. If I didn't hand the Ridge over, he would make a court case out of it just to make me and my family suffer, because he knew I didn't have the guts to come clean about my paternity."

Paternity.

Alan's and Joe's faces popped into my head, followed by Julie's and Lily's. Paternity could sure make a mess of things, I reflected. Reminding myself that, aside from the striking physical resemblance, Alan had no proof that Joe was his son, I realized that even suspected paternity could wreak havoc in the lives of all those involved.

"You were one hundred percent positive that Ron was your son?" I pressed him. "I mean, did you run a paternity test to prove it? He wasn't just some con artist taking advantage of a wealthy bank president?"

Warner sighed. "I wish that had been the case, Bob. Then none of this would have happened. Fact is, I didn't need a paternity test to know Ron was my son. He may not have looked like a Warner because he had his mother's raven hair and those high cheekbones, but he had something I couldn't deny: a birth certificate with my name on it as the father."

"But anyone can—"

"No buts, Bob. It was legal. I tracked down the hospital in California that issued it and had it verified. My name on the certificate and a birthdate nine months after Ron's mother left Flagstaff. She never told me, never contacted me. By the time I met my son, he'd legally changed his name from William Warner, Jr., to Ron Walking Eagle, and he'd stored up enough resentment towards the father he'd never known to make my life a walking nightmare."

Yikes. At least Alan had found out now that he might have a son. I couldn't imagine how difficult it would be to learn you'd fathered a child after that child had become an adult. I figured that would be enough fodder for counseling sessions for life.

"I never knew what happened to Ron after the court ruled in my favor," Warner said. "I didn't hear from him again, and, to be honest with you, I was so relieved, I didn't care. Over the years, I kept wondering, though, if he'd show up again some day to blackmail me or make some other kind of trouble, but he never did. I thought it was all over, until that Corwin fellow showed up in Flagstaff to research his book. Wilson got wind of it, and next thing I knew, he's got a drinking problem."

"I'm sorry to hear that, Bill."

Like it or not, I was so deep into counseling listening mode, I couldn't have said anything else if my life depended on it. My invisible neon "talk to me" sign was clearly blazing at full intensity. Sometimes, I feel like I should just carry a portable tape recorder with me, and when someone wants to talk, I could just hand it to him, and tell him to have at it, and I'd come back and pick it up after I get coffee.

Or after I ran errands.

Or after I went birding in Jamaica.

Jamaica.

That was a thought.

I wondered if Luce might want to try Jamaica for our honeymoon.

We'd already agreed we wanted to go somewhere tropical for our honeymoon, which we were postponing from right after the wedding to during my winter break from school. I was going to have to get a birding guide . . .

"Not as sorry as I was to see it," Warner confessed. "But that was nothing compared to the downhill slide Wilson's taken since Julie Burrows came to town. He needs to dry out, bad. And I don't know if he's behind these attacks on Julie and your sister, but if he is, we need to find out and put a stop to it."

"Sounds like a plan," I said.

Warner's eyes went wide and his face froze.

Oh, no.

All of my interior alarms began clanging wildly.

I knew it. The old man was about to have a stroke, after all, right here in front of me. Mouth-to-mouth resuscitation I could manage, but raising the dead was way out of my league.

Warner's mouth opened.

"Behind you," he breathed.

Taking the chance that he wouldn't fall down dead while I checked over my shoulder, I wasn't sure what to expect waiting behind me.

Bigfoot?

Nope.

Just a picture-perfect Scott's Oriole.

Posed amidst the bristly branches of a pinyon tree, the oriole was an incandescent burst of yellow. His sunny belly, back, shoulder and tail patches were starkly defined by the surrounding black feathers. I realized it was like looking at an Orchard Oriole, except in all the places the Orchard was orange, the Scott's wore yellow. At an inch longer than its cousin, this oriole also seemed substantially bigger, though that impression might well have been the result of his brilliant yellow coloring which made him stand out with even more definition from the dark needles around him.

I interrupted mentally cataloguing my observations to turn around and check on Warner. I didn't want him dying while I wasn't looking.

"Are you doing okay?" I whispered, careful to keep my voice low do I didn't scare off the Scott's.

"I'm not dead yet, if that's what you're asking," he whispered back. "Really, I'm fine," he added when I gave him a questioning look. "Watch your bird."

So I did. I studied the bird in silence, happy to have the chance to add it to my life list. A Scott's Oriole was a good find, even for a local Arizona birder. Another minute of posing, and then it flew off.

"Nice," I told Warner.

"Too bad your fiancée missed it."

I cringed. Luce was going to be ticked. I'd flat out forgotten she wasn't right there with us.

Maybe I wouldn't tell her. What she didn't know wouldn't hurt her, right? Besides, I figured that if she were still a little angry with me about the delay in my white knight duties at the ledge, missing the oriole was not going to help me regain her unqualified favor.

Silence really is golden.

"Hey, there!" Warner called out. "You just missed the Scott's Oriole!"

I looked over my shoulder to see Luce and Gil closing in on us through the pines.

Thanks, Bill.

"You're all right!" Luce exclaimed, her eyes on Warner. "I was so worried!"

"It was the beef jerky again, wasn't it?" Gil admonished his grandfather. "Stubborn old man."

He clapped his arms around Warner and gave him a hard hug.

"You scared the life out of me, Granddad. Don't do that again, you hear me?"

Warner smiled at me over his grandson's shoulder. "I'm just playing with you kids. A little shot of adrenaline never hurt anybody. Believe me, I'm not ready to pack it in yet, Gil. I'm still building my legacy."

Luce turned to me.

"Did he say you saw a Scott's Oriole?"

That's my Luce. She doesn't miss a thing.

I was going to tell her, anyway.

Really.

In a few years, maybe.

"Yes, we did," I told her. "And it flew that way."

I pointed in the same direction that Warner had indicated before his choking episode. I took Luce's hand. "Come on, we'll find it."

I looked at Gil and Warner.

"I think we'll take it from here. Thanks for showing us around the Ridge."

"Anytime," Gil said. "Thanks for taking care of my grandfather. I know he looks like a tough old coot, but he's a teddy bear inside. I hate to think what might have happened if you hadn't been here."

His voice hitched just the tiniest bit, betraying a well of emotion that he was working hard to cover. "Peas in a pod," his father had slurred out at the restaurant, a note of resentment in his tone. Watching Gil with his grandfather here at the Ridge, I suddenly realized I'd misinterpreted Wilson's comment.

Wilson Warner didn't resent his father's and son's close relationship at all.

He envied them.

"Say, Bob," the elder Warner asked just as I started to turn away. "I know you're interested in that old court case because of your sister and her husband, but do you know why Julie Burrows is so hell-bent on finding out whatever happened to Ron Walking Eagle? Far as I know, he didn't have any . . . family...waiting on him. There were a lot of reporters sniffing around back then, trying to stir up the sacred Indian lands angle into a full-fledged conflagration, but from what I've seen of her, Ms. Burrows looks way too young to have been one of those bottom-feeders. So what's her connection?"

I looked from Warner to Gil and back again to the old man.

"Ron was her friend. He cared for her when no one else did." I gave Luce's warm hand in mine a squeeze. "I think he was, for a while, her dad."

And with that, Luce and I went in search of the Scott's Oriole.

Chapter Eighteen

"HE'S LYING," JULIE SAID FOR ABOUT the twentieth time in five minutes. "Ron was a Native American. He was a member of the Yavapai community. He cared passionately about tribal culture and rights. Warner is lying."

I was sitting at her kitchen table where the four of us—Joe, Luce, Julie, and I—had just devoured the veal medallions in fig and almond cream that Luce had adapted from an item she'd seen on the lunch menu at the restaurant. Alan and Lily were hunkered down at the inn on campus, eating a dinner prepared by students in the college's culinary program. I didn't know what their entrée was, but I was pretty sure it wasn't as good as what Luce had prepared. Some days, I have to kick myself for being so lucky with Luce. She's my ideal woman. She birds, cooks, and puts up with me.

Although she does have this fear of empty air, I'd recently discovered. I may have to rethink that "ideal woman" part. I thought nothing could scare Luce.

Then again, I may already be in too deep. The wedding invitations went in the mail last week. Guess I'll have to sell all my mountain-climbing ropes and pitons and cancel my subscription to *Free Fall, the Magazine for People with a Death Wish.*

"But do you have any real proof of Ron's membership in a tribe?" Luce was asking Julie. "Warner has a certified birth certificate. Think about it," she said. "If Joe told someone he was Native American, why would they question it? Especially when he's here in Flagstaff with other Indian students. If Ron, with his classic Native American looks, judging from that photo of the two of you in your office, said he was Yavapai, and was working as an activist for Indian rights, who would think twice about his heritage?"

"But why would he do that if he weren't Native American?" Julie persisted.

"Because he wanted to?" I suggested. "Look, Julie, there are a lot of people who support a cause because they believe it's right, and not necessarily because it's part of their birthright or heritage. As to why Ron said he was Yavapai, maybe he thought it would play better if he had a blood connection to his cause."

"Or maybe his mom was a member of the Yavapai band," Joe interjected. "Mr. Warner didn't say who Walking Eagle's mom was, did he? He said she was just passing through town, right? There's a Yavapai community not that far from Flagstaff, and maybe she was running away from home, Mom, just like you did when you were a kid. And then, maybe she didn't want her baby to know he was a half-breed, because she knew how hard it would be for him, so she raised him as a Yavapai."

Joe's eyes pleaded with his mother.

I thought of our conversation this afternoon, and his desperate need to have Julie acknowledge the reality of his life as a half-breed. Her refusal to see his life through his eyes was already driving a wedge between mother and son as evidenced by Joe's reluctance to share with Julie the real source of the hate mail they'd received; as a counselor who had years of experience with drama queens, troubled teens, and everybody in-between, I shuddered to think how that wedge could ultimately drive them apart. I could feel the words on my tongue, ready to jump to Joe's assistance.

But I kept my mouth shut.

This was between Joe and his mom.

Come on, Julie, I prayed. *Listen to what your son is saying.*

Julie studied Joe's earnest face.

"And when Ron grew up, and found out he wasn't who he thought he was, he wanted to meet his father, so he could figure out who he really was?" she asked him. "Because he felt like a part of him was missing. Is that it?"

You could have heard the proverbial pin drop in the kitchen as Luce and I watched mother and son in silence. We all knew that the topic under discussion was no longer Ron Walking Eagle's tribal affiliation.

This was about Joe's dad.

His real dad.

Who might be Alan.

Or not.

"Yeah, Mom, that's exactly it," Joe said, standing his ground.

Go, Joe!

Julie turned to Luce and me.

"Would you excuse us for a moment?" she asked.

No! No! I want to hear this, too!

I wondered if anyone else in the room could hear me yelling inside my head. I looked at Luce, hoping she would say some woman thing that would allow us to stay in the room and hear the answer to Joe's unspoken, but very loud, very crucial, question.

"Of course," Luce said. She grabbed my arm and dragged me out the back door of Julie's little bungalow.

"What are you doing?" I asked in dismay as soon as we were out of listening range of the kitchen. "I want to know the truth, too! Is Alan Joe's dad or not?"

"Julie's already told us he's not," she reminded me, dropping onto an ancient metal lawn chair on the tiny brick patio.

I spotted a fleck of lime green paint on the chair and figured that it must have originally been that color back when it was produced in the Pleistocene Age. Now, eons later, it was just dull metal gray.

"I know," I argued. "But what if that wasn't the truth? Alan said she's always had some control issues. And one way to control a situation is to manipulate the truth."

Luce patted the chair next to hers. It didn't look quite as aged as the one she was sitting on. I guessed it was a relic from the Bronze Age, but I could have been wrong.

It's been known to happen.

On occasion.

A lot.

"First of all, it's really none of your business if Alan fathered Joe," Luce pointed out. "It's not going to change your relationship or your history with Alan. The only way it might affect you is if Alan came to you for advice on how to handle a long-distance adolescent son."

Oh, man. What would that be like? Teens were tough enough to deal with when you lived with them all the time, according to parents I met at the high school. The Lab Mouse Liberator came to mind. Parenting a child who lived in another state would have to be impossibly difficult. If Alan wanted assistance for that, he was going to need professional help I wasn't qualified to give.

He was going to need a psychiatrist.

Not for Joe.

For Alan.

Because knowing Alan, he'd drive himself crazy worrying about the boy.

"Do you think Julie would consider moving to Minnesota?" I asked Luce.

Luce shook her head.

"Bobby, don't you think you're borrowing trouble here? I repeat, Julie says that Alan is not Joe's father."

"Now, see, this is the problem," I tried to make her understand. "Saying that 'Julie says,' is not hard evidence. In fact, 'Julie says' a lot of things that aren't exactly true. Alan told me he has his doubts, too, by the way. There's only one way to settle this once and for all: a paternity test."

Luce laughed.

"Oh, and you're the one to ask Julie to have it done? I don't think so."

"It's got to be Alan," I said. "He's got to ask her. He has rights in this case."

"There is no case!" Luce retorted. "She says he's not the father, and Alan isn't going to make a case of it, if for no other reason than to refuse to embarrass her in front of Joe, her son, by insisting that she's lying."

"People should be DNA sequenced at birth," I mumbled. "Then this would never happen."

"What in the world are you talking about?"

"Tracking bloodlines," I replied. "Warner was telling me that scientists tried to analyze the DNA of Gyrfalcon communities to try to identify subspecies, but they couldn't do it. Too many genes in the pool, apparently."

"So you think babies should have their DNA profiled and put on file? Would you want our children to have that done?"

Whoa.

Our children.

Our. Children.

My head started spinning.

"Put your head between your knees and breathe deeply, Bobby. You've got that glassy stare coming on," Luce warned.

I closed my eyes and put my head in my hands.

Children.

As in *my* children.

No wonder Lily had had a hard time getting Alan to discuss the topic. Thinking about that much responsibility in very personal terms and possibly in the short term, as well, just about made me pass out, and I didn't even have an unannounced love-child waiting in the wings.

Or did I?

Our. Children.

My lungs quit working.

I risked a look at Luce through my fingers. My voice was a croak. "You're not, like, trying to tell me something, are you?"

"Of course, I'm trying to tell you something."

My head spun faster, and I closed my eyes again.

"I'm trying to tell you that you are worrying over nothing. This is Alan's issue."

Air rushed back into my lungs. My heart started pumping again. The darkness lifted from my eyes.

Okay, that last part was probably due to the fact that I opened my eyes and not to a cosmic experience of reprieve. But you get the idea.

I was relieved.

I looked up at Luce who had a frown tugging at her lovely mouth.

"Bad choice of word," she noted. "I mean, it's Alan's life, not yours, Bobby."

Praise be to God.

Luce looked at me suspiciously.

"You thought I was going to say I'm pregnant, didn't you?"

"No!" I'd forgotten her uncanny ability to read my mind at the worst possible moments. I braced myself, totally uncertain how she was going to respond.

"Yeah, the idea scares me, too," she admitted, laying her hand on my arm. "I definitely want us to have kids, but not for a little while. I need to get used to being married before I make that leap. Do you mind?"

"Mind?"

I practically choked on the word, I was so grateful.

"I'm in no rush. I'm more than happy to let Lily provide my parents with their first grandchild."

The suspicious look was back on Luce's face.

"Are you saying that Lily's pregnant?"

"No!"

I could feel a fine sheen of sweat on my brow, and it wasn't a result of the dry Arizona heat. I needed to find something else to talk about before I jammed my foot any further down my throat. Lily would shoot me if I told Luce what she'd shared with me about her attempts to talk to Alan about starting a family. Lily and Luce were good friends, it was true, but no way was I volunteering that information. My shins were already banged up enough from today's impromptu rock-climbing.

Now there was a topic. Our excursion to the Ridge.

Including Luce's fall to the ledge, her incipient panic, and my tardy response.

On second thought, maybe that wasn't such a good idea. I'd tried to make it up to her by finding the Scott's Oriole, but that had been a bust, too. We'd spent an hour looking through the pines, but the sunny-bellied bird didn't make a return showing.

I put my hands on my thighs to heave myself out of the decrepit lawn chair, thinking that if I walked around Julie's sparsely vegetated back yard, some other topic of discussion might miraculously present itself. Instead, a sharp edge caught at my palm through my jeans pocket.

"Ouch."

Then I remembered the little artifact that Khan had inadvertently picked up from the old nest on the alcove above where Luce had been stranded on the ledge. I dug in my pocket and pulled it out.

"What is that?" Luce asked.

I turned the jagged tube around in my hand.

"I'm not sure. Khan had it in his toes when he flew back to Warner this afternoon. It must have stuck on his foot when he'd perched on that abandoned eagle nest."

She gave me a funny look.

"The Gyrfalcon. Not Warner," I clarified. "I've read that Gyrfalcons in the wild will often use abandoned eagle nests for their own, so maybe it was instinct that attracted Khan to the nest. But Khan's never been wild because he was bred for competition. He was raced by a wealthy Saudi Arabian before Warner got his hands on him. On Khan, I mean. Not the Saudi Arabian."

Luce smiled. "And this is going . . . where?"

I held up the scratched plastic tube.

"That's how I got this," I said. "Khan must have picked it up from the abandoned eagle's nest near where you were on the ledge. That was the only place I saw him land, so I assume that's where it came from."

She held out her palm, and I gave it to her.

"Careful. The one end has jagged edges."

She studied it for less than three seconds and said, "It's an inhaler. I used one when I was a kid when I got bad cases of hay fever. That's really odd."

"What?"

She rolled the cracked tube in her hand.

"Gil and I were actually talking about the pollen counts on the Colorado Plateau before I slid down the slope. I told him how I'd always heard that Arizona was a good place for people with allergies, because the air was so dry, but he told me there were plenty of other things to be allergic to in the state, like junipers, honey mesquite and Palo Verde trees. He said he and his dad can hardly stand to come out to the Ridge when the Rocky Mountain junipers flower in the spring. Wilson has such bad allergies, Gil can't remember a time when his dad didn't always have an inhaler in his pocket. "

She handed the faded piece of plastic back to me.

"This one's an old model of inhaler. It's just like the ones I used twenty years ago, which would make it almost as old as Gil. Maybe it was one of Wilson's."

I stuck it back in my pocket.

"So why did you pick it up?" she asked.

I shrugged.

"I don't know. It just seemed out of place. I didn't want Khan littering the Ridge, I guess."

I didn't add that it reminded me of something that was still niggling, unformed, at the back of my mind. I stood up and looked at the back door to Julie's kitchen.

"You think we can go back in, yet?"

Luce lifted her hands and laced her fingers into mine, and I pulled her up from her own relic of a lawn chair.

"I think we should make a discrete exit and leave them to their own devices," she said.

Then she leaned into me and laid a nice, long, warm kiss right on my lips.

"Okay," I agreed when she broke our lip lock. "I gotta tell you, you're a much better kisser than Bill Warner. Although, I have to admit, he was unconscious. So maybe it's not a fair comparison."

I caught her fist on its way to my shoulder and brought her knuckles to my lips.

"I think we should pursue this topic back at the inn, don't you?"

"You are such a sweet talker," she said and then added, "and so easily distracted, too."

"I'm not distracted," I corrected her. "I'm just good at prioritizing. I can talk to Joe tomorrow and find out what his mom told him. But tonight—"

I could have sworn I felt the earth move under my feet.

Funny. I wasn't even kissing Luce. I was just holding her hand to my lips. Must be the trains passing through town.

"Yes?" Luce asked expectantly. "You were saying?"

"Tonight, I'm—"

Again, I felt a tremor move up my legs.

I looked at a wooden swing Julie had suspended from an old oak in her tiny backyard, and it was clearly swaying. In the same instant, I heard tinkling noises like a window cracking from around the side of the house.

"Having an earthquake," I told her, pulling my suddenly speechless fiancée into the open middle of the yard.

Chapter Nineteen

"It's an earthquake!" Joe whooped as he ran out the back door, Julie close on his heels.

"How cool is this?"

"Not at all," Julie answered, wrapping her arms protectively around her son, who was too busy checking out the backyard in motion. "That tinkling sound was the rest of our broken window falling out of its frame, I think. Just pray that's all the damage we're going to have."

A sharp crack rang out, and we all watched a line etch itself in the house's plaster exterior from the top of the kitchen door to the roofline.

"Someone's not praying hard enough," Joe observed.

And then it was over.

The night was still, the trees stable.

"So, does this happen often?" Luce asked.

I noticed she looked a little stressed around her lovely blue eyes.

"Actually, it happens a lot in Arizona, but the epicenters aren't usually so close to Flagstaff," Julie assured us. "The geology department here at the university is the home of the Arizona Earthquake Information Center, and they get in the news once in a while, especially when some huge quake has hit somewhere else in the world."

"They recorded more than fifty earthquakes in Arizona just last year, Mom," Joe told her, "but most were in the one to two range on a twelve-point scale."

He turned to me and Luce, his face lit up with enthusiasm.

"One of the geology professors came to talk at a session yesterday at the conference. He had really cool pictures of collapsed buildings and mountains falling away."

I thought Luce went a shade paler.

"Ixnay on the mountains falling," I whispered to Joe. "It's a little too personal for Luce right now."

His brown eyes fixed on Luce for a moment, then swung back to me. He nodded in understanding.

"Oh, my gosh," Julie breathed, laying her hand on her son's shoulder. "Joe, did the geologist say anything about small tremors preceding bigger ones? You know, like warning signals?"

"He said it happens all the time. A bunch of other stuff can happen, too, like the air temperature rises, or animals start acting weird, phones malfunction, and people with respiratory illnesses experience increased discomfort."

Joe swept his hair off his face with both hands.

"Although the professor said there's no scientific proof of any of that except for the small tremors that might indicate a bigger shift in tectonic plates is coming. He said that earthquake prediction isn't exactly down to a formula yet."

I looked at Julie.

"Are you worried about aftershocks, or a bigger quake?"

"Neither," she replied, a hint of excitement creeping into her own voice. "I'm wondering if a little tremor is what caused the rockslide that caught Alan and me at the Ridge two days ago. And I'm also wondering if that's why the rock face just didn't look the way I remembered it from twenty years ago when Ron went into the cleft."

"There could have been some rock falls from tiny tremors," Luce suggested.

"And they disguised where I thought Ron went," Julie concluded.

I tried to visualize the ledge and the alcove at the Ridge. During dinner, Luce and I had described the spot to Julie, and she'd affirmed that was where she and Alan had been climbing, though she was certain there'd been no alcove exposed to the ledge.

Yet that alcove and its abandoned eagle's nest had been plainly in sight when we'd arrived at the precipice.

But, I suddenly recalled, Gil had said it looked different to him from just a few days earlier.

Had the rockslide that injured Alan removed boulders from a previous, similar event? An event that had occurred sometime after Ron's disappearance?

It was my turn to catch the excitement quietly building in the yard.

"I know where the body's buried," I announced.

Joe gave me a quizzical look.

"So does everybody in town. Around the campus. They told us about the three cemeteries on the college tour," he reminded me.

"Not bodies," I told him, "Body. Singular. As in Ron's body."

"Oh, my God," Julie whispered. "In the alcove. It has to be."

She looked at me, her eyes wide, and the same color as my sister's.

"I just remembered that he had a name for that cleft, because he said it was his sacred space, so it deserved its own name."

I waited for her to finish.

"He called it 'Eagle's Nest.' I thought he meant it was his—Walking Eagle's—nest. I never realized he was referring to the jumble of sticks out in front."

If Ron had been looking for a secret spot in the preserve he could use as a spiritual retreat house, he hadn't selected a very private site. Anyone who knew the Ridge back then must have known exactly where that eagle's nest was located, along with the alcove behind it. The main trail in the preserve led right to it.

He might as well have hung out a shingle on the alcove with his name on it, I reflected, or marked the rock cliff with his hand like the rock men did back at the petroglyphs in Minnesota every time they disappeared into the earth for some contemplation. Sort of like the In-Out board we use to keep track of everyone's whereabouts in the counseling office at Savage High School.

Only instead of moving magnets from In to Out, Ron could have used hand prints. One hand print, and Ron Walking Eagle was "in" his sanctuary. Two hand prints, he was "out." Three hand prints, back in five minutes.

A sudden chill went down my spine.

According to Julie, Ron had never come out that last time he went in. And unless there had been a seismic disturbance that same night that sealed him into the rock, something else had kept him there.

"Julie," I said. "There wasn't an earthquake the night Ron disappeared, was there?"

She shook her head, her eyes still wide.

"No. But what if he was injured somehow going down, and then he couldn't climb back up?"

I could see the terror growing in her expression.

"What if he starved to death in that alcove, and no one knew? I camped out at the preserve that night, waiting for him to come back. In the morning, when he didn't show up, I went to that cliff, and I called for him, but he never answered."

She looked up at me, a remembered pain in her eyes.

"I went to where he'd parked the car, and it was gone. I hitched back into town, but he wasn't at the apartment, either. A day later, I left."

She turned her face away from me.

"I was a runaway, and I couldn't risk someone grabbing me and turning me into the police. I didn't know what had happened to Ron, but I knew he wouldn't have abandoned his apartment—or me—like that."

She returned her eyes to my face.

"Earlier, Bob, when you suggested that maybe Ron had done that very thing—just abandoned me—"

I interrupted. "I am so sorry, Julie. It was a thoughtless, heartless thing to say. I was . . . stressed."

"Well, so was I. But it got me thinking and remembering how those two days felt before I left for California, what it was like to suddenly feel adrift again after I thought I'd figured out who I was and where I belonged."

She draped her arm around Joe and gave his shoulders a squeeze.

"It wasn't a good feeling, and I realized that you were right: Joe needs me to listen more carefully." She dropped a kiss on her son's dark hair. "He needs to know who he is."

And that would be . . . ?

I didn't say a word, but Luce shot me a deadly look. Man, sometimes I hate that psychic thing of hers.

I backed off, and noticed that tears were running down Julie's cheeks.

"So now I'm wondering," she said in a hushed voice, "what if I'm to blame for Ron's death? What if he starved to death because he was injured and couldn't get out?"

"You said his car was gone," Luce pointed out. "Of course you'd assume he'd taken it back to Flagstaff. You did what anyone would do in that situation."

Julie sniffed, and being the well-trained counselor that I am, I automatically dug in my pocket for a tissue, but instead jabbed my hand into the jagged tube I'd stashed there. I pulled it out and looked at the faded plastic again.

"It's just like the ones I used twenty years ago," Luce said.

Call me unimaginative, but there was only one way I could think of that an old inhaler would make its way into an abandoned eagle's nest on the edge of the Ridge.

Someone had dropped it there, which meant that at least one other person had visited Ron Walking Eagle's secret nest.

Someone, I guessed, who had known that Ron would be there, too.

Someone who knew the Ridge.

Someone like Bill or Wilson Warner.

"Whoever it was, moved the car," I said, thinking out loud, "to hide the fact that Ron had been there."

And I could think of only one reason why someone would want to hide that particular fact.

No one could trace Ron Walking Eagle's last steps if they were erased.

"You're right, Julie," I said, still staring at the ancient inhaler in my palm. "Ron was murdered."

"We have to go look in that alcove," she said.

I shook my head.

"Not tonight. If Ron's there, he'll still be there tomorrow."

"But what if more rocks have fallen?" Joe asked.

"Then we'll have to dig around them," I said. "We're not going out there tonight. That cliff is hard enough to navigate in broad daylight." I threw a quick glance at Luce. "Believe me, I know from experience."

"Hello? Anybody home?"

The four of us looked in the direction of the voice that was coming from around the corner of Julie's house. A moment later, Professor Corwin appeared, breathing hard.

"Are you all right?" Julie asked in alarm.

"Fine," he replied, wheezing. "I was concerned about you."

Wheeze.

"The earthquake."

Wheeze.

"Your little old house."

Julie took his arm and led him to the troglodyte chair I'd used. The professor sat and took a handkerchief from his jacket to mop his shiny brow. He not only looked winded, I realized, but like he was in real discomfort. His eyes were squeezed tightly shut and the skin around his mouth and nose looked blue. For a split-second, I even wondered if I was going to have to repeat my earlier performance as a first responder at the Ridge, but Corwin finally seemed to catch his breath.

Thank goodness.

One mouth-to-mouth in a day was already more than enough for me.

Unless it was with Luce, of course.

Gee, maybe I was easily distracted after all.

"I was worried that your home might sustain some kind of damage," Corwin told Julie. His thin shoulders relaxed under his jacket, the sides falling open across the rickety arms of the old chair. I noticed that his chest seemed sunken, his collarbone prominent. "I wanted to be sure you and Joe were all right."

Julie knelt in front of the old man and took his hand in both of hers. "We're fine, Charles. I really appreciate your concern."

Except I didn't think that was simply concern that was lighting up Charles Corwin's face.

Unless I was totally off base, the professor was in love with Julie.

"We have to take off," I announced, grabbing Luce's hand, practically dragging her out of the back yard. "I'll call you tomorrow, Julie," I called back over my shoulder as I hustled us around the corner of the house and towards our car parked on the pine-lined street.

"What has gotten into you?" Luce asked as I stuffed her into the rental. "One minute you want to stick around and pry into Julie's privacy, and the next, you can't wait to get away."

I swung around the back of the car and folded myself into the driver's seat of the compact.

"I hate these tiny cars," I complained, turning on the ignition. "Now that Lily's got a big guy like Alan traveling with her, I hope she starts renting mid-size cars."

"Bobby?"

I turned to face her. "What?"

She tipped her head to one side and lifted her eyebrows. Thanks to my astute observation of Luce's body language over the years of our relationship, I knew what that particular expression meant: "What's going on in that red head of yours?"

Well, technically my hair is red, but it's really more of an auburn color now. Kind of like the rust on the troglodyte chair in Julie's back yard, now that I think of it. The same chair in which the professor was probably still sitting at that very moment, ardently gazing at Joe's mother.

"Bobby!"

"I think Corwin's in love with Julie," I said, "which helps to explain why he's been helping her out so much with this book of hers."

"You just now figured that out?"

I shot her a glance.

"You knew this?"

"All you had to do was see the way he looked at her during lunch," Luce replied. "He would definitely like to be more than her mentor."

"But he's got to be at least thirty years older than she is," I pointed out. "Maybe more. When he was wheezing, he looked like he was on his death bed."

Luce shook her head.

"He's fifty, Bobby. That's only fifteen years older than Julie. And what difference does age make anyway?"

I turned the corner and headed back toward the inn on campus. I thought again about Corwin and his prematurely aged appearance, his sunken chest, his bald head, his shortness of breath.

The man was not well.

"He's dying," I told Luce in a flash of insight. "I bet you that Charles Corwin has lung cancer."

CHAPTER TWENTY

LUCE WAS QUIET FOR A BLOCK OR TWO.

"I think you may be right," she said, her voice soft in the car. "When we first met the professor at lunch, I thought there was something familiar about him, but I couldn't put my finger on it. Now I know what it was," she added. "He reminded me of Aunt Min before she died."

She reached over to place her hand on my thigh, and I covered it with my own. I'd only known Luce's aunt for a year before she'd been diagnosed with lung cancer; within six months, she was gone.

"Aunt Min lost her hair from chemo," Luce recalled, "but she refused to wear wigs. Instead, she wore all those colorful scarves wrapped around her head, even when she was in the hospital. Near the end, she could hardly draw two breaths in a row without turning blue. And she lost so much weight, her clothes were huge on her."

I tightened my hand on Luce's. Min's passing had been especially hard on her family.

"That's what looked familiar to me about Corwin," Luce explained. "The way his jacket hung on his body, like he'd suddenly lost a lot of weight. And he was taking pills at lunch— probably for pain."

He'd told me it was for headaches, I remembered. He'd used an inhaler a few times, too, during the meal.

The inhaler.

I thought of the old plastic tube in my pocket. That was why it looked familiar to me when I saw Khan drop it on the ground at the Ridge.

It had reminded me of seeing Corwin using his own inhaler during lunch.

"That would explain why the professor is pushing Julie to solve the mystery of Ron's disappearance, too," Luce mused. "Maybe he doesn't have a lot of time left, and he wants to make sure she has all the information she needs from him. Plus, it gives him an opportunity to spend more time with her, especially if his condition is worsening. Do you think Julie knows?"

I pictured Julie carefully seating Corwin in the old lawn chair, then taking his hands between her own. There had been tenderness in her manner, care and gentleness.

"I think she does," I said, "but I'm not sure that she's in love with him."

"She's not."

I shot her another look as I pulled into the parking lot at the Inn. "And she told you this?"

Luce unsnapped her seat belt. "Yes, she told me this."

I was beginning to feel like the odd man out . . . again.

Usually, it was Luce and Lily trading information that left me feeling left out. I hadn't known that Julie had joined the club, although I should probably have expected it, based on the camaraderie I'd seen between my sister and Julie at lunch. The only time that I knew of that Luce had been alone with them was when Alan and I had taken the elevator up to the conference office after lunch.

Cripes! How long did it take these women to bond? Five seconds? Even super glue takes longer than that to stick.

"Is there anything else Julie's told you that you might want to share with me?" I asked.

"No."

I eyed her suspiciously. She'd had that "no" ready too quickly.

"No, as in 'no, she hasn't told you anything else,' or 'no, you don't want to share with me'?"

"That's right," she said.

I had to think about it for a minute, but I still didn't know if I'd gotten an answer—or, at least, an answer I could understand.

I got out of the car and snagged her around the waist as she headed for the inn's front door.

"Do you know something I don't?"

Luce dropped a kiss on my mouth.

"Bobby, I know a lot of things you don't. I went to culinary school, remember?"

"Besides in the kitchen," I clarified. "Do you know something about Julie I don't?"

"Yes, as a matter of fact, I do," she said.

Finally! An answer I could understand.

"And that would be?"

"Private," she replied. "I don't betray confidences."

I groaned just as my cell phone started to chirp. Defeated, I dug it out of the jeans pocket that didn't hold the old inhaler.

"Hello?"

"How would you like to add a Mexican Spotted Owl to your life list, Bob?"

It was Bill Warner. We'd traded business cards this morning at the Arboretum, when my only connection to him had been as a fellow birder. Of course, now we had a lot more in common: an afternoon at the Ridge, a mutual interest in a missing person, a near-disaster experience (Luce's), a near-death experience (Bill's), and an earthquake. I'd even breathed into the guy's mouth.

Maybe I should make him take me to dinner.

"Where are you?" I asked him.

"I'm at my son's place. Wilson's home," he added. "Go west on Business Route 40 until you see the exit for North Belle Springs Road. Hang a right and follow it all the way to the end. It turns into a private driveway. Take that all the way to the house."

"Forty west to North Belle Springs, then right," I repeated. "Got it. We're on our way."

"We're on our way where?" Luce asked when I stuck the phone back in my jeans.

I gave her a grin. "To see a threatened subspecies, my dear. With any luck, you and I are going to score a Mexican Spotted Owl tonight."

Her eyes lit up like blue fire.

"That was Bill Wilson," I told her. "He's at his son's place outside town. Are you game?"

For just a second, I thought she might hesitate. After all, I'd promised her a Scott's Oriole this afternoon and come up empty-handed. For all my reputation as a skilled birder in Minnesota, I wasn't exactly burning it up in Arizona.

Yet.

Instead, she gave me a smug smile.

"Honey," she said, "I'm already gone."

And with that, she turned on her heel and sprinted back to the car.

"It's time to fly, Bobby," she called back. "How fast can you drive?"

I took off at a run after her, my grin getting wider.

"I thought you'd never ask."

Chapter Twenty-One

The rental car's speedometer was just hitting 100 miles per hour when Luce spotted the exit off the business route. I took the turn tight and shot up to the yield sign where it intersected with North Belle Springs Road. Almost immediately, the scenery around us changed. Where we'd just been zipping along an open highway, now pines closed in on us on both sides of the road. The further we drove, the older the trees seemed to get until we were completely surrounded by old-growth forest.

"This certainly looks promising," Luce noted. "These are mature trees, which is exactly the kind of habitat the owl prefers. My guess is this area hasn't been logged, either, judging from the thickness of vegetation. Another point in our favor."

Luce was right. The walls of trees around us were perfect stomping grounds for the Mexican Spotted Owl. Forested mountains and canyons all the way from southern Utah and Colorado to west Texas and even central Mexico qualified as nesting locations for the bird, though in recent years, the owl's distribution range was shrinking in large part as a result of climate change as the region got hotter and drier. For a long time, the logging industry had been the owls' primary adversary as companies cut down the forests—much like the Northern Spotted Owl's situation up in the Pacific Northwest—but that had changed when the Mexican subspecies was included in the Endangered Species Act in 1993. Nowadays, the owl was especially threatened by drought, which led to wildfires, and subsequent starvation.

"Those daily afternoon rains they get here in Flagstaff are probably the Mexican Spotted Owl's best friend," I observed. "All that precipitation keeps the vegetation growing, which means more little critters are thriving around here, which translates into more meals for the owls."

I slowed down as the paved road narrowed into a private driveway. Around us, dusk was fading into darkness, and without the presence of streetlights illuminating the drive, it was like sliding into a black hole. My headlights caught a rabbit bolting across the road ahead of us, and I was pretty sure I saw a couple of bats winging through the trees.

If I were a Mexican Spotted Owl, this would have been an all-you-can-eat buffet. No wonder Bill had located an owl out here.

Up ahead, soft landscape lighting traced a path from a four-car garage to a sprawling, two-story log home. Most of the windows were dark, though some light filtered out into the night from around curtains pulled shut on the ground level.

"I guess this is the place," I said, easing the car to a stop in front of the big garage. Just as I put the car in park, though, one of the garage doors lifted, and a jeep backed out. Luckily, it was two doors away from where I sat, so it didn't back directly into the front end of Lily's rental.

That would have been a drag.

Or more likely, a whopping tow-truck bill, not to mention an insurance hassle when we tried to turn in a car that was suddenly two feet shorter in length than it was when Lily had rented it.

It wouldn't be a compact any more—just compacted.

The jeep pulled up next to me and the driver popped his head out the window.

It was Gil Warner.

"Hey, Bob," he said. "You here for the owl?"

"Yup," I responded. "Your grandfather made me an offer I couldn't refuse. You see it already?"

Gil laughed. "Only about a thousand times. My dad's had a nesting pair back in that steep little canyon on the edge of his land ever since I can remember. You should hear them calling during the breeding season—they sound like little dogs barking. Pretty creepy if you don't know what it is, but great for spooking girlfriends right into your arms."

"Ah, yes," Luce added. "Birding does have that romantic allure, doesn't it?"

"I've got to run into town for my dad. He forgot some papers at the bank he needs to review tonight, so I'm the designated errand-boy," Gil explained. "If you're gone before I get back, have a good trip home to Minnesota."

He checked his rearview mirror, and I thought he was going to take off, but he leaned his head out the window again.

"Say, Bob, about your sister, the one who looks like Julie Burrows."

"I think he's talking about Lily," Luce added helpfully from the seat next to me.

"Thank you, Sherlock," I replied, then waited for Gil to continue, but he was suddenly preoccupied with adjusting his side view mirror.

"I have to apologize for my dad," he finally said, not looking at me. "He shouldn't have been driving this afternoon."

I waited again. As I've already pointed out, I know how to play this game.

"I was with him in the Porsche. He saw your sister and thought she was Julie, and he just lost it."

He turned to me then.

"I'm so sorry. I had no idea he'd try to hit her. My dad's gone totally berserk over Julie Burrows digging into the family history, but I never imagined he'd try to hurt someone. As soon as I realized what he was doing, I grabbed the wheel from him and took the car around the corner. I made him get out and switch places with me, and then I drove him home to sober up."

Gil hung his head in shame. "I understand if your sister wants to press charges. Maybe she should, because then Dad would have to clean up his act. I've really been hoping this whole thing would just go away, but it's only gotten more and more out of hand."

I felt sorry for him. Having an alcoholic in the family was never easy, I knew from my counseling experience, but when that addiction threatened the safety of others, it was past time to take action.

"I don't know what my sister wants to do, Gil. Mostly, I think she wants to go home. Regardless of her decision, though, you need to get your dad some help."

He nodded in agreement.

"That's why Granddad's out here tonight," he told me. "He's going to try to get Dad to check himself into rehab. Maybe that's why he called you to come on out for the owl—maybe you can help. He thinks the world of you since you saved his life this afternoon."

Aw, shucks, it was all in a day's work.

"I've got to go," he said, and with that, he peeled out of the drive.

"Oh, boy," Luce commented. "I bet you didn't know you were headed for an intervention tonight, did you? I think you should consider billing the Warners for all your services rendered. At this rate, you'd probably make enough to cover our plane fares."

"Which reminds me," I said. "We need to rent our own car to drive to Phoenix's airport, because I'm sure not flying out of Flagstaff."

"Chicken."

"As I recall, you already promised me we were going to take the land route to Phoenix," I reminded her.

"So I did."

"Okay, then," I said. "Now let's go get us some owl."

We walked up to the front door of the house and rang the doorbell. A moment later, Bill Warner opened it up and invited us inside. His tanned face was lined with worry.

"Is the owl gone?" I asked.

"No, no," he reassured me. "The owl's back in the canyon where he always sits. A real creature of habit. He's been nesting in the same spot with his mate for years. They've got two owlets this year. You can see the daddy bringing them prey most every evening, usually for a couple hours after sunset. Takes his parental responsibilities pretty seriously. Unlike some fathers I know," he added, his voice laced with an emotion that I couldn't quite identify.

Which fathers? I couldn't help but wonder. Was Bill referring to himself and his disastrous relationship with his firstborn, Ron? Or was he thinking about Wilson, and his drinking problem?

He ushered us across a wide expanse of polished pine floor in the foyer and then led us through a living room to a wall of sliding glass doors.

"We saw Gil leaving," I told him, deciding to force the issue. "He said his dad was the one who almost hit Lily this afternoon."

Bill slid a door open and stood aside for Luce to step out ahead of us.

"My son is a wreck," he said. "I know Gil makes apologies for his father, but I won't. I raised that boy to shoulder his responsibilities. 'You do what it takes,' I taught him. That's what I always did. I worked my tail off to build this family's fortune. Wilson just had to stay the course. That's all. I don't know where it went wrong, but it did. He did."

"Gil wants his dad to get help," I told him. "He said he thought you came over here tonight to persuade your son to go into treatment for his alcoholism."

Bill looked at me for a moment in silence.

"I did," he admitted. "But as soon as I mentioned rehab, Wilson walked out of the house, and now I can't find him."

He closed his eyes and shook his head.

"Seems like I've got a problem with sons who disappear, wouldn't you say?"

Luce stuck her head back inside the open doorway. "Are you coming out?"

"Yes, ma'am, we are," Bill answered her, his enthusiastic tone not fooling me for a minute. The man was more than distraught, from what I could see.

He was afraid, but I wasn't sure of what.

Chapter Twenty-Two

Bill Warner took the lead across the wooded property, easily navigating the forest of mixed conifers and pines in the deepening dusk. Pinyon and junipers slowly gave way to stately ponderosas, and the earth beneath us became more rugged the further we walked. Almost without warning, we found ourselves in a small canyon with steep sides and plenty of habitat that any Mexican Spotted Owl would appreciate.

"Watch your step," Warner cautioned Luce. "We don't have the drop off here like you saw at the Ridge, but you really don't want to take a ride on your rear end down to the creek."

I slipped my arm around Luce's waist and pulled her tightly against me.

"I won't let you go sliding anywhere," I told her, just as my own foot slid on a slippery patch of pine needles.

"Why am I not reassured?" she muttered.

"Sshh!" Bill commanded in a whisper. "The owls should be right ahead of us. Look up and to your left about ten yards. There's a big old hole in a tree, and if we're lucky, we just might spot the youngsters perching on branches near it, though I have to say, I only saw the one baby the last time I was out here."

We crept closer to the towering pine, its uppermost branches forming a broad canopy over the steep side of the canyon. Sure enough, a thick body sat on a limb not far from the tree's cavity, its large white spots giving it a lighter appearance than the coloring of its northern and western cousins. But even from our distance, I could clearly make out the dark eyes of the Mexican Spotted Owl, a feature that set it apart from most other owls with their yellow or orange eyes.

"He's a big guy," Luce whispered next to me.

"One of the biggest owls in the United States," Bill noted softly. "And pretty tame, too. I don't think they've ever scattered when I've been here."

I lifted my arm and pointed at a smaller figure perched on another branch on the opposite side of the tree cavity.

"Right there. A juvenile."

The fluffy youngster sat like a statue on the branch, its dark eyes unblinking, its white-splotched feathers contrasting with its overall ashy brown coloring. Bill's timing had been perfect, I thought. Another fifteen minutes, and the owls would have become invisible to us, blending in perfectly with the surrounding natural camouflage of bark and branches. Despite his familial trials—or maybe because of them—Bill Warner was a skilled birder. He wouldn't be the first person to welcome his birding pursuits as an escape from stress, either.

Did I mention I dealt daily with teenage drama queens?

"Of course," he was telling Luce in a low voice, "I don't come tromping in like an elephant, either. I respect their privacy."

"They're among the lucky ones, then," Luce said. "A protected habitat, a hospitable climate, lots of food sources. If only all the threatened and endangered birds could find a spot like this, we wouldn't be losing species at all."

"And don't forget the hunters," Bill added. "No hunting around here."

A gun shot rang out into the fading light.

The owls took flight.

I threw a look of alarm at Bill.

"You were saying?"

My foot slipped on another patch of slippery pine needles as we followed our path back to the house, but it didn't slow us down.

Bill had us hustling, and since I wasn't familiar with the territory, I gladly left it to him to lead the three of us back to the security of the big log house. Night had fully fallen on us, and with no stars visible through the canopy of the old-growth forest above us, I didn't think I could have found north, or any other direction, if my life had depended on it.

"Damn poachers," Bill hissed as he set a brisk pace through the pines. "It's been a long time since I've heard gunshots out here, and unless I miss my guess, those shots were definitely on this property."

"What would someone be shooting at?" Luce asked.

"Eagles," Bill replied. "There's a couple of nice nesting spots for Bald Eagles just around the corner from the little canyon where we just saw the owls. Somebody must have been out scouting around here during the day, and they sighted a nest. There's still a lucrative black market trade for eagle feathers, you know. Eagles may be sacred to Native Americans, but their feathers are a hot commodity for dancers who want to put together winning costumes for tribal dance competitions."

I recalled seeing the fancy dancers on campus when we'd first arrived, as well as our conversation earlier today about the illegal trade in Gyrfalcons and the enormous amounts of money involved. I hated to think that there might be a connection between the cultural celebration of powwows and the destruction of eagles for profit, but unfortunately, I knew better.

"What's the price tag for an eagle feather, Bill?"

He made a growling noise that reminded me of an angry bear.

Not that I'd made the acquaintance of any angry bears, thank goodness, but I did get within conversational distance of one during my search for a Boreal Owl up in the north woods of Minnesota once. Fortunately, that particular member of the ursine genus decided his grunts and growls would be wasted on me, and he took his attentions elsewhere, but not before I developed a life-long appreciation of the size of his canines.

Flag's Number One Fan came to a stop on the trail and turned to face me and Luce.

"The price tag is about what you'd expect for an illegal transaction: outrageous. Last I heard, one perfect feather from a Golden

Eagle could go for more than $250," Bill said. "So when you figure that an entire bird could furnish about fifty-two feathers for powwow regalia, you can see why some folks decide it's worth the risk to take eagles. It's easy money if you can get away with it."

A second shot split the night.

Only this one was closer.

Much closer.

"I thought you said those nests were back there," I said, pointing back in the direction of the canyon.

"They are!"

"Someone's shooting near the house," Luce said, her voice hushed in the sudden stillness of the night.

And then that same someone came crashing through the pines, the long barrel of a rifle dark in his hands.

I grabbed Luce and pulled her behind me, letting my own body act as her shield.

The man came to an abrupt halt, and then leveled his gun at my head.

I hate it when that happens.

Chapter Twenty-Three

"What the hell are you doing, Wilson?"

Bill Warner reached out and grabbed the rifle's barrel, jerking it down and away from me, but Wilson immediately pulled the weapon back up to stare in my face.

"What the hell are you doing, Dad?" Wilson retorted, his words slurring together.

He didn't take either the gun or his eyes off me. I could feel Luce's fingers digging into my sides, trying to move me back a step.

Not that one step would matter, I reflected. I needed to be a whole lot of steps—like on the other side of the house—if I wanted to survive this shotgun's blast.

"Give me the rifle, son," Bill said, his voice surprisingly gentle after his previous outburst.

That's right, Bill, I silently encouraged him. *Talk Wilson off the ledge here.*

Crap. What was it with ledges out here?

"I think you and I need some help, Wilson," Bill continued, his voice still mellow and even, "and I want to listen if you're ready to talk about it."

"In front of them?" Wilson asked.

A light breeze stirred the pines around us, and I caught a potent whiff of bourbon.

"I've got nothing to hide, son."

"Oh, yeah? Tell it to a judge, Dad."

His eyes flicked away to his father's face, and in the next second, he was laid out on his back on the ground, with Luce's knee planted in his chest, the rifle still rocking on top of a brush pile where she'd thrown it as she'd tackled him.

"Wow," I said to her. "They teach you that in culinary school?"

"I'm not the one you need to worry about," Wilson gasped out as he struggled to catch the breath that Luce had knocked out of him. "I'm not the one who killed Ron."

Luce slowly stood up, her eyes locked on the wheezing man. I could tell from the tension in her arms and legs that my fiancée was ready to kick more . . . ah . . . rear end . . . if need be.

"Who killed Ron?" I asked Wilson, just as I sensed his father coming up behind me.

"Just do what it takes, right, Dad?" Wilson said, his eyes closing. "I saw you there that night. You didn't know I'd followed you out to the Ridge. You went over the cliff, and I knew where you were going. To talk some sense into my long-lost half-brother in his secret sanctuary. Your first-born."

"Wilson, you don't know what you're talking about, son," Bill told him. "Let's go on up to the house and I'll call the rehab center, tell them we're coming right now."

Wilson tried to pull himself up on his elbows, but kept falling back onto the rough earth. Finally, on his third attempt, he managed to support himself and stared at his father.

"No one ever saw Ron again after that night, Dad," he said. "You wanted that run for mayor so bad, you decided to donate the Ridge to the county so everyone would see you as this local hero, but it backfired, didn't it? Your illegitimate son showed up with a plan of his own, but you shot him down, so he figured he'd hit you where it would hurt the most: your almighty public image. You couldn't handle the bad press of Ron Walking Eagle, Native American imposter and activist, so you got rid of it. You got rid of it all. Your own son. And all I've ever done since is try to keep your dirty little secret for you. And what do I get for it?"

He laughed bitterly.

"A son who's ashamed of me and a father who wants to put me into treatment for a mess of his own making."

Wilson swung his head in Luce's direction and then in mine.

"Did he tell you all that when he took you birding?" he asked, his voice loud and filled with contempt. "Well, Dad, I finally took your advice. I did what it takes. I wanted every last bit of Walking Eagle out of our lives for good, so I let that eagle of Gil's out of his cage. Gave it a headstart. And then I shot it. Now we're just alike, Dad. We've both killed a Walking Eagle."

Bill took a step closer to where Wilson lay on the ground.

"You shot Gil's eagle?" His voice was thick with dismay.

Wilson laughed again.

"You see how this goes?" he asked me, his words slurred. "I tell you my father is a cold-blooded murderer, and he's upset about a bird."

Bill moved faster than I could have imagined.

Well, maybe not that fast, but for an almost eighty-one-year-old, the man was incredibly quick. He dropped to one knee beside his son and grabbed him by the lapels of his jacket.

"You fool!" he shouted in Wilson's face. "I didn't kill Ron! Yes, I was there! Yes, I tried to make him back down! But I didn't kill him. I left him there, stubborn and defiant."

He shook his son in fury.

"And when he disappeared, I thought *you* were responsible for it. When Ron took us to court, I told you the reason why—that he was my son, that he was angry, that he was blackmailing me. And for some reason, you were jealous of him! Why, I'll never know, but it was plain as day that you felt threatened by him."

"He was your son. Your first-born," Wilson repeated, his own anger spent, his voice heavy with emotion. "I always wondered why no matter what I did, it wasn't good enough for you, and I finally knew why. You had another son."

"A son I never knew." Warner almost choked on his words. "And when you, the son I did know, the son I thought I knew, went so silent after Ron disappeared, I was afraid. I knew you'd been hurt, angry. I thought it was because you couldn't stand the idea that I'd been unfaithful to your mother. You hated me for that, and you hated Ron. And then he disappeared. I never asked you if you knew anything about it, because I didn't want to know."

"Thanks for the vote of confidence," Wilson sneered. "My own father thought I was a murderer."

His voice was thick with pain.

"Gee, Dad," he said, "we're more alike than I realized. Both of us thought the other was capable of killing a man. We're just icons of the perfect father-son relationship, aren't we?"

I heard a rustling noise approaching from the direction of the house and turned away from the two Warners to peer into the darkness beneath the pines.

Walking Eagle limped into view.

"Bill," I said. "It's Gil's eagle. He's injured."

Warner's head snapped around and he jumped to his feet.

"I can't even kill a bird," Wilson moaned and dropped his head back to the ground.

"He knows my voice," Warner said, relief pouring into his own voice as he slowly advanced toward the big bird. "I've worked with him with Gil, so he must have been near here, hiding. Come here, baby."

The Golden Eagle stood its ground, teetering a little to the left.

"We've got to get him back to the house and then over to Blue Sky Raptors," Warner said. "Suzie will get him fixed up."

He turned his attention back to his inebriated son, who had begun to snore loudly enough to wake the dead.

"Maybe we could hook him up with Elvira," I whispered to Luce. "Whenever she needed to call up her zombies, she could just ask Wilson to pass out and snore."

I felt fingers pinching my side in the darkness.

"It was just a suggestion," I said.

"And Wilson is getting checked into rehab tonight if it's the last thing I do," Bill added.

His voice softened.

"No," he corrected himself. "It's going to be the first thing I do."

His eyes moved from Wilson to me and Luce.

"Think you two can give me a hand here? I need to get my boy home."

Chapter Twenty-Four

The sun was shining brightly on the wrought iron tables set out in the inn's courtyard patio the next morning when Luce and I filled our plates with cantaloupe, eggs, and freshly baked cinnamon rolls from the outdoor breakfast buffet line. Alan and Lily were already seated at a table that was partially shaded from the sun by a neighboring olive tree; Joe was sitting between them, devouring a plate of pastries as only a preteen boy could do. I wove my way through the crowded patio of patrons until I reached their table.

"You got room for two more?" I asked.

In answer, both Lily and Alan scooted their chairs a bit closer to Joe's, and I pulled over an unused chair from another table to make a fifth seat for Luce, who was still back at the buffet, carefully considering her fresh-squeezed juice options.

"You hear anything yet?" I asked Alan as I sat down.

Last night, while Luce and I had helped Bill Warner move a boneless Wilson up to his house, I'd finally had a chance to tell him about the conclusion that Julie and I had reached in regards to Ron Walking Eagle's final resting place. Warner's response had been encouraging and determined. He'd recalled several small quakes in the last twenty years that had caused some rockslides at the Ridge, and promised to get a crew out first thing in the morning to the ledge where we'd discovered the old eagle's nest. If Ron's remains were back in that alcove, Warner was going to bring them out and give them a proper burial.

If, instead, Warner's crew found nothing to retrieve, the mystery of Ron Walking Eagle's disappearance would remain just that—a mystery. Julie Burrows would never complete her investigation or write her book about a murder, and Bill Warner would wonder for the rest of his life what had really happened to his first-born, and mostly unknown, son.

Warner had even promised to call Julie personally, after he got Wilson checked into the clinic, to invite her to join him at the Ridge for his crew's search. Since she already knew the truth about Ron and the elder Warner's relationship, Flag's Number One Fan had figured there was nothing to lose by asking her to come along. In fact, since Julie had been living with Ron at the time, Warner was hopeful she might supply him with some details about his estranged son that might provide them with further avenues for investigation into his disappearance.

I guessed that was why Joe was here with Alan and Lily this morning—because Julie was out at the Ridge with Warner and his crew. I could see where it might not be the greatest idea in the world to have an almost thirteen-year-old boy present at the exhumation of a decaying corpse. Assuming, of course, that Warner and Julie got lucky with our reasoned conclusion, and did, indeed, find Ron—or what was left of him—in the alcove.

Given what a decaying corpse might look and smell like, I wasn't at all sure that "lucky" was really the operative word there. Even prepared adults had a gross-out threshold, and I would guess that finding an old dead body might just push someone well past that boundary.

I knew I wasn't volunteering to go out and look in any creepy alcoves this morning. My plans for the day were to stay on flat, open surfaces in bright sunshine, and avoid even thinking about graveyards.

Okay, so it wasn't the most exciting day's agenda I'd ever planned.

But at this point, it sounded really good to me.

In any case, I mentally congratulated Julie for passing her son along to Alan for the morning. I was sure my best friend and his young charge could find something equally interesting, though perhaps less macabre, to do.

I had a sudden memory of Joe's excitement during the small quake we'd had last night. Maybe he and Alan could go to the earthquake lab on the NAU campus and simulate massive destruction with computer models. Maybe the professors there would share more footage of collapsing buildings and colossal landslides with them. In an earthquake lab, I bet the possibilities for apocalyptic scenarios were mind-boggling. Guaranteed to keep a preteen fascinated for hours.

I, on the other hand, would not have been fascinated. Experiencing yesterday's little quake first-hand had been more than enough for my lifetime. The idea of mulling over the multitude of possible ways to be swallowed up by the earth wasn't exactly on my must-do list for this morning.

Like I said, flat land and sunshine.

Make that stable flat land and sunshine.

The possibility that had kept me awake for most of the preceding night, though, hadn't had anything to do with seismic reoccurrence.

Instead, it had been the possibility—make that possibilities, plural—of what had really happened to Ron Walking Eagle.

Based on Bill Warner's admission to his son, Ron was still alive when he left him in his secret cave that fateful night, yet Ron's car ended up back in his apartment parking lot the next day—without Ron—according to Julie. The solution to that part of the equation was clear: someone else must have met Ron in the rocks even later that night and taken his keys to return the car.

If I could trust the confessions of the two Warners, neither of Julie's prime suspects had moved the car, much less killed Ron. That meant that Julie would have to look elsewhere for a potential murderer, and twenty years after the fact, that sounded like an impossible task. From what she and Corwin had told us about the angry atmosphere in Flagstaff during the court case, there were plenty of folks in Flagstaff who might have held a serious grudge against Ron: tour operators, local Native Americans, environmentalists, souvenir key chain suppliers.

All things considered, disappearing sounded like it would have been a smart solution for the defeated Walking Eagle.

But if that were the case, where had Ron gone?

As both Warner and Julie had insisted, Ron had never resurfaced anywhere, which led me to assume that someone or something had prevented him from making a reappearance during all those years. Without a doubt, the obvious answer was that Ron had been disposed of.

I had another vision, but this time it wasn't of Joe sitting across the table from me with his mouth full of food. This time, I pictured a man's body being tossed off that rocky ledge at the Ridge in a fatal fall. Could someone have forced Ron over the edge, or heaved his unconscious body off into space just feet from where Luce had been trapped on the ledge yesterday?

Memo to me: stay away from all precipices for the rest of my life. And if you happen to be on one, don't look down. You may not like what you see.

"Hey, look at that! There's a big pile of bodies down there! Gee, could this cliff be dangerous?"

I reached under the table to grab Luce's knee, my stomach tipping a little at the thought of Luce out on the ledge yesterday.

She gave me a curious look.

"Just making sure you're still here," I whispered. "Delayed reaction."

She shook her head and rolled her eyes, then went back to eating her breakfast potatoes.

"No word from anyone," Lily finally answered my question. "I don't know if that's good or bad news."

"Good," Alan declared.

"Bad," Joe annouced at the same time.

"You first, Joe," I said. "Why is it bad?"

"It's bad because if they don't find Ron, my mom is going to go crazy wondering whatever happened to him."

"And I say it's good we haven't heard anything," Alan explained, "because that means they're too busy to call us. If the cave were empty, they'd let us know right away, but if there's a body in there, they're going to have to call in a whole bunch of other people. Depending on what they find, it might be a crime-scene, which means the whole Hollywood treatment—forensic techs, police, detectives, reporters, live interviews."

"I wish Mom had let me go with her," Joe said wistfully. "She took the professor along. She said he deserved to be in on it, since he'd been such a big help to her in tracking down court records and locating people to interview about the old court case. I think she feels kind of sorry for him, too," he added.

"You mean because of his poor health?" I asked.

Joe nodded.

"I can tell he's pretty sweet on her, too," he added, "but she's not interested in him like that. She says he's not her type, that no one is her type since my dad died."

My mouthful of scrambled eggs almost fell back onto my plate. "Your dad?"

"Joe was just telling us what Julie shared with him last evening about his biological father," Lily said. "He was killed in Afghanistan. He was in the Marines, and he met Julie before his platoon was deployed there. They'd talked about getting married when he got back, but he didn't make it home."

I threw a quick glance at Alan, wondering what he thought about this revelation, but he was wearing his best poker face, giving nothing away. Was he trying to determine, as I was, if this was another of Julie's fabrications?

A father who'd died before her son's birth was surely a convenient story if Julie didn't want Joe to keep asking about his paternity. Then again, I'd counseled a few kids over the years who'd found themselves in that very situation—making their grand entrance into the world just as a parent was exiting. No kid should have to go through that, but I knew it happened.

The real question here, I had to remind myself, was Julie's honesty; though I was beginning to better appreciate her reasoning when it came to Joe, I still wasn't sure about her methods. Before my suspicions could multiply any further, however, Joe offered a self-revelation of his own.

"My mom had told me that part before, but I didn't want to believe it," he confessed. "I didn't want to think I didn't have a dad somewhere. It was bad enough being a half-breed, but a half-breed without a dad was even worse."

He dropped his eyes to the last pastry on his plate.

It looked like a cherry Danish.

"So when we found out that Alan was going to be here for the seminar, and my mom said she'd known him in Seattle before she met my dad," Joe explained, "I just wanted to . . . I don't know . . . pretend like I had a real dad for once."

Alan draped his arm around the boy's shoulders and gave him a hug.

"I'd be proud to be your dad, Joe. Any man would be. And I'm sure your dad is watching over you all the time, helping you grow into the man he knows you're going to be."

Looking at Alan comforting Joe, I could feel heat at the back of my eyes.

Damn Hawk.

He was going to make me cry in another minute.

I hate being a sensitive guy.

And then Joe dropped the bombshell.

"So I told my mom that I want me and Alan to get a paternity test, just so he's all clear that there's no question that he's not my dad." He suddenly looked unhappy.

Lost.

"But she said no."

Chapter Twenty-Five

I EXCHANGED A SHOCKED LOOK with Alan, and I swear we were connected to each other's brains for that moment, because I knew exactly what he was thinking.

She's hiding something.

And the only thing she could be hiding was that Alan was, indeed, Joe's father.

Luce, bless her heart, jumped into the conversational vacuum that had sucked up anything Alan and I could possibly say in response to Joe's announcement.

Lily, oddly enough, didn't seem in the least perturbed.

"So did your mom find the documents she needed at the courthouse yesterday?" Luce asked Joe.

His brown eyes—so like Alan's—clouded over.

"No, she didn't, and she wasn't happy about it, either," he reported. "She said that every tip Professor Corwin had given her so far had panned out with good information, but she couldn't find the property documents he'd told her about. Of course, by then she was pretty steamed about Lily almost getting hurt, and then when she talked on the phone with that lady from the Yavapai tribe, I thought she was going to explode."

"What lady?" I asked.

Joe finished off the cherry Danish. I think I'd counted five on the plate when we sat down. A sudden vision of an older Joe attending prom and stuffing food in his mouth while singing a rap song filled my head.

Please, God, I prayed, don't let me have chaperone duty for prom this coming school year. I'd like to enjoy eating food for a few more years yet.

"The lady from the tribal registry. Mom's been trying to talk with her for the last couple weeks to verify Ron Walking Eagle's status. And she finally got her on the phone last night after you and Luce left," Joe explained. "The lady said the same thing you told Mom: Ron wasn't a Yavapai. At least, not by birth."

"What do you mean?" Alan asked.

"The registry lady told Mom that Ron's mom, who wasn't an Indian, had married a man who belonged to the tribe, but it was when Ron was a kid. So he grew up in a Yavapai community, but he wasn't Yavapai."

Joe turned to me and flashed a grin.

"How do you like that? People were talking down Ron because they thought he was a half-breed, and it turns out he's all white. You just never know, do you? People aren't like your birds at all. You said all you need are field marks, and you can identify one bird out of all the others, but people fool each other all the time about who they are."

Alan gave Joe's shoulders another squeeze.

"How'd you get so smart for a kid?"

"I'm not a kid," Joe replied. "I'm almost thirteen."

"Did your Mom find anything else out from the tribal registry woman?" Lily asked. "We were hoping they might have a family contact for him," she told the rest of us.

"No," Joe answered. "That was the other part that ticked my mom off. The lady started ragging at her, saying that nobody in the community wanted anything to do with Ron Walking Eagle, that they'd been glad when he'd left because he was bringing shame to them. That if he wanted to be so important, he was choosing the wrong way to go about it. "

"What way was that?" Alan's voice was carefully neutral.

"She wouldn't say," Joe said, tossing his napkin on his empty plate. "She hung up on my mom."

My phone vibrated in my pocket, and I pulled it out. I checked the caller ID, but didn't recognize the number.

"Hello?"

"He's here," Julie's voice sounded tired and flat. "We found Ron's body. And then some."

I wasn't sure I wanted to know what the "then some" meant, but she plowed ahead before I could stop her.

"He was killing eagles. For their feathers," she explained. "There are four bodies back in that alcove, Bob, and only one is human."

Chapter Twenty-Six

Alan was right. By the time we got out to the Ridge, it was crawling with all the characters from a primetime crime show. Two media vans were disgorging satellite dishes and cameramen in the trailhead parking lot, while a small squadron of police and state patrol cars were pulled onto the sparse grasses beyond the lot.

"This must be the place," I said, sliding Lily's rental into an open space near a van sporting the logo of Blue Sky Raptors.

Last night, after we'd lugged Wilson back to his house, Gil had returned just in time to load his dad into his grandfather's car; as soon as the two older Warners were backing out of the driveway, Gil had raced into the back yard to find Walking Eagle. Cradling the big bird in his arms, he'd directed me to go get the eagle's carrier from the garage, while he had Luce call Suzie McDaniels at Blue Sky's rehab hot line to let her know that Gil was bringing in his Golden Eagle for immediate attention.

"I wonder if Suzie's here," Luce said, echoing my own question. "I guess that would make sense, if there are eagle bodies in the alcove. I expect someone has to take responsibility for them until a decision is made about where they should go."

"They'll go to the National Eagle Repository in Denver," Alan noted. "It's the law. After the bodies arrive, the technicians there will evaluate the condition of the eagles and their feathers. If they're in good condition, the feathers will be made available to Native Americans for use in religious and cultural ceremonies."

"Thank you, Professor," I said.

"I'm not finished," he replied, angling his wrapped knee carefully out of the car's front passenger seat. "You have to have a permit from the U.S. Fish and Wildlife Service to have an eagle feather in your possession, and in order to get that, you have to be an enrolled member of a tribe that has been recognized by the American government, and you can only use the feathers for religious purposes."

"Now are you done?"

"Yes."

"So I can't buy Luce an eagle feather to place in her wedding bouquet?" I asked.

"Not unless you've got a couple pints of Indian blood hiding in that White body of yours," he replied.

"It depends on the tribe, doesn't it, Alan?" Joe asked. "Some tribes say you're a member if you've got one great-grandparent who was Native American, while others say you've got to have at least one parent from the tribe to be enrolled."

"And others don't look at blood at all, but you have to be able to trace your ancestry directly back to the original members enrolled in the tribe," Lily added.

Luce, Alan, and I all stared at Lily.

"Julie and I were talking about it yesterday while I was waiting to be examined at the hospital after my almost hit-and-run accident," she defended herself. "You know . . . just talking."

I eyed my sister suspiciously.

Lily was "just talking"?

Not in a million years.

She'd been pumping Julie for information.

Information about Joe, and probably about Joe's father.

I'd known she was up to something, but it hadn't occurred to me that my sister had joined forces with Julie to give her the opportunity to ferret out the truth about Joe's immediate ancestry.

But it did explain why she hadn't seemed as shocked as Alan and I when Joe announced his mother's refusal to schedule a paternity test.

Lily had already known that would be Julie's decision.

And she was okay with it.

She trusted Julie.

So what else did Lily already know about the Burrows family that the rest of us didn't?

"Hey, Bob!"

I looked away from my sister and caught sight of Gil Warner coming towards us from the pine stand that marked the beginning of the trail back to the cliff with the alcove.

"You here to join the party?" he called.

"I guess so," I replied. As soon as he got within non-shouting range, I introduced him to Lily, Alan, and Joe.

He colored under his tan when he realized that Lily was the woman his father had almost run down with his Porsche.

"I'm really sorry about what happened to you yesterday," Gil told her. "My dad's got a long road of rehab ahead of him, but at least he's taking the first steps today. I know that doesn't make up for what he tried to do, but I want you to know we're not going to let anything like that happen again. If you want to press charges, you should do that."

Lily shook her head.

"I won't, but thanks for the apology."

"Are you here with Blue Sky or with your grandfather?' Luce asked.

"With Granddad," he replied. "I didn't like the idea of him being around that dropoff without someone keeping an eye on him, so I tagged along. Then, when we found the eagles, I called Suzie, and she drove on out. She's back there now, making arrangements and signing receipts with the police to take custody of the birds. You can't believe what good condition those feathers are in. It must have been like an airless vault in there."

His words made me cringe.

I'm not too fond of small spaces to begin with, but picturing an airless one was even worse, not to mention that this particular space also held a dead man.

I didn't suppose that Ron was in as good a condition as the feathers, either. Twenty years of decomposing would do that.

"So your guess was right on the money when it came to where the body was buried," Gil continued. "That alcove's been sealed up for quite a while, thanks to the little seismic shifts we get out here. One of the work crew that Granddad hired said he could tell by the sharp edges on the faces of the rocks below the alcove's ledge that those stones had just recently tumbled. Basically, the stones rolled away and the tomb was opened."

Great. We had moved from a geological apocalypse to a biblical one. If I saw chariots of fire descending from the sky I was going to throw Luce on the ground and pray for deliverance.

"Cool," Joe said.

"Not really," Gil told him. "A dead body is pretty gross up close. Especially one that's fairly dried out."

"I want to see it," Joe said.

"He's almost thirteen," I told Gil by way of explanation. "Gross is cool."

"Nobody's seeing it now," the youngest Warner informed us. "The police already have the body bagged, and they're loading it into a helicopter they brought in to land in the meadow. The only bodies in the alcove now belong to the police and the detectives who are collecting evidence and taking pictures."

"To document where they found the eagles?" Luce asked.

Gil shook his head.

"To document the scene of a crime. The medical examiner found a big hole in Ron's chest. Somebody clearly put a bullet into him."

He looked up at the sun-washed morning sky.

"My uncle," he added. "I didn't even know I had an uncle, and now I find out he's been dead for twenty years."

His eyes caught mine.

"No wonder my dad was messed up. He thought that his own father was capable of murder."

I didn't tell him that his dad wasn't the only one who had harbored that suspicion. Julie Burrows had virtually been banking on it, staking her career as an investigative journalist on the possibility that she was closing in on a killer in Flagstaff. Encouraged by Corwin and the personal attacks she'd endured, Julie had been confident she was nearing the end of her search.

Well, she had the body now, so the police couldn't dismiss her claims of a crime, even if it had happened two decades ago.

But as for the identity of the murderer, Julie was going to have to start over, just as I had feared, which meant that Joe was going to have to live with his mom's obsession for a while longer yet.

"You should still come and see this circus," Gil invited, herding our little group of five towards the pines. "Julie and Granddad are going to be interviewed by some reporters right above the dropoff. I'm sure it'll be the big story on all the television channels by tonight."

"Murder and illegal eagle feathers," Alan commented. "Yup. That's probably a guaranteed viewing audience around here."

He took a few long strides with his damaged leg, then slowed down.

"On second thought, maybe I'll just wait for the news at ten."

"Give me the keys, Bobby," Lily commanded me, her hand out. "I'm taking Alan back to the inn. Joe, you get a ride home with your mom, all right?"

"What about me and Luce?" I asked as I dropped the keys into the palm of her hand. "Are you just abandoning us out here?"

"I'll give you a ride back," Gil offered. "We can even go by Blue Sky, if you're interested, and you can see how Walking Eagle's doing this morning."

"Works for me," Luce agreed. "But I think I'll skip the circus."

She turned to me.

"How about you and I take another shot at the Scott's Oriole? You owe me, and this might be our last chance."

"Done," I said. "We'll deliver Joe to his mom, and then we'll try for the oriole until Gil's ready to leave."

"I'm booking our flights home," Lily called to us from where she was trying to fold Alan back into the little rental car's front passenger seat. "Which do you prefer—morning or afternoon departure?"

"Neither!" I shouted back. "Luce and I are taking the scenic route. We're driving to Phoenix to catch a plane."

"Chicken!" my sister yelled at me.

"So sue me!" I yelled back.

"Can we get going?" Joe asked. "I don't want to miss my mom's interview."

"Sure," I told him.

Out of the corner of my eye, I noticed that both Luce and Gil were trying to hide laughter.

"What?" I demanded. "You don't think that was an adult exchange with my sister? You didn't hear me say 'Am not,' did you? That would have been juvenile."

I put my arm around Joe's shoulders.

"Let's go find your mom and get her autograph before she becomes too big of a local celebrity."

"You think she'll get famous?"

"You never know," I told him.

I didn't add that famous or not, I was pretty sure she was going to be steamed, because Julie Burrows was just like my sister—once she got her teeth into something, she didn't let go. And Julie Burrows had her teeth into Ron's murder so deeply, nothing short of finding his killer —even twenty years after the fact—was going to make her happy.

And I had the distinct feeling that if Julie wasn't happy, nobody around her would be happy, either.

Especially Joe.

Chapter Twenty-Seven

After turning Joe over to his soon-to-be-interviewed mother, Luce and I retraced our steps across the meadow which was still playing host to an assortment of camera crews, policemen, and other interested parties. Off to one side of the clearing, I spotted Suzie McDaniels from Blue Sky Raptors talking with a man wearing the uniform of the U.S. Fish and Wildlife Service. She obviously spotted me, too, because she immediately waved Luce and me over to where she stood with the federal official.

"You heard the news, I take it," Suzie said after she'd introduced us to her companion. "But what you didn't hear was this: Ron Walking Eagle was the reason I came to Flag twenty years ago."

I glanced again at the uniformed man beside her.

U.S. Fish and Wildlife Service.

Suzie had come to Flagstaff working undercover for the U.S. Fish and Wildlife Service to break up a poaching ring.

A ring she never caught.

"You didn't know it was Ron," I said.

Suzie shook her head.

"Every time I thought I had a lead on who the poacher was, it dried up," she said. "None of my informants could quite pin him down, and I finally ran out of patience about the same time that my field office ran out of funds. We called off the case, but I liked Flagstaff too much to leave, so I retired."

She smiled at her companion.

"David was just coming on board with the Wildlife Service when I left. He's stuck it out, still making the world safe for unsuspecting wildlife."

"Do you do undercover work?" Luce asked David.

"Not so much anymore," he replied. "With all the funding cutbacks we've had, we're lucky to be able to do even a small portion of what we should be doing."

He nodded in the direction of the precipice where news crews were still posing reporters to film segments.

"Ron Walking Eagle sure had the sweet set-up here, I have to say," he noted. "His alcove was a perfect hide-away for an eagle poacher: it gave him almost unlimited access to prime nesting areas for eagles in the Ridge, and it was remote enough to avoid any eyes prying into his business. He was one smart thief, I'll give him that."

"And his cover was perfect," Suzie added. "I was right here in town when that court case was underway, and I never caught on to the whole 'sacred land' subterfuge. Really, I don't think someone engaged in the illegal eagle feather trade could have found a better place to set up shop."

Nor could they have asked for a smoother excuse to claim a "sanctuary" in the Ridge, I reflected. As a disgruntled son demanding his inheritance, Ron had effectively misrepresented to Bill Warner his real objective for wanting the land, and when that ploy failed, his back-up plan to make the Ridge a tribal preserve had been just as successful in getting him what he wanted: a reason for him to camp out in eagle territory. The fact that he'd been hunting had been easy to disguise, as long as no one climbed into his alcove. And as Julie had attested, Ron protected his cleft in the rocks as his spiritual retreat, a place that was forbidden to other visitors.

Yet, I knew of one person who had actually entered Ron's secret alcove: Bill Warner.

"But Gil's grandfather knew that Ron Walking Eagle was using that space," I pointed out to Suzie. "He told me he went into the alcove once."

"And saw nothing more than bundles of cloth along a back wall," David reported.

He moved aside and motioned at the three large bags behind him.

"Walking Eagle knew enough to keep the dead birds under wraps in case someone did stumble into his lair."

I looked at the row of sacks on the ground.

Bird in a bag, anyone?

"If you weren't thinking about the possibility of illegal activity, you wouldn't be looking for it," Suzie said. "From what Bill told us, the last thing on his mind during his visit with Walking Eagle was a suspicion of eagle poaching.

"And while Bill Warner is really involved with our birds and the local birding community now, he wasn't plugged into that scene back then," she reminded me. "He's only been birding for the last ten years or so."

I glanced again at the row of bags.

"Was Bill the one to discover the eagles?" I asked.

"No, thank goodness," Suzie replied. "I think it would have broken his heart if he'd had. Bill himself didn't go into the alcove this morning. His crew did, and then they called the police as soon as they found Ron's body. It wasn't till the crime scene technicians came and started cataloging evidence in the alcove that they found the eagles."

"Poor Bill," Luce said. "What an awful day for him."

Yeah, I figured today was ranking right up there as Worst Day Ever for Flag's Number One Fan. Bill Warner had finally learned what had happened to his missing illegitimate son: he'd been murdered, but not until after he'd gone on a spree of killing eagles. I'd say that was a clear reminder to be careful of what you wish for, because you just might get it.

And then really not like it.

"Do you think the poaching had anything to do with Ron's murder?" Luce asked Suzie and David. "Could it have been a sale gone sour?"

"You'll have to ask the police about that," David replied. "Though I would expect if the eagle feathers were the motive for the killing, those birds wouldn't have been left behind."

"Nice try, Sherlock," I told Luce. "Cross off all those illegal feather dealers we had on our list of murder suspects."

She threw me an icy look. If we'd been alone, she probably would have socked me in the arm for impugning her reputation so casually. But with a Fish and Wildlife officer in attendance, Luce was restraining herself.

Nice to know my federal taxes were good for something, even if it was just saving me from a sore arm.

"Do you need help getting those eagles to your van?" I asked Suzie.

"We've got it covered," she assured me, "but thanks. Actually, we're waiting to give an interview to the media. It didn't take them long to sniff out the fact that there's more than one story here today, and eagle poaching is a hot button around here, as you can imagine. There's always a reporter or two who fancies he or she is going to be the ace investigative journalist to break some big black market feather ring, and change the world for the better."

"Then we'll leave you to the paparazzi," I said. "Don't let them pick your bones clean," I added.

"Not nice, Bobby," Luce said as we left Suzie and David. "Reporters are just doing their job."

"If it bleeds, it leads," I reminded her. "Why can't the news stations broadcast happy stuff, like—I don't know—puppy shows, or family reunions?"

I remembered the last White family reunion I had attended. The potato salad spoiled and everyone came down with food poisoning.

"On second thought, forget the family reunions," I said. "Give me cute puppies."

"Animal Planet. They've got the Puppy Bowl every year."

"They also have 'When Wild Pets Eat Their Owners' Extremities,'" I pointed out.

I looked back briefly to see a flock of . . . media people . . . descending on Suzie and her old coworker.

"Why would anyone choose a career in journalism?"

"Ask Julie," Luce said. "Or Professor Corwin. He had a long career in it, so it must have made him happy."

"Or not," I noted. "He said it just wasn't the same as when he'd been young and hungry."

"And you don't think you'll say the same thing about counseling when you're his age?" Luce challenged me. "I can hear you now—'oh, for the days when all I had to deal with were girl fights during cafeteria duty.'"

I covered my ears with my hands.

"I can't hear you. I'm on vacation. La la la la la."

Luce laughed and pulled me onto the trail into the pinyon and juniper pine forest where I'd seen the Scott's Oriole with Warner yesterday.

"I don't see how Julie will ever find out who killed Ron," she mused out loud. "At this point, she'd have to find a journal of Ron's that documented his every move that last evening, along with everyone he talked with. As a witness, she can't provide anything—she was right here at the Ridge, but she wasn't even aware that Warner was here, too."

I abruptly stopped on the trail as something in Luce's comment triggered that nagging feeling I sometimes got that I was missing something that was staring me in the face.

"Bobby?"

I looked at Luce.

She was staring me in the face.

And the nagging sensation flew out of my head.

Damn.

"Keep walking," I told her.

"I was," she countered. "You're the one who stopped."

"Right. I did."

I tried to call the nagging sensation back, but it wouldn't oblige.

"And now," I said, taking another step, "I'm walking again."

"You're trying to remember something," she accused me. "I know that look on your face —the one where your right eyebrow goes up and your left eyebrow goes down."

"What an observant observer you are," I observed.

Luce smiled.

"That's why I'm such an awesome birder. And that's why I can see the Scott's Oriole sitting up in that pine behind you even though a clump of needles is almost hiding it."

I slowly turned my head to follow her gaze. The sunny bird was right where she'd said, perching motionless on the high branch.

"Score," I said. "You got your Scott's."

And I suddenly remembered what that nagging sensation was trying to tell me.

Julie hadn't seen Warner at the Ridge that night.

She hadn't seen Wilson tailing his father.

She hadn't seen anyone.

Because she hadn't been there.

"Son of a gun," I whispered. "She's lying."

Chapter Twenty-Eight

I grabbed Luce's hand and took off for the clearing at a brisk pace.

"You want to tell me what we're doing?" she asked.

"Tracking down the truth," I told her, my eyes focused straight ahead as I tried to control my rising frustration with Julie Burrows's apparently malleable sense of honesty.

If Julie had lied about being at the Ridge that night, what other falsehoods had she been feeding us? I mentally reviewed the facts—or what I had thought were the facts—and realized there were a few gaping holes in what I knew of Julie's investigation.

Hole Number One: If Julie wasn't a witness to the events of the night Ron disappeared, how could she have known for certain that Ron had even gone to the Ridge? For all she knew, he could have had a friend pick him up around the corner from his apartment and then hightailed it out of town in search of greener pastures, or bigger scams.

Hole Number Two: If Julie wasn't a witness who saw Bill Warner approach Ron's hide-out, why had she been so intent on making contact with him when she'd begun investigating Ron's disappearance—intent to the point that she'd incurred harassment? Warner, after all, had won the court case. Why would Julie think he'd have any information for her about his former opponent? She'd clearly been shocked to learn that Warner was Ron's father, so the idea of a biological link between the two couldn't possibly have sent her in Warner's direction.

Hole Number Three . . .

"Watch out!" Luce hissed, jerking me away from the lip of Hole Number Three. I stopped scrutinizing Julie's tactics and found myself staring at a small crater in the trail.

"No matter what we're rushing back to the clearing for, it isn't worth a sprained ankle," Luce said. "You trip in that hole, and it's going to be a long hobble back to the car."

"Julie's lying," I told her. "She wasn't a witness to anything."

And that would explain, as Joe had mentioned to me yesterday, why Julie had been close to calling it quits with her investigation into Ron's disappearance. She didn't have any proof that Ron had been murdered because she didn't see him go over the cliff to his so-called sanctuary. No matter what she suspected had happened to him, she had no evidence, and had apparently run out of leads to track down.

Until she met Charles Corwin at the youth conference's opening banquet.

He'd given her some information he'd uncovered during his own book research, Joe had said. And when Julie became a target of harassment—not the hate mail, because Joe knew whose work that was, but the slashed tires and broken window—the professor had assured her she was onto something, or someone.

I looked into Luce's blue eyes.

"I think Corwin has been manipulating Julie. For some reason, he's been pushing her to solve Ron's disappearance."

"Why would he do that?"

"Because he's a really nice man, and he knows he's dying," I improvised, "and he wants to help her get her book written before he's dead?"

Yeah, that sounded brilliant.

More like a stupid stab in the dark.

I had no idea why Corwin would be pushing Julie to solve a murder. I thought he was in love with her, but maybe I'd misread the look in his eyes. Maybe it wasn't love at all, but the prospect of co-authoring one last book before he died. Everybody wanted to be immortal, right? I couldn't imagine his treatise on preservation politics had made much of a splash in the minds of the reading public, but to be the co-author of a potentially explosive true crime book?

He'd be famous, even if he weren't alive to see it.

Kind of like saying if a tree fell in a forest, and no one was around to hear it, it didn't make any noise.

Well, maybe it was not like saying that, but if someone wasn't around to reap the reward, why would that person care about the reward in the first place?

I picked my way carefully along the rest of the trail to the place where it opened out to the meadow.

"Maybe Corwin's the witness," Luce said, her hand shading her eyes as she scanned the clearing.

"What?"

"Think about it," she said, her voice humming with growing excitement. "He gave Julie leads she hadn't been able to turn up through her own efforts. He pointed her in the direction of the Warners, right? He sent her to the courthouse to review documents he had to have known didn't exist, because he'd done the same research for his own book. Why would he do that, unless he wanted her to start asking very specific questions about the connections between the Warners, the Ridge, and Ron?"

Her warm fingers tightened around mine.

"Corwin knew things no one else did about the case, Bobby. Things that only someone could know if he'd been directly involved with Ron."

I heard a soft whistling noise above me and looked up in time to see Khan zipping past. At the precipice side of the meadow, Bill Warner was talking with Julie, his gloved fist in the air. Like a white ghost, Khan landed gracefully on his master's wrist. I could just make out something in the bird's beak. He must have found another interesting artifact to bring home to his owner.

The inhaler.

Khan had retrieved the faded remainder of an old inhaler from the abandoned eagle's nest on the alcove ledge.

Charles Corwin used an inhaler.

Along with about a million other people.

One of whom was Wilson Warner, according to his son.

And that got me . . . nothing.

Nothing but a beat-up piece of plastic in my pocket, and a whole lot of wondering if Julie wasn't the only world-class master of smoke and mirrors in Flagstaff.

I looked at Bill Warner standing beside Julie.

The fact was, he'd admitted to seeing Ron right there in the rocks the night he disappeared. No one saw Ron afterwards, so who was to say that Warner hadn't shot his son, eliminating any future risk of blackmail or scandal? The man had wanted to be mayor so badly, he'd donated a sizable piece of real estate to the county, and even his legitimate son, Wilson, assumed that committing murder was within his father's repertoire of power plays.

And what about Wilson himself?

The man was in rehab today, but where was he twenty years ago after he watched his dad go over the edge of the cliff to visit Ron? True, he'd denied killing Ron, but could I trust the word of a drunken man? A drunk who'd stood to lose his position as the only son—and heir—of a very wealthy man? And that wasn't even including the scandal about Ron's illegitimacy that Wilson would have had to endure on his father's behalf. If anyone had had a motive for killing the ersatz Yavapai Indian rights activist, it had been his half-brother.

But that still didn't explain Corwin's egging Julie on to find out what happened to Ron.

Unless Corwin had seen both of the Warners at the Ridge the night Ron permanently disappeared.

I turned to Luce as a new configuration of the facts began to assemble in my mind.

"I think you're on to something," I said. "Wait here."

Chapter Twenty-Nine

I MADE A BEELINE FOR THE EDGE OF the cliff near where Julie and Bill were standing. As I crossed the meadow, Gil fell into step next to me.

"I want to thank you for helping Granddad with my dad last night," he said. "I never knew why their relationship seemed so strained, but now I get it. I always thought that my dad figured he could never live up to his father's expectations—you know, he'd never carve an empire out of the wilderness the way Granddad did. And that's why they were so cold to each other."

He hesitated a moment before he went on, and I could feel my 'Confide in me—I'm a counselor' sign lighting up.

"I felt sorry for my dad as it was," Gil continued. "But when Julie started pushing him to see Granddad, it made Dad a wreck, and I couldn't handle it any more. I just wanted him to be okay, you know?"

I stopped my stride and looked the younger Warner in the eye, all my counselor instincts buzzing.

"What are you trying to tell me, Gil?"

He hung his head in embarrassment.

"I slashed Julie's tires and broke her window. I just wanted her to leave my dad alone so he'd quit the drinking."

"But it didn't help," I said.

He shook his head. "No, it didn't."

"You have to tell Julie," I told him.

"I know. My Granddad's going to be disappointed in me."

I put my hand on his shoulder.

"I have a feeling there's a lot of that going around right now," I said. I looked up to see Warner and Julie approaching us. At least now I knew who'd vandalized Julie's home and the motive behind it. That was the good news.

The bad news was that the slashed tires and broken window had nothing to do with Ron's murderer, which meant that Julie was still no closer to identifying his killer than when she and Alan had set out to explore the Ridge and found themselves caught in a rockslide. Granted, she now had a spot on the evening news with her and Warner's discovery of Ron's body and the poached eagles, but if she was looking for personal closure, it hadn't shown up yet.

But I was pretty sure I knew where to find it.

"Tell them about the tires and the window," I told Gil, just before Warner and Julie came to a stop in front of us. "Everyone needs to clear the slate, so you can start over and do it right this time. Trust me, Gil. It's going to be fine."

I caught Julie's eye.

"Where's the professor? He came out here with you this morning, didn't he?"

"He's back on the alcove ledge," she replied. "It turned out that he knew some of the crime scene technicians from a long time ago, so he's shooting the breeze with them. I think he's hoping they might let something slip that we can use for a new lead to keep looking for Ron's killer."

And I thought Alan and Lily were stubborn. Clearly, they had nothing on Julie Burrows. Twenty years after the fact, she was still optimistic she could run a killer to ground. Tenacious lady.

She would have made a good Gyrfalcon.

I headed for the precipice, where technicians were hauling the tools of their trade back up over the rim. A stack of bagged items and cameras sat on the ground, far enough from the lip of the dropoff to guarantee that nothing got accidentally knocked off the cliff and into all that vertical space. An older detective, his shirtsleeves rolled up in deference to the day's building heat, stood by the pile of equipment.

"I wanted to talk with Professor Corwin," I told the man. "I understand he's down by the alcove. Any problems with me going down to see him?"

"No. We're just wrapping up," he answered. "It was a surprise to see Charles here, I have to say. I think I'd heard he was back in Flag, but I didn't know he was up to his old tricks."

"You know the professor?"

"Did, a long time ago," the man said. "I was a rookie at the department, and he was a reporter for some small newspaper somewhere in the state. He was investigating some black market eagle ring, as I recall, but nothing ever came of it."

The detective squinted up at the sun, then wiped his hand over his sweating brow.

"Looks like we finally found his ring, though," he added. "Just goes to show you, I guess. All things come to he who waits."

"You sound like a birder," I told him. "Only we'd change it to 'all birds come to he who waits.'"

"You're a birder, huh? Then you must know Bill Warner. He's the best friend any bird could have in the northern half of Arizona. Says it's his legacy to make sure our birds stick around for generations to come." He wiped his forehead again. "I hear he's thinking of funding a fancy new raptor center to replace that little double-wide trailer that houses the Blue Sky rehabilitation program."

"I'll have to ask him about it," I said, then pointed to the edge of the cliff. "Did you guys rig up a grid to make it easier to get down to the ledge?"

"You bet. That earth is unstable enough over there without all of us climbing up and down. It's secure, now, but I'm just as glad to be done with it. Talk about being between a rock and a hard place."

"Don't I know it," I muttered, recalling my solo descent down the rough slope to rescue Luce not even twenty-four hours ago. If anyone had told me I'd be back here today, actually asking permission to repeat the trip, I would have said that was crazy.

Crazy is as crazy does, I guess, because here I was, about to go over the lip.

Again.

So much for my day's agenda.

I squatted down on the precipice and looked at the ropes securely attached to the rocky face of the same slope where I'd maneuvered my way down to Luce yesterday. The rigging reminded me of a giant spider web on steroids. Below and to my right, Charles Corwin sat on the ledge of the alcove, his back to the abandoned eagle's nest, his eyes focused on a ragged piece of rock that he was turning over and over in his hands.

Come into my parlor, said the spider to the fly.

Gotta love those happy old nursery rhymes, right? Good thing I hadn't recited one to Luce yesterday when she was out on the ledge. If I'd crooned "And down will come baby, cradle and all," I would probably have been nursing a broken engagement, if not a broken bone, today. Luce normally had a great sense of humor, but yesterday would not have been the best moment to test it.

"Got a minute?" I called to Corwin.

"I've got a few, actually," he called back, laying the nasty-looking rock aside. "No seminars to teach today."

No bodies to find now, either, I silently added.

I went over the lip and used the rope grid to make my way onto the ledge.

"That wasn't a bad idea," I said, once I sat down next to Corwin, "having Julie protect you by saying she was the witness, and not you."

To my surprise, he didn't react. No gasp, no dropped jaw, not even a blink of his eyes in their deep hollows behind his glasses.

"It was her idea," he said.

I noted a hint of a wheeze in his breathing.

"She was afraid that if I went to Warner and said I'd seen him here that night, I'd be in danger. She knows my health is frail. She didn't want me walking into the hands of a potential murder suspect."

"And you didn't object."

"She insisted. She's a very strong woman."

"Especially when she was doing exactly what you needed her to do," I pointed out. "You're quite a talented manipulator, Charles."

This time he did react. It was just a tiny flinch at the corner of his eyes, but I saw it, and it told me loud and clear that I was on the right track.

I sent a silent thank you to my professor in grad school who mercilessly hounded us to become adept at reading body language.

"Every verbal nuance means something," she'd hammered into us, "but a person's body gives it all away if you know what to look for."

So I'd mastered the meanings of the various tics, the eye dilations, the muscle movements that made up the physical language of the body. True, it hadn't landed me a whole lot of hot dates over the years, but it sure came in handy when you were feeling your way to the truth.

Like I was now.

I smiled. "But Warner wouldn't see her. And the problem with that, for you, was that there was no way to find out, then, if Bill Warner, or Wilson, had seen you here at the Ridge that night. Had seen you *after* Warner had seen Ron, that is," I added.

Corwin tipped his head to the side, studying me.

"Go on."

"You needed to be sure neither Warner nor Wilson could identify you as the last person to see Ron alive," I speculated. "Because after Warner left, you confronted Ron in his cave. I'd guessed that you—the hungry young reporter who wanted to change the world—went to get the real scoop about why the white man was passing himself off as a Yavapai activist, but now I know better."

I pointed my finger up towards the cliff edge.

"Your old buddy up there told me how you crossed paths twenty years ago. You were hunting Ron, not because of his Native American masquerade, but because of the eagle poaching. Exposing the black market operation was going to be your claim to fame."

Corwin coughed, then closed his eyes. When he opened them again, his gaze was fastened on the past.

"And to fortune, with any luck," he said. "I was going to be golden. The journalist who cracked the Southwest's biggest black market feather ring."

His eyes drifted shut and he lifted his lined face to the sun.

"When I walked into the alcove, he was wrestling a bald eagle into a bag. It was dead, of course. He pulled a gun on me, I jumped for him, we struggled, the gun went off. I was twenty-six years old, my fingerprints were on the gun, and a man was dead. Not to mention there were dead eagles in the cave. I wouldn't have believed a man innocent who came to me with that story, myself."

"So you took off."

"I did," he agreed. "I knew I had Ron pegged as the feather supplier, but when I saw Bill Warner, big man in Flag, show up for a chat, and then leave, I wondered how big the poaching ring was. If Bill Warner was involved, I figured I was dead one way or another. I had no clue about their blood relationship until I started researching my book a few years ago. I ran across some court documents that made me wonder about Ron's tribal affiliation. By the time I put it all together, I realized that Ron was a bigger schemer than I had ever imagined. It was a great story, but if I told it, I was going to jail for Ron's death."

He pulled a yellow inhaler out of his shirt pocket and took a hit of medication. I didn't tell him how a Gyrfalcon had dropped a clue to a killer at my feet.

"How long do you have, Charles?"

His tired eyes locked on mine.

"A few months, max. I'll be dead long before I come to trial."

"Does Julie know? About your prognosis, I mean."

He nodded.

"She's a good woman. Once I realized why she was asking the questions about Ron, I felt awful. Ron might have been a crook, but he took care of Julie, and when he was gone, she had no one again. All she knew was to run away, so she just kept on running. What a lousy way for a kid to grow up."

He took out a handkerchief to wipe his bald head.

"It was my fault she was abandoned, and I wanted to make it up to her. I was convinced that if I guided her investigation in the right direction, she'd figure it all out. She can write the book, Bob. It will give her—and Joe—job security. It's the least I can do for her."

"You're going to tell her the rest of the story? Your part of it?"

He nodded again.

"The Warners, too," he added. "They deserve to know the truth, and I'll take the consequences. I may have lived with a lie for the last twenty years, but I'm not going to die with it."

He took a deep breath, coughed, and stood up.

"We all want to be immortal, Bob, but the only thing that really endures is the truth."

From a distance, I could hear Julie calling for us.

Corwin smiled at the sound of her approaching voice.

"I'm in love with her, you know," he confessed. "She was the last thing I expected when I signed on to teach at the conference, but she's been the best thing that's ever happened to me. And that's the truth."

He looked at the rigging up the slope.

"Can you give me a hand? I'm not the mountaineer I was twenty years ago."

I reached out and steadied the ropes as Ron Walking Eagle's killer began his slow climb back up to the top of the Ridge. Once he was up over the lip, I took a final glance at the ledge of the alcove that had been hidden for years under various rockslides, and could just make out some fresh graffiti etched into the stone near the opening into Ron's hiding place. I moved closer to read it.

RIP.

Rest in peace.

Corwin had left a message for Ron.

Considering the two men's stories, I hoped it would apply to them both.

Chapter Thirty

I HELD MY BREATH AND LIFTED my binoculars to my eyes.

"Well?" Luce said beside me. "Have you got your Minnesota record?"

We were back in the grasslands in the southwestern corner of the state, making one last try for the wayward Gyrfalcon that had continued to appear in the Iowa farm field while we'd been in Flagstaff. Next week, I'd be back at Savage High School, preparing for the new academic year, listening to the lovely droning voice of our assistant principal as he reviewed the student dress code which nobody ever enforced except for him.

I could hardly wait.

So when I saw the email early this morning from my birder buddy across the state border, I picked up a sleepy Luce at her place, and we headed out for our final attempt to score the bird.

"I think I do," I told her, my excitement at the prospect making my hands a little less steady than I would have liked. "But he needs to glide a little further north to cross the state line."

I pointed to a stand of trees south of where we stood.

"That's my marker," I said. "If he's on the far side, he's in Iowa. This side, he belongs to us."

We watched the big bird's slow wingbeats as it made a long pass over the open prairie.

Unlike Bill Warner's majestic white Khan, this falcon was mottled brown, although his leg feathers tended more towards white, especially when he turned into the morning sunlight. Suddenly, he swooped low over the ground and disappeared from my view.

"Late breakfast," Luce noted.

I continued to observe the spot where I'd seen him dive to the earth, hoping he'd make quick work of his prey and return to the skies.

The Minnesota skies, if at all possible.

"I wonder how the Warners are doing," Luce said as we waited for the Gyrfalcon to reappear. She must have been thinking about Khan, too. "Didn't you tell me that Wilson was now volunteering at Blue Sky Raptors with Bill and Gil?"

"That's what Warner said in his last email a couple of days ago. Wilson isn't exactly crazy about handling any birds yet, but apparently he's throwing himself into getting the new rehab facility off the ground. The Blue Sky rehab facility, not the people one where he's still in treatment," I clarified.

The Gyrfalcon rose above the grasslands and turned north.

"Come on, baby," I whispered. "Just a little further."

Like an arrow from a quiver, the falcon suddenly sped over the state line.

"Yes!" I pumped my fist in the air, then wrapped my arm around Luce's waist and lifted her off the ground in a celebratory hug.

"Is that like a happy birder dance?"

I turned to see Joe Burrows standing a little ways behind us, his new binoculars hanging on his chest.

"Absolutely," I agreed. "I'm thinking of making my debut at a local powwow soon. But my costume won't have any eagle feathers on it. I'm going to use tissues instead."

He gave me an odd look.

"Tissues?"

"It's standard equipment for high school counselors," I explained.

I pointed to the Gyrfalcon who had already headed back to Iowa.

"So what do you think of that guy?" I asked.

"Big, for sure, but not nearly as impressive as the Golden Eagles back home."

"You want Golden Eagles? We've got Golden Eagles," I assured him. "You come visit your grandmother over winter break, and I'll introduce you to a friend of mine at the National Eagle Center in Wabasha. He lives for Golden Eagles."

"I don't know if Mom will let me come twice a year," Joe said. "Alan had to twist her arm to get her to let me come back with you guys this time. If she wasn't going to be so busy with her book and making Professor Corwin comfortable, she would've put up more of a fight, I think."

"But she did agree with Lily that it was time for you to meet your dad's relatives," Luce reminded him. "And since Alan's your second cousin, she knew you'd be in good hands out here."

That particular agreement, I found out later, was what Lily had wanted when she'd glued herself to Julie back in Flagstaff. She'd decided to trust Julie's denial of Alan's paternity, but the striking physical resemblance between Alan and Joe had nagged at my sister until she was convinced that they really were related somehow. And once my sister is convinced of something, not even wild horses could drag her away.

Kind of like the same way wild horses couldn't drag Julie Burrows away from her objectives, either.

So Lily had worked diligently to breach all of Julie's defenses while Luce and I were out birding, and the end result was the revelation of Joe's dad's identity: Sam DuChien, Alan's cousin, who, it turned out, had fallen hard for Julie when he met her briefly at a party at Alan's place when he'd lived in Seattle. Sam had enlisted in the service, and his short stay in town was enroute to his first deployment. By the time Julie knew she was pregnant, Sam was overseas. When he didn't make it back, she'd decided Joe was all the family she needed.

And all the family Joe needed, too. The fact was, Julie had never known what a real family could be like.

But it sounded like that was going to be changing for both her and Joe.

"Oh yeah, I'm in good hands all right," Joe laughed while we walked back to where we'd parked my car along the Jackson county road. "Every time I'm at my Grandma's house, she can't stop hugging me long enough to let me breathe. And Lily keeps giving me these funny looks like she's memorizing what I look like. To tell the truth, I'm ready to fly back home tomorrow. A guy needs some space of his own, you know."

Gee, hadn't that been a part of that phone conversation I'd had with Lily just a few weeks ago, not that far from this very spot, when she woke up and discovered that her new groom was missing in Flagstaff?

A guy just needs some space of his own.

In Alan's case, the space he'd found in Flagstaff had turned out to be more vertical than horizontal, and he was still limping with that bum leg of his from his fall in the rockslide.

Space, I decided, was vastly overrated.

"Like she's memorizing what you look like?" Luce asked Joe.

He nodded.

"Yeah, really weird."

Luce shot me a meaningful look across the top of the car, and I could see her thoughts as clearly as if they were suspended in a balloon over her head.

Lily's thinking about babies. In particular, what her and Alan's babies might look like.

I wondered if Luce could read my thoughts just as well. The words in the balloon over my head read: *I don't want to know.*

"Hey, look at this!" Joe said, bending down to brush some dirt off a slab of stone near the car. "It's a petroglyph! Alan talked about this in one of his sessions at the conference."

Luce and I both stepped over to take a closer look at the rock face that lay partially covered in late August grasses.

The more Joe brushed, the clearer the image became.

It was a handprint, like the ones we'd seen at the Jeffers site before our trip to Flagstaff.

"Someone wanted to leave his mark," I told Joe.

"Alan said it's human nature," he replied, "that we all want to be important, to claim a little bit of time and space—history—for ourselves."

I looked past him to the endless sea of grass that stretched out across what remained of Minnesota's ancient prairie. Compared to the majesty of nature, who didn't feel insignificant in the universe?

Professor Corwin's words floated back to me.

"We all want to be immortal."

Yes, we do.

But that isn't always a bad thing, I reflected. Sure, there will always be some bad apples in the bushel, but the good ones are still in there, too. I thought of Bill Warner and the legacy of habitat preservation he hoped to leave behind—a legacy that would benefit generations of both humans and wildlife to come. I thought of Jeffers Petroglyphs and the records in stone that told us human nature really hadn't changed in five thousand years—that we all have stories we need to tell.

Truths to share.

Birds to score.

Okay, so maybe that last one wasn't a universal human drive, but it sure got me out of bed in the morning.

Especially when there was a chance to claim a Minnesota record.

Now there was a legacy.

I clapped my hand on Joe's shoulder.

"What do you say we make a run up to Jeffers so you can see those petroglyphs your second cousin lectured you about?"

Joe lifted his brown eyes to mine and smiled.

"Cool."

He brushed his black hair off the sides of his face in a gesture that was, according to his giddy new grandmother, the mirror image of his father, Sam, and his cousin, Alan.

"Do you think we can, you know, maybe look for some more birds there, too? I mean, it's my last chance to get Minnesota species on my new life list before I leave tomorrow."

"You got it, buddy," I told him.

"Cool," he said again.

Very cool, I decided, putting the car in gear. I glanced at my fiancée beside me and then at Joe Burrows in my back seat. We had a new birder on board.

Very cool, indeed.

BOB WHITE'S "FALCON FINALE" BIRD LIST

Swainson's Hawk
Grasshopper Sparrow
American Kestrel
Upland Sandpiper
Horned Lark
Mourning Dove
Townsend's Solitaire
Stellar Jay
Red-tailed Hawk
Dark-eyed Junco
Spotted Towhee
Sage Thrasher
Bullock's Oriole
Mountain Bluebird
Black-headed Grosbeak
Broad-tailed Hummingbird
Black-chinned Hummingbird
Western Bluebird
Canyon Wren
Wild Turkey
Mexican Jay
Scott's Oriole
Mexican Spotted Owl
Gyrfalcon

Acknowledgments

Though I have barely scratched the surface of his expertise, I want to thank Scott Mehus of the National Eagle Center in Wabasha, Minnesota, for sharing some of his insights about Golden Eagles with me. Actually, I want to thank the whole staff at the NEC for their warm hospitality every time I attend their SOAR events in March—if you ever have the chance to visit the NEC, it's a gorgeous facility that provides excellent educational programming about eagles while working to enlarge our store of knowledge about these magnificent birds. I have no doubt that I'll be revisiting raptors in a future Bob White adventure, so I'm sure I'll be tapping Scott and friends again for more details.

While I do place my novels squarely in real places, I occasionally take some literary license with locations. The Inn at NAU no longer exists—students in the School of Hotel and Restaurant Management are now placed in other venues for hands-on hospitality training. The campus is still surrounded by cemeteries, however, and while I didn't see a single zombie when I last visited some eight years ago, it did inspire me as a perfect location for a murder mystery. My thanks goes to Gabe Fribley, a former Flagstaff resident, for updating me on campus and city news, including tipping me off about the ongoing Snowbowl controversy and its parallels with my fictional Ridge dispute.

About the Author

Jan Dunlap divides her time between birding, teaching, and writing. While she admits to being nowhere as skilled at birding as her fictional protagonist Bob White, she is an optimist and hopes one day to be able to identify all the birds showing up at her back porch feeders. Her first Bob White Birder Murder Mystery, *The Boreal Owl Murder*, won a silver medal in the 2008 Midwest Book Awards. She lives in Chaska, where she is working on her next Bob White book, and she welcomes visitors at her website

www.jandunlap.com

You can also find Jan on her Facebook Author Page.

Can't get enough of Bob White?

Keep up with Bob and his friends by visiting Luce Nilsson's new blog Me, Bobby, and the Birds at

www.cooksleepbird.blogspot.com.

Luce will post about what's happening between the books, including birding tales, travel highlights, favorite recipes, and life with Bob White.